The Protectors Series

Duncan

BY

Teresa Gabelman

THE PROTECTORS

DUNCAN

Gabelman, Teresa (2013-7-20).

DUNCAN (THE PROTECTORS SERIES) Book #3.

Kindle Edition.

Editor: Hot Tree Editing

Photo: www.bigstockphoto.com

Cover Art: Indie Digital Publishing

Acknowledgements

I wish I could thank every reader by name. You have given me the courage to continue to do what I love and that is to tell stories. Until you, the awesome readers, tell me to stop, I will continue to write. Thank you for reading my stories. If I can make you have just one strong emotion while reading, I have achieved my goal, and that is to take you out of reality if only for a second or two. Your support means more to me than you will ever know. And to the Warriorettes, well, what can I say about these crazy women except every single one of you ROCK!

Special thank you to my editor, Becky Johnson, at Hot Tree Editing for your understanding and being patient with me. It's a pleasure and blessing to work with you. Anyone not using your service is truly missing out on working with the best!

Chapter 1

Duncan Roark sat staring at his cluttered desk without seeing anything at all. Three months he had searched for her, and…nothing. Not even a hint of where she had disappeared to. The low growl escaping his lips rattled papers on his desk. He had failed her in more ways than any man worth having her should. His arms rested on the edge of the desk as if ready to dig into the pile of work that waited for him, but his clenched hands said otherwise, as did his darkening eyes.

Slowly, his hand reached for the drawer on the right; he then opened it cautiously, almost as if something would jump out. His fingers stretched to touch the silky black hair still bound by a simple rubber band. Anger gripped him without warning, causing him to slam the drawer shut. Picking up the closest object, he hurled a stapler at the wall in front of him.

Jared Kincaid opened the door to Duncan's office at that exact moment. "Like what you're doing with the place." Jared eyed the stapler sticking out of the wall before looking back at Duncan.

"What do you want, Kincaid?" Duncan growled, running his hand through his shoulder-length blond hair that was coming loose from the leather tie. "I'm not in the mood."

"Obviously." Jared walked in and sat in one of the two chairs in front of Duncan's desk, stretching out his long, muscled legs - settling in, totally ignoring Duncan's foul mood.

"I'm in the middle of something, so spit it out, and then get out." Duncan shuffled papers around not even knowing what they were.

Damon and Sid walked in also catching sight of the stapler sticking out of the wall. "Nice. You gonna frame it?" Sid walked over and sat in the other chair leaving Damon to lean against the wall.

"What is this?" Duncan leaned back in his chair, eyeing each Warrior.

"Tea time." Sid's smart-ass answer echoed in the room as he kicked his feet up on Duncan's desk.

"The women are worried about you." Damon's deep voice broke the sudden silence.

Duncan sighed, shaking his head before his eyes zeroed in on Sid. "First off, get your big-ass feet off my desk before I break your legs." He knocked them off anyway before Sid could comply. "Second of all, I'm fine. So go and tell your women *thanks*, but…butt out."

Jared snorted. "You can tell them that yourself."

"Well, we had a pow-wow and decided that you need to stop being an asshole and get your shit together." Sid didn't pull any punches. He thought about putting his feet back on the desk, but stopped at Duncan's look.

"I've always been an asshole, and my shit *is* together, now get the fuck out of my office," Duncan growled, getting tired of the game.

"There's talk that this may not be your office much longer." Jared sat up straight, all fun and games gone.

"So be it." Duncan shrugged his shoulders. He had figured as much. A lot had slipped in the three months she had been gone. He really didn't care anymore. He had given his life to the Council, his life was now hers.

"So be it?" This time Sid sat up. "What the fuck do you mean, 'so be it'? It took me months to get used to working under you, being the asshole that you are. I sure as hell am not going to get used to someone else coming in here changing shit."

"I never asked for this job," Duncan replied, no emotion in his voice.

"Okay, enough with the bullshit." Jared slammed his hand on the desk. "We're all worried about Pam and we *will* find her, but until then, you need to step up and get your head out of your ass. We need you in this position so we can get shit done. We're losing the war out there, buddy, and we need our leader."

Duncan growled his frustration. He knew they were right, but his focus was on her, only her. "What the fuck do you want from me?"

No one said a word, just stared at Duncan. Sid finally broke the silence by standing. "I may sound like the biggest pussy by saying this, but it needs sayin'." He leaned over the desk, staring directly into Duncan's eyes. "I have never had a family, even as a human. Everyone in this room, I consider my family, my brothers, and I would give my life for any one of you. I am behind you, in whatever you decide to do. You leave the Council, I walk behind you. We *are* going to find her, Duncan."

Everyone watched a little wide-eyed as Sid finished and calmly walked out of the room, without slamming the door behind him.

"What a pussy," Jared snorted then grinned, uncrossing his feet to stand. "Though I do second what he said. You walk - I walk." He leaned over, slapping Duncan on the shoulder before following Sid out the door.

Duncan glanced at Damon who still leaned against the wall, arms crossed. "You think Jared's going to give Sid hell for his little speech?"

"Without a doubt." Damon grinned. "Never heard Sid talk like that before. Seriously didn't know he had it in him."

Running his hand down his face, Duncan sighed. "You need to take over for me until I find her."

"No." Damon's answer was firm. "I will help you, but not by taking your place. You're our leader, and that will *not* change."

Anger flashed across Duncan's features. "How can I be a leader when I don't care about anything other than finding Pam?" Looking down at his desk littered with notes, files and shit he had no clue about, he pushed them aside. "Fuck!" That one word held so much pain and frustration, Damon flinched.

"We *will* find her," Damon replied, still in the same pose he was in when he first came into the office. "But I have one question."

Duncan's head came up in a snap, his mood foul. "What?"

Damon's large frame moved away from the wall, his arms dropping to his sides. "Once you find her, then what?"

"What in the hell do you mean, 'then what?'" Duncan was doing his best to hold his anger in check. "What fucking difference does what I'm going to do make?"

"Because Pam is my mate's best friend, and if you are just going to find her to break her heart, then you need to sit back behind that desk and let us take care of her." Damon's answer was firm and point blank.

Duncan's only answer was a growl, his fist closing tight.

"Answer my question," Damon said, his voice calm. "Because if we do get a lead on her, your answer is going to determine whether you're going to be informed."

Duncan flew across the desk, stopping inches from Damon. "Then I'll beat the information out of you if it comes to that."

A slow smile spread across Damon's mouth but didn't reach his eyes. Warriors they were, brothers they would always be, but their alpha ways were always at the surface - always ready for a good brawl.

"My mate's wishes come before yours in this case." Damon's eyes darkened to match Duncan's. "I hope sitting behind that desk hasn't made you soft, because if you don't answer my fucking question, you won't be told anything."

Both men roared as Duncan tackled Damon, taking him to the ground. Duncan's fighting skills far exceeded any of the Warriors in their group, but Damon wasn't a slouch. He gave as good as he got.

"Stop it!" Nicole rushed in, trying to break them up. Running to Duncan's desk, she started throwing things at them. She may be a vampire now, but she was a smart woman and knew not to get in the middle of two fighting Warriors. Jill followed her, dodging the men as they rolled toward her, swinging. "I said stop it!" Nicole yelled louder.

Jared and Sid ran in, moving Jill out of the way of the rolling Warriors. "I'll take Damon for a hundred." Jared stood with Jill at his back.

"Pfft...Duncan is going to tear him up. Hell, I'll even raise it a hundred." Sid snorted watching the men.

A book hit Jared in the chest. "Break them up, Jared." Nicole shouted. "What the hell is wrong with you? They're going to kill each other."

"Ah, come on Nicole," Sid sighed. "Lighten up. They're just letting off some steam." Sid growled when a book bounced off his shoulder.

"Break them up!" Nicole demanded, running out of things to throw. "Or I swear I will tell everyone what I caught you watching the other day." She directed that threat to Sid.

Jared's eyes widened as he looked over at Sid. "What were you watching?"

Shooting a nasty look at Nicole, Sid headed toward the fighting Warriors. "Shit! Girls take the fun out of everything."

When both men were broken apart, they sat panting, their eyes glaring at each other. Damon's grin spread first with Duncan's following. "I think you broke my jaw, asshole." Damon worked his jaw back and forth with his hand.

"Serves you right." Duncan rubbed his shoulder. "You're lucky that's all I broke."

Nicole frowned, watching the four Warriors laugh, slapping each other on the back. "Are you kidding me?" Nicole threw her hands on her hips. "You beat the crap out of each other then walk around congratulating each other?"

"Honey…" Damon tried to stand, but his leg gave out.

"Don't you 'honey' me, Damon DeMasters." Nicole walked toward the door. "I can't believe you guys."

"Dog house for you tonight," Sid chuckled. "Guess you got a lot of sucking up to do. You guys make me nauseous. No woman will ever pull me around by my dick."

Those words stopped Nicole cold. "I found Sid watching Rachel Ray." She smirked at Sid.

"Who and what the hell is Rachel Ray?" Jared frowned.

Nicole put her hand on her hip, liking the nauseous look on Sid's face. "It's a chick talk show."

"Dude!" Jared took a step away from Sid, his eyes narrowing. "A chick talk show?"

"She's a cook," Sid replied but snarled at Nicole. "She has good recipes. I was getting ideas for-"

Nicole walked up to Sid, leaning in close, cutting him off. "A woman may not be able to lead you around by your..." she glanced down then back to his face, "...*dick*, but one sure can make it shrivel up."

Nicole, proud of herself, walked out of the room, shoulders back, her head held high. Jill followed, her hand across her mouth, trying to hold back laughter. It didn't matter to Nicole that she knew what Sid had been doing, which was actually writing down recipes since he cooked most of their meals. He was an excellent cook, but anytime she could put the arrogant Warrior in his place, she would do it.

Sid turned to glare at Damon, stabbing a pointed finger toward Nicole's retreating back. "She is evil."

Damon grinned proudly, watching his mate walk out the door. "No, she just put you in your place, and very well at that."

The three Warriors laughed and snorted at Sid's expense. "What the hell are you laughing at?" Sid punched Jared in the shoulder. "You owe me two hundred dollars. Duncan had his ass."

"Bullshit." Jared followed Sid out. "Damon was all over him."

"Pay up, bitch," Sid snarled.

"Not happening," Jared laughed. "Come on. I think there's a Martha Stewart marathon on today."

"Fuck you." Sid slammed out of the room with Jared's loud laughter following him.

Duncan cursed as he picked himself off the ground once they were alone. Reaching down, he held his hand out to Damon, helping him to his feet. "I love her, brother." Duncan's eyes didn't waver.

"I know you do." Damon gave him a nod. "I just wanted to make sure we were both on the same page. Just don't let her go this time."

"I made a lot of mistakes where Pam was concerned." Duncan admitted, taking responsibility for his inactions. "Mistakes I won't be making again. She is mine."

Damon nodded, understanding completely. "We'll find her, brother." He grabbed Duncan's shoulder in comfort. "We *are* going to find her."

Chapter 2

Jared found Tessa and Nicole in the kitchen, their heads together, which meant impending trouble for him and Damon.

Walking up to Tessa, Jared grabbed her from behind, kissing her soft cheek. "What trouble are you two brewing up?" He frowned when they both jumped, looking guilty. Glancing closely at them both, he cocked an eyebrow. "Seriously, what trouble are you two getting into now?"

"Nothing." Nicole cocked an eyebrow back at him. "Are you boys done beating the crap out of each other?"

Jared eyed them a second longer before pulling Tessa against him tighter, wrapping his thick arms around her waist. "You need to get used to that, Nicole. We Warriors get a little…" he grinned as he searched for a word, "heated sometimes, but it's always good in the end."

Rolling her eyes, Nicole started out of the room. "Heated, my butt," she snorted, glancing at Tessa. "I'll see you in half an hour."

Tessa nodded as Jared turned her in his arms. "What's going on in half an hour?" Jared tilted her chin up when she continued to watch Nicole walk out of the room.

Hesitating for a second before answering, Tessa tiptoed to kiss his chin, avoiding any eye-contact. "Just girl stuff."

"What kind of girl stuff?" Jared wasn't falling for it. He knew Tessa well and knew when she was lying.

Grasping the back of his head, she moved to his mouth. Jared let her have her moment, because in all honesty, he loved her mouth on his and anywhere else her mouth found on his body. He never knew he could love so deeply, but damn, this woman had him wrapped around her little finger. Before long, his body had hers pressed against the wall, his hand working eagerly up under her shirt.

"My God, would you two give it a break!" Sid groaned as he walked in. "I can't walk anywhere in this damn place without you two slobbering over each other. It's downright disgusting."

Pulling his hand out of her shirt, Jared snarled, "Get out of here, Sid."

"No, you get the hell out of here," Sid snarled back. "This is my domain, and from here on out, anything but eating in this kitchen is against kitchen law."

"Kitchen law?" Jared tilted Tessa's chin for one more kiss before turning to face Sid.

"Yeah, Sid's Kitchen Law will be posted by the end of the damn day. Now, get the hell out of my kitchen and find a private room." Sid slammed a few pots around. "But before you do that, Duncan wants to see you. He wants you to take his classes tonight."

"Shit." Jared frowned. "We had plans."

"It's okay." Tessa fixed her clothing, her cheeks flushed from Jared's heated kiss and embarrassment at being caught once again by Sid. "We can do dinner and a movie another night. I'm going to check on Gramps. I'll talk to you later tonight." She touched his cheek before hurrying out of the room.

Sid and Jared both watched her closely as she left. "She didn't seem too broken-hearted," Sid snorted.

Jared frowned. "I found her and Nicole in here with their heads together, which usually means trouble."

"You poor bastards," Sid chuckled, adding oil to a skillet.

"Sid." Jared glared. "Shut the fuck up."

"Just sayin'." Sid grinned, chopping onions. "Women are nothing but trouble." His comment was made to an empty room since Jared had already slammed out the door.

*****

Nicole pulled into Pam's old apartment building, parking in the back. Clicking off the lights, she shut off the car with a long sigh. "You ready?"

Tessa flipped the hood of her black hoodie up. "Lead the way."

Glancing around as they made their way across the parking lot, Nicole walked to the sliding glass door knowing it would be locked, but tried it anyway. Next, she tried a window, and sure enough, it opened, as Pam said it would.

"Hope my ass fits through that," Tessa whispered, eyeing the window.

"You and your ass will fit." Nicole laced her fingers together. "Come on, before someone sees us."

Putting her foot in Nicole's cupped hands, Tessa grabbed the windowsill and slid the window open. With one heave, Tessa was half in and half out of the window, her ass flashing out into the parking lot. Thank God, the window was above the sink. Placing both hands down on the counter, Tessa shimmied her way in, but ran out of counter space and fell the rest of the way through the window, landing on the kitchen floor in a clumsy heap.

Nicole hopped through the window with ease, landing with grace. "You okay?" Nicole whispered, reaching down to help Tessa up.

"Well, that was graceful. Yeah, I'm good." Brushing off her pants, Tessa frowned. "Some days I guess it pays to be a vampire."

"Yeah, it does come in handy." Nicole grinned, handing Tessa a mini flashlight. Being a vampire, she could see perfectly at night. "Come on, let's get busy."

"What exactly are we looking for?" Tessa kept her voice low, testing the flashlight, but keeping it from shining toward the windows.

"A syringe vial." Nicole headed out of the small kitchen. "I'll check the bedroom. You check the bathroom."

"That sounds familiar." Tessa rolled her eyes. A syringe vial is pretty much what brought Tessa and Jared together.

"It does. I forgot about that," Nicole snorted. "So I guess you don't need a description."

Tessa followed Nicole, stopping at the bathroom door. "Why didn't you tell the guys that Pam contacted you?" Tessa herself had just found out before Jared had interrupted them in the kitchen.

Stopping, Nicole turned to look at Tessa, her face lined with worry and stress. "Actually, I was going to tell them, even though I promised her I wouldn't, but Damon and Duncan were too busy beating the crap out of each other." Nicole shrugged her shoulders. "I know I should have, but they pissed me off fighting, and the more I thought about it, I have never broken a promise to Pam. She said she isn't in any danger, but was dealing with something and needed this vial if I could find it."

Tessa nodded in understanding, wanting to help Pam as much as Nicole did. "Well then, let's find that vial." Tessa ducked into the bathroom and started rummaging through drawers and cabinets.

Nicole walked into the bedroom and stopped. The scent of old blood hit her highly-sensitive nose as soon as she walked in the room. Looking around, her eyes zeroed in on the bed. Making her way closer, she spotted two chains locked onto the head post. Her stomach clenched.

The bed was a mess of covers and a few clothes, Pam's clothes. Grasping the edge of the cover, not really wanting to see what the cover hid, and even knowing exactly what is was, she flipped the sheet back. Her eyes welled up at the sight of old brown blood stains that told the horror of what happened in this room. "Oh my God." Nicole felt the room closing around her. She had to get out of here.

"Don't move." A man's voice and the click of a gun echoed in the silent room.

*****

"If you knew they were up to something, why the hell did you leave them alone?" Damon slammed into the Cincinnati Police Department with Jared hot on his heels.

"I didn't leave them alone," Jared defended himself as he passed Damon. "I caught them talking in the kitchen, and they looked guilty as hell. Nicole left and then…"

Damon stopped, a suspicious frown forming on his lips. "And then what?"

Jared thought about the 'then what,' which was Tessa's sweet mouth.

"Wipe that goofy-ass look off your face and come on." Damon gave him a disgusted look before heading to the front desk.

"Oh, like Nicole hasn't turned your brain to mush with her sexy little…" Jared chuckled when Damon flipped him off over his shoulder.

Stopping, Damon loomed over the counter, glaring at the officer who was unlucky enough to be the one on shift.

"Can I help you?" he asked, looking back and forth between the two huge Warriors.

"Buzz them through," Officer Pete Rosen ordered before Damon could answer.

Damon and Jared passed through the door. "Where are they, Pete?"

Frowning, Pete tilted his head for them to follow him. Stepping into a room, he closed the door. Pete Rosen had been on the Cincinnati police force since he was twenty-one years old. He was six months from retiring at the age of fifty-five. He had seen a lot of shit during his years on the force, but nothing had prepared him for working with vampires. To his surprise, he had enjoyed his short time working with the Warriors and respected them deeply. So when he saw Nicole come in handcuffed with another woman he didn't know, he had called Damon right away. Nicole was well known around the police station, and he always had a soft spot for her; she was the best when it came to the kids she worked with. She was always hitting up the police department for charities.

Pete leaned against the closed door and sighed. "Detective Ferguson is interrogating them."

"Who the fuck is that, and why is he interrogating my wife?" Damon growled taking a step toward the door.

"What the hell did they do?" Jared crossed his arms, not sure he wanted to hear the answer to that question. The only thing that Pete had told them over the phone was that they had Nicole and another woman in custody, which Jared assumed was Tessa.

"They broke into Pam Braxton's apartment," Pete replied. "And Tom

Ferguson is lead detective on Sheriff Bowman's murder."

"Dammit!" Jared rubbed his hand up and down his face.

"Dammit is right." Pete frowned. "Ferguson is an asshole and will do anything to close a case. Rumor has it, he plans on running for mayor, so the more bad guys he puts away, the more votes go in his pocket."

"So in other words, he'd make a deal with the devil." Jared knew the type all too well.

"If he hasn't already." Pete opened the door and headed down the hall to another room where two men sat watching a monitor.

Jared and Damon both looked at the screen, seeing Nicole and Tessa seated at a small table that was attached to the wall. A tall balding man in a suit stood in the middle of the room, his hands clasped behind his back.

Damon noticed Nicole wincing. The man moved, and he saw why. Her hands were in front of her on her lap, handcuffed. "Those better not be silver handcuffs."

One of the men sitting at the monitor snorted. "She's a fucking vampire, of course it's silver." His laugh died a quick death when he turned and met the black eyes of Damon DeMasters.

Jared stepped in front of Damon. "Well, since she is a vampire, as dumbass over there has pointed out, we have authority." He nodded toward Pete and the door. "Lead the way, Pete."

Damon growled, flashing his large fangs at the man who was visibly trembling in fear. His partner quickly pushed his own chair out of harm's way, clearly stating his partner was on his own.

"Come on, bro." Jared pushed Damon toward the door. "You can decapitate the asshole later. Let's try to get the women out of trouble."

Two doors down, Pete gave a one-knuckle knock before opening the door. The older officer headed toward Nicole and unlocked her handcuffs. Damon and Jared followed, filling the tiny room.

"What the hell do you think you're doing?" Detective Ferguson stepped in front of Pete before he could unlock Tessa's handcuffs.

"The VC Warriors are here, so there is no need to handcuff these women." Pete stood his ground with a half grin on a weathered face that had seen too much. "I'm sure they'll protect you."

"I wouldn't bet on it," Jared mumbled, his eyes leaving Tessa's handcuffed hands to shoot a nasty glare at the detective.

"You have no right coming in here, Officer Rosen." Detective Ferguson looked quickly away from Jared's intense glare, putting his focus back on Officer Pete. "I could have your badge for this."

"The Sargent is in his office." Pete nodded toward the door. "Be my guest."

With one last hard glare at everyone in the room, Detective Ferguson stormed out, slamming the door behind him.

"You have ten minutes tops before he's back." Pete headed toward the door.

"Thanks, my man." Jared slapped him on the shoulder.

"Yeah, well, you owe me one." Pete grinned closing the door behind him.

Once the four of them were alone, Jared turned toward Tessa and

Nicole. "So who's going to start?"

"Don't need an audience." Damon nodded up toward where the camera was hidden behind a fake smoke detector.

Walking over, Jared gave a hard glare into the smoke detector that held the camera before taking the face-front off. With a twist of a wire, the red recording light went dark. "Secure." Jared turned back around.

Both women sat staring at the Warriors. "What?" Nicole broke the silent staring contest they were having.

"You know exactly what," Damon growled, looming over his mate.

Nicole stood quickly. "Don't you growl at me, Damon DeMasters," she hissed standing toe-to-toe with him.

"What were you two doing in Pam's apartment?" Jared glared at Tessa, giving Damon and Nicole some cooling off time.

"We were getting some clothes for-" Nicole answered, still having a stare down with her mate.

"Bullshit." Jared didn't let her finish.

"I will call Adam if I have to." Damon pulled out his phone. Adam was Tessa's brother who had been turned into a half-breed. He had the power to read people with just a touch, no matter how hard they tried to block him.

Nicole wrinkled her nose at him before plopping back down in her chair. "We were looking for a vial."

"Why?" Damon's tone hadn't changed. He was pissed, and it showed in his voice, body language and scowl that slashed across his

17

handsome face.

"I'm not sure," Nicole replied then frowned when they both continued to glare at her. "I don't know."

Damon rubbed his hand down his face, clearly irritated. "Why didn't you come to me with this? Duncan has been looking everywhere for her, and here you are talking to her." Damon shook his head, disappointment radiating off him in waves.

Nicole looked away for a second, but her eyes quickly found his again. "She is my friend and asked me not to say anything."

"Where is she?" Damon's tone deepened, his eyes narrowed.

"I have this under control," Nicole replied, standing her ground. "She's fine."

"I demand you tell me where she is." Damon's voice rose with each word.

"Okay, why don't we just calm down." Jared tried to smooth the situation over, but Nicole stood again, this time knocking her chair over.

"You demand?" Nicole tilted her head, looking up at her mate. "You demand?" She shouted this time, her voice trembling with anger.

"Shit." Jared stepped in front of Tessa who had also stood.

"You have no right keeping this information from Duncan, Nicole," Damon shouted back; he never shouted and definitely not at his mate. "And you know it!"

Nicole gave him a deadly glare. "What I do know is my friend trusts me, and I'm not breaking that trust."

"Call Adam," Damon growled at Jared, but his eyes did not leave Nicole. "And Duncan."

"Screw you." She emphasized each word with a hard point of her finger to his chest before walking around him.

"Where do you think you're going?" Damon went to grab her arm, but she snapped it back.

Nicole stopped and slowly turned around. "Away from you."

"I don't fucking think so." Damon took a step forward to grab her again, but she smacked at his hand.

"If you touch me, you are going to have your hands full, Damon DeMasters," Nicole hissed.

"You are *not* leaving." He loomed over her, bent slightly to glare down at her.

"Is that a demand?" She stretched up so she could go nose-to-nose with him.

Before Damon could respond, Tessa pushed past Jared. "Stop it. Just stop, both of you." She walked between the two, pushing each of them back. "I know where she is. Nicole, I understand why you haven't told Duncan, but I never promised Pam anything. You can stay here while I tell them what I know, or you can leave."

Nicole stared at Tessa for a few seconds before nodding her head. Without looking at Damon, she walked out the door, closing it softly.

Tessa watched Damon stare after Nicole, his face changing before her eyes. He hated himself for fighting with his mate and it clearly showed. She almost felt sorry for him…almost.

"You're an asshat." She pointed at Damon. Before he could open his mouth, she continued. "You of all people should understand Nicole. She is loyal to a fault."

"She should be loyal to me. Her mate…her husband." Damon frowned, becoming angry again. "She should not have kept this from me."

"This isn't about you," Tessa sighed. "This was about Duncan. You said so yourself."

"But you both put yourselves in danger." Jared pointed out with a frown of his own. "That makes it about us."

Tessa snorted. "Breaking my damn neck was the only danger I was in." Seeing Jared's concern, she waved it away. She didn't need to go into her embarrassing fall through the kitchen window. "I actually didn't know until today about Nicole and Pam having contact, but I was there when Pam called. She asked Nicole to go to her apartment to find a vial. It was a quick call. Nicole is supposed to meet her with the vial."

"Where?" Damon demanded impatiently taking his phone out.

"Are you going to apologize?" Tessa crossed her arms; she could play stubborn with the best of them.

A loud sigh escaped his lips. "Sid's right. Women will drive you nuts," Damon growled. "Yes, I will apologize."

"Good, 'cause you were being an ass."

As Damon's growling grew louder, Jared wrapped his arms around

Tessa. "Tell him where, Tessa. The faster he calls Duncan, the faster he can apologize to Nicole."

Tessa glared back at Damon in warning before rattling off what she knew and where Nicole was to meet Pam.

Damon punched in a number on his cell. After a second of silence, his voice echoed in the small room. "We found her."

Chapter 3

Newport, Kentucky, was Pam's stomping grounds. She grew up here, along the Ohio River. For a brisk November night, Newport on the Levee was bustling with activity. Restaurants were overflowing as well as the shops that had sprouted up overnight. Flipping the hood up on her lightweight jacket, Pam scanned the crowd looking for trouble. In every face, she expected to see Kenny scowling back at her. She spooked herself so much, she was afraid to look at anyone, but she had to be prepared. He was out there, and she knew, without a doubt, he was looking for her.

Two women walked close by talking and laughing, reminding Pam of better times when she and Nicole would walk the Levee. They would talk about their day as they headed toward their favorite place to eat, Dewey's Pizza, then go to Club Zero for a beer and some dancing. Shaking the memories away, she hurried her pace. She didn't have time for memories.

Seeing the spot she was to meet Nicole, Pam headed toward the bench and sat, huddling into her jacket. It wasn't overly cold for November, but the weather in Kentucky was never what it was supposed to be. Her eyes focused on the strong current of the water; the Cincinnati skyline across the river reflected in the rippling water as pieces of driftwood skirted past. Her eyes lifted to stare across the water; her stomach fluttered. Duncan Roark was there somewhere. He might as well be a million miles away rather than a short drive across the river. There wasn't a second that went by that she didn't think of the Warrior. He probably hated her now. Not liking the thought, she stood, nerves and aggravation radiating off her. Even though she had talked to Nicole, she never let the conversation become personal.

A feeling of being watched shivered through her body. Slowly, she turned, scanning the area. "Come on, Nicole," she whispered, shuffling from foot-to-foot and feeling more nervous than usual. Something didn't feel right, and lately her instincts were dead on.

Checking her phone again, she looked back up, spotting a tall man with long hair. She only knew one man who towered over people with hair like that. "Dammit!" She turned to head in the opposite direction, but stopped. She should have known Nicole wouldn't keep her big mouth shut. Damon DeMasters was at her back and Jared Kincaid was at her front. With nowhere else to go, unless she wanted to take a cold swim, she turned again to walk between the two Warriors before they got any closer.

Before she could take two steps, her eyes found his golden gaze staring intently at her as his long legs ate the distance up between them. Feeling cornered and panicked, Pam glanced quickly for an escape, but she knew it was useless. Her heart and body took over, sending her moving toward Duncan, but her head screamed for her to run.

As if in a daze, her body kept moving toward what she wanted more than anything in the world, but seeing the look on his face stopped her. His mouth opened in warning, his hand shooting out toward her. Snapping out of her dazed state, Pam let her eyes roam the area. She and the Warriors were surrounded by more uniformed police officers than she could count, all pointing their guns on her.

A tall man walked toward her, flashing his badge. "Pam Braxton." He put his badge back in his coat pocket, nodding toward an officer who proceeded to handcuff her. "I'm Detective Ferguson. You are being brought in for questioning on the murder of Sheriff Bowman."

"This is bullshit. You get off handcuffing women?" Jared growled, moving closer to Pam. "She is no threat."

"This time you have no jurisdiction." Detective Ferguson smirked. "I suggest you Warriors go on with your business before you're arrested and taken in with her."

Duncan looked at both Jared and Damon. "Call Sloan." Before anyone could question why, Duncan punched the detective square in the face.

*****

As Pam was led away to a police car, Duncan followed, pulling the officer who handcuffed him along with him. After they carefully placed Pam in the backseat, the officer closed the door.

"Uh, sir." The officer holding onto Duncan's arm nervously cleared his throat. "You need to come to my car."

Duncan looked down at the man and frowned. "I'm riding in this car." He nodded to where Pam sat.

"But, I don't think Detective Ferguson will be happy with that decision." He shook his head, trying not to seem too terrified. "Please, I don't want any trouble. I'm just doing my job."

His face softening slightly, Duncan looked over to where Detective Ferguson stood with his head held back, trying to stop his bleeding nose. The bastard was lucky he still had a nose. "I don't think he cares who goes in what car at the moment."

Knowing he wasn't going to win, the officer looked at the other one who shrugged his shoulders. "Okay, but don't cause problems."

Duncan nodded, and then with a slight tug, he broke the handcuffs off his wrist handing them to the surprised officer. "Didn't want it to look like you took these off me, and they're not silver." Duncan patted him on the shoulder before walking around the car to open the door and climb in.

"Are you nuts?" Pam frowned at him after he slammed the door shut. "You just hit a detective."

"After three months, that is all you have to say to me?" Duncan frowned back at her.

"At the moment...yes." Pam looked away.

"Lean forward," Duncan demanded, but when she ignored him, he grasped her shoulders, moving her in the position he wanted her. Just as he did with his handcuffs, hers were broken and tossed onto the floor.

Pam rubbed her wrists glancing up at him. "Thank you."

"You're welcome." Duncan's golden eyes roamed her face, and his fingers burned to touch the softness of her cheek. "Why did you run?" The deepness of his voice filled the police cruiser.

Wrapping the too-large jacket around herself like a protective cloak, Pam shivered. "This isn't the time or place, Duncan."

"This is definitely the place, and three months ago was the goddamn time." Anger vibrated from his voice. "I have been searching everywhere for you. Not a minute has gone by that I wasn't looking for you."

Turning from him, she watched an officer walk toward the cruiser. "Then you wasted your time because as soon as possible, I'll be gone again." She finished the cruel words, squeezing her eyes tight.

"The hell you will," Duncan growled down the back of her neck. "You are mine, and I *will not* let you go this time."

Her lips curved sadly. "Soon, you'll be the one tossing me away." Her words were spoken with such conviction it surprised Duncan.

"Never!" The word was spoken softly, but with certainty before he moved away as the officer got in the car.

*****

Pam followed the officer, who had not said a word about her no-handcuffed state, into what she figured was an interrogation room. She sat in the chair Duncan pulled out for her.

"Mr. Roark, you can't stay in here," the officer stated, looking up at the camera, hoping to find some help with the situation.

Pulling out a chair across from Pam at the small table, Duncan made himself at home. "I'm not going anywhere."

"Listen, sir, I don't want any problems, but you cannot stay in here. I have the utmost respect for you and the Warriors, but it's the rules. You hit an officer and have to be processed," the officer stated, starting to sweat in earnest. Taking his hat off, he swiped his forehead.

"What is *he* doing in here?" Detective Ferguson demanded, sounding funny with what looked like two Kotex stuck up his nose. "Get him out of here, now. I'm pressing assault charges."

"Then you better bring an army, because I'm not budging from this room." Duncan stood, rolling his shoulders.

Armed officers rushed into the room with guns drawn. Pam also stood, taking in the situation. "If you release him and drop all charges, I will tell you everything you want to know." Pam took a step toward Duncan.

"Get back." Duncan nudged her away, his eyes daring anyone to make a move while she was in the way.

"Shut up, Roark," Pam growled as she walked forward again.

"You're crazy," Detective Ferguson sneered. "I'm not dropping charges on this maniac. He attacked me."

"No, he punched you in the face." Pam shook her head. "If he would have attacked you, you'd be dead."

"Get him the hell out of here." The detective stepped out of the way so the officers could do their jobs. "I don't care how you do it, but get him behind bars now."

Pam walked forward, her hands outstretched. "You do, and I will go to my grave without speaking a word about what I know, and what I know is something that no one else does."

Detective Ferguson's eyes brightened. With his run for mayor, something like this could boost his votes. He wanted the son of a bitch that killed Sheriff Bowman behind bars, but anything extra could seal the deal on him becoming mayor. "We can make you talk."

Pam frowned, shaking her head. "For almost a year I was tortured by the man you're looking for. You can make me do *nothing*."

The officers dropped their guns slightly at her words, looking at the man calling the shots. "Take him out and drop all charges," he told the officer that brought them on.

"I want to see it in writing." Pam didn't back down. "And I want him out of here, but not until I see that you have dropped all charges."

"Now wait a minute." Duncan was stuck between being a proud son of a bitch, watching her call the shots, but annoyed as hell that she was calling his shots. "I'm not going anywhere."

"Then I say nothing," she tossed over her shoulder at him. "And what I have to say, the Warriors also need to hear. So, it's my way or no way."

"How do I know this isn't just a ploy for me to drop charges?" Detective Ferguson eyed her suspiciously.

Duncan watched as Pam's back went stiff before she glanced over her shoulder at him, an apology in her eyes. Slowly, her eyes lowered as she looked away and faced front, pulling the large jacket off with shaking arms. She held the jacket with one hand, her head down toward the floor. He watched her take a deep breath before lifting her head to a proud angle.

Detective Ferguson looked down at her stomach then back to her face. "What does your being pregnant have to do with anything?"

Frowning, because from the back she looked as she always had, Duncan took a step to the side, and sure enough, her stomach was rounded. He lifted his gaze to her face, watching as she lifted her hand. Duncan couldn't see what she was doing, but when she dropped her hand, every officer in the room gasped and stepped back, as well as Detective Ferguson.

Duncan grabbed and turned her to face him, her eyes downcast. Slowly, her gaze again came up to meet his. "I'm so sorry. I never wanted to hurt you." A single blood tear slipped from her one golden eye.

Chapter 4

"Tell me again." Sid walked next to Jared as they followed Damon and Sloan into the police station. "Because I don't believe that Duncan 'Do Everything By The Book' Roark punched a detective. I mean, I seriously think I have a man crush going on here."

"Will you shut the fuck up, Sid?" Sloan growled, stopping at the front window and slamming his hand down hard on the counter. "Where in the hell is the officer in charge?" His growl sent the clerk running for whomever she could find.

"You know, if you guys don't start treating me right, I'm putting in for a transfer." Sid leaned against the wall, arms crossed. "I really feel harassed with all the 'shut the fuck up, Sid' comments. I mean, where's the brotherly love stuff we're supposed to have for each other, because I sure as hell ain't feeling it."

"Does he ever shut the fuck up?" Sloan asked Damon and Jared, his legendary temper bubbling just below the surface.

"Nope," Jared answered, not even looking at Sid, whom he knew was grinning like an idiot.

The clerk rushed back, breathing hard. "I'm sorry, I can't find him anywhere. Can I help you with something?"

Sloan sighed in aggravation. "One of my Warriors was arrested…"

"Yes, but the charges have been dropped on Duncan Roark." She hurriedly informed them.

"Dropped?" Sloan frowned.

"Yes, Detective Ferguson dropped all charges," she replied, looking a

29

little more at ease.

"Then where is Duncan Roark?" Sloan demanded.

"I swear I'm seeing more of you Warriors today than I have in the whole time we've been working with you." Officer Rosen walked up behind the clerk buzzing them in. "How you doing, Sloan?"

"Actually, Pete, I've been better." Sloan followed him. "What the hell is going on?"

Pete actually chuckled. "Now ain't that the question of the day."

The Warriors followed the older officer down the hall to a room where Duncan stood bent with both hands on a table, staring intently into a computer screen.

No one said a word. By the look of Duncan's profile, they knew something was seriously wrong. The four Warriors surrounded him, looking over his shoulder. Pam sat; her chair scooted back from the table to make room for her growing stomach.

Of course, Sid was the first to break the silence. "Son of a bitch. Who's the daddy?" Jared and Damon grimaced, waiting for Duncan to blow. When Duncan remained silent, not even acknowledging their presence, Sid decided to take it a step further. "At least now you know what kind of woman she is. I mean, you wasted three months of your forever life looking for a woman who screwed-"

Duncan had him up against the wall with a knife to his throat so fast the others were just now reacting. Nose-to-nose with Sid, Duncan's eyes flashed black instantly.

"You will never speak of Pam without respect again, you son of a bitch." Duncan nicked Sid's neck with the knife. "I will slit you from ear-to-ear without hesitation. And to answer your question of who the father of her child is, well, he has a knife held to your fucking throat. Any more questions?" The last words were hissed as the knife pressed a little deeper.

"Ah no, think that covers everything." Sid's eyes also turned black, but his tone held no aggression. "Now can you remove that blade from my throat?"

With one last warning glare, Duncan removed the knife, flipping it easily in his hand. No one was more adept with knives or swords than Duncan Roark was, and when he brought them out, everyone who knew him knew it was serious business.

Damon was at the monitor, ignoring the drama behind him. He knew Sloan and Jared would not let Duncan kill Sid even if the dumbass deserved it. Leaning closer, he frowned. "Jesus!" His eyes met Duncan's. "She's a half-breed."

Sloan pushed him out of the way. "That's impossible." At that moment, Pam looked up at the camera for a split second as if hearing him and showing him how possible it really was.

*****

Pam looked away from the fake fire alarm where she knew the camera was, and wondered absently why they tried to hide it - everybody knew they were being taped. God, she felt sick, but she willed it back. She knew Duncan was watching. She didn't want him to know what she went through. Even knowing it wasn't her fault, she felt ashamed and didn't want to see the look of pity in his golden eyes. She loved him, had loved him after he took such good care of her during her recovery from the car accident she and Nicole had been involved in. Her feelings for him had happened so fast, totally taking her by surprise because Duncan was so not her type. He was gorgeous, yes, but he was too subdued for her tastes, or so she thought. Where he was quiet and responsible, she was loud and an in-your-face type of girl…or had been that way before things went bad.

"Can you turn that off?" Pam nodded toward the camera.

"No, Ms. Braxton." Detective Ferguson peered down his long nose at her. "I cannot. From here on out, I will be the one asking the questions."

Not comfortable with his attitude, Pam clasped her hands together tightly. The old Pam would have told the arrogant ass to curb his attitude, but that Pam was buried deep. She would find that part of herself again, but today wasn't going to be the day. Today she felt too raw.

"Who is the father?" Detective Ferguson stood close to her, crowding her with intimidation. "Is it Kenny Lawrence's?"

"What does that have to do with Sheriff Bowman?" Pam frowned, her arm automatically going to her stomach.

"Answer the question, Ms. Braxton." He regarded her critically.

"I refuse to answer that question as it has nothing to do with Sheriff Bowman." Pam stood her ground, but jumped when he slammed his hand down on the table in front of her.

"You do not have the right to refuse anything." His loud tone made her cringe.

"And that is where you're wrong detective." Sloan Murphy walked into the room like he owned the place. "She has every right to refuse to answer any question. As she is a half-breed, she is under the VC Council Protection. I will be sitting in on the rest of this little interview. I suggest you stick with your questions about the murder of Sheriff Bowman, or this interview is over."

Detective Fergusons eyes narrowed in disdain. "You have no right barging in here. I'm conducting official business which does not involve the VC Council."

"As stated, she is a half-breed and is under our protection, so ask your questions, but be very careful of the subject," Sloan warned, his eyes also narrowed.

"I am really starting to not like you Warriors very much," he spat out in disgust.

"The feeling is mutual." Sloan's lip curled. "At this very moment, three Warriors are holding back one seriously upset Warrior who wants to tear you apart. I believe you've already met him when his fist connected with your face. So I suggest you be more polite and respectful to Ms. Braxton with your questions."

"When was the last time you saw Kenny Lawrence?" Detective Ferguson touched his swollen nose before he spat his question out, his focus back on Pam.

"The night of Sheriff Bowman's murder," Pam answered, feeling a little more at ease with Sloan in the room.

"You have not had contact with him since that night?" His eyebrows rose unbelievably. "Not even to tell him about the baby?"

"Interview is over." Sloan walked up to Pam to pull her chair out for her.

"If I find out you are lying and have seen Kenny Lawrence, I will lock you up to where you won't see the light of day for a long time." The detective pointed at her.

Pam stopped in front of the detective. "If I see the bastard, you will be the first to know." Pam took a step closer with a hiss. "I will have his bloody corpse brought to your doorstep."

Feeling a tug on her arm, she let Sloan Murphy lead her away and out of the room. Turning the corner, she came face to face with Duncan. Wrapping her arms around her stomach, her eyes automatically went to the floor, shame flaming across her face.

"Bring her back to headquarters…soon," Sloan said from behind her, before walking away.

A large hand gripped her chin gently making her flinch. "Never look away from me in shame." His deep spoken words penetrated her fear. "And know, I would cut off my own hands before they would ever bring you pain."

Raising her mismatched eyes to his, she couldn't hold back the flood of tears. She swiped them away angrily, hating them. She was sick of tears. She was just so sick of it all. "Are you just going to be something else I have to try to survive? Because in all honesty, I don't think I can survive much more."

Duncan's eyes darkened slightly at her words. "I will remove myself from you if I ever cause you pain of any kind." He backed away slightly as if waiting for her to make the final decision - if she was going to accept him.

For the short time she had known Duncan Roark, the one thing she truly knew about him was that he was a brutally honest and honorable man. If there was anyone she could trust, it was him. Knowing the only way to find her way back to herself, she had to take the first step in healing. Holding in the sobs of fear, anger, wanting and pain, she rushed to him. Wrapping her arms around him tightly, she let everything go.

Duncan held her just as tight, absorbing her sobs of pain, all the while keeping his own emotions in check. Never had he wanted to kill anyone more than he wanted to kill the son of a bitch who had broken this woman. "I've got you," he whispered. "I've got you."

*****

He didn't know how long he stood holding Pam in his arms. It was as if time stood still. His large hand cupped her head to his chest while his other rubbed small comforting circles on her back. He had never been a sensitive man, but with her, this felt so right. She was where she belonged, in his arms.

Feeling the presence of someone, he glanced up to look into Sid's eyes. "What do you want?"

Sid actually seemed to be without words as he shuffled from one foot to the other, his hands deep in the pockets of his jeans. "I just wanted to apologize." Sid slid his gaze from Duncan to Pam. "Sometimes things just come out of my damn mouth before I can pull them back. I never meant anything…"

"It's forgotten." Duncan nodded, but frowned when Pam started to pull away from him. He wasn't ready to let her go. "Can you drive my car back and we'll catch a ride with Jared?"

"Not a problem." Sid caught the keys Duncan tossed at him. Taking one last glance at Pam, Sid looked like he wanted to say something more, but he turned and walked away.

Duncan kept his eyes on Pam who had wiped her tears away, and stood staring at his chest. He gave her a minute to compose herself, but as soon as Jared walked up, she stiffened, and her composure crumbled.

"Hey, Sid said you wanted to ride with me." Jared spoke to Duncan, but his eyes were on Pam's back.

Before Duncan could say a word, Pam turned so fast and was in Jared's arms, hugging him so tightly, it surprised both Warriors. "I'm so sorry," Pam pleaded. "Please don't hate me."

Jared's eyes met Duncan's briefly before he pulled Pam away from him so he could look down into her face. "I could never hate you, Pamster." He smiled when she snorted at the nickname he had started calling her before all hell broke loose. "You saved lives the night at the Sand Trap and that of my mate, so if anything, I thank you."

Duncan watched Pam fight with her emotions. "Come on." Duncan wrapped his arm around her. "Let's get out of here."

Pam nodded, still not looking either of them in the eye.

"You want me to take you to your place?" Jared let them pass.

"Yes." Duncan opened the door, but stopped when Pam shook her head.

"No." Pam answered right after. "I heard Sloan say he wanted me at headquarters, and the quicker I can get this over with, the faster I can get my life ba-" Pam looked down at her hand resting protectively over her protruding stomach. "Started."

"Are you sure?" Duncan and Jared asked at the same time, both sounding protective and wanting what was best for her. Duncan frowned at Jared.

"Yeah, I'm sure." Pam replied, sounding a little more like herself. "It's time I face this. I'm tired of running."

As soon as the three walked out the door of the police station, bright flashes and a rush of reporters pressed forward with cameras and microphones, all shouting at once.

"Is it true you're a half-breed and pregnant?" One man asked, shoving his microphone past other reporters and almost hitting Pam in the face.

"Ms. Braxton." Another reporter yelled over the group. "Are you keeping the baby? Is it going to be human?"

"Who's the father? Is he human?" A woman reporter, not caring she was being shoved and pushed, shouted above everyone else.

Duncan shielded Pam, pushing her behind him. Just behind the reporters, Duncan spotted Detective Ferguson standing a few feet away. Their eyes met, and with a salute of his hand, the bastard turned away, getting into his car wearing a smug grin that Duncan swore one day soon he would be wiping off the bastard's face.

Chapter 5

Finally, they made it to headquarters. Jared had sped, ran red lights and broke every traffic law known to man to get away from the reporters. "I think we lost them." Jared parked, glancing at Pam and Duncan in the rearview mirror. "What the fuck was that?"

"It was the detective. He's trying to flush out Kenny." Pam answered, looking at Duncan. "I'm right, aren't I?"

Duncan cursed but nodded. "That's exactly what the bastard is doing."

"I have to get out of here." Pam went for the door, struggling to get it open, but Duncan stopped her. "He'll find me here. I have to go."

"You're not going anywhere." Duncan held her tighter when she struggled. "You're safe. He's not going to get anywhere near you."

"No, you don't understand. He swore to me if I went to you, he would kill you." Her whole body shook. Her eyes, wide with fear, looked from Duncan to Jared. "All of you."

"I hope to hell the son of a bitch tries." Jared smirked, but it didn't quite reach his eyes.

"Why won't you listen to me?" she pleaded with Duncan. "He *can* and *will* kill you."

Anger slashed across Duncan's face. Did she have such low confidence in him to keep her safe? "You're wrong, Pam." Duncan tried to keep the anger out of his voice. "Kenny comes anywhere near you, he's as good as dead."

"It's not me I'm worried about." Pam gritted her teeth with frustration. "He won't kill me now, not with me being pregnant, but he will kill anyone who helps me."

"What makes you so sure the bastard can take us out?" Jared had turned to look at her, his tone angry.

Pam swallowed hard, glancing away. "Because, he almost did."

"What?" Jared shared a look with Duncan.

Rubbing her stomach, Pam nervously glanced out the back window. "I left him when I found out what he had been doing, but he caught me. I was coming to you to tell you what I had found out." Pam stared at Duncan, her eyes caressing his face. "He warned me that if I ever betrayed him, he would kill every Warrior as well as their mates. He had pictures of you all."

The silence in the car was deafening. "What were the pictures, honey?" Duncan reached out and squeezed her hand gently.

The pained expression on her face wrinkled her forehead "He had pictures of all of you with a red laser mark on your head. He said that if I left him or said a word about what I had found, he would kill you all. I couldn't let that happen." Her eyes finally met his. "I couldn't let that happen. I had to stay."

Jared's black eyes met Duncan's once again before he climbed out of the driver's seat, slamming the door.

Pam jumped at the noise. "I'm sorry." Her head bowed before his. "I wanted so much to come to you, but…"

Duncan grasped her chin bringing her face to his. "Listen to me." He waited until she looked up. "Nothing is going to happen to any of us. We are going to find him, but until then, you are safe and you are not going anywhere."

"But…" Pam's eyes once again widened with fear.

"You have protected us, even saved our lives once." Duncan stroked her chin with his thumb as a small smile tilted his full lips. "Now it's time for us to return the favor."

"Why are you doing this?" Pam shook her head in disbelief. "After everything that's happened, how can you even stand to look at me?"

"You are burned into my memory. Everything I look upon, I see you." Duncan leaned closer, slowly so not to frighten her. "Not even removing my eyes would take your image from me. I love and have loved you, Pam Braxton. I was a fool to let you walk away from me."

Pam's hand reached up to his face, but stopped before touching. "I'm not the same." Pam pulled her hand back. "I've changed. I don't know if I can love again." She caught the sob that escaped her trembling lips.

Duncan reached out and grasped her hand, placing it on his cheek. "I don't care."

"I don't want to hurt you." Her voice was pleading. "I'm so afraid. I don't want to be afraid anymore."

"I've got you." He repeated his oath to her, his large hand gently grasping the back of her head, cradling her next to his chest.

*****

Pam was barely holding herself together. Emotions trembled through her body, making her legs shaky. She hated the helpless feeling that plagued her. Her mental state wasn't much better; it flitted from wanting to be strong then back to wanting to run and hide so everything just went away. Her hopes were that everyone forgot what had happened, and that no one would see the weakness she had displayed in her relationship with that bastard. What she wouldn't give to turn back the hands of time so she never would have gone on that first date with Kenny Lawrence. Soon everything was going to come out, and she was afraid she wouldn't be able to handle it; she was barely hanging on as it was. Glancing down at her growing stomach, she knew without a doubt, she had to hang on. She had to be strong…she had no choice. She had to handle it. This wasn't just about her anymore.

Feeling the strength of Duncan's large hand where it rested on the small of her back gave her mixed emotions. Would he hate her once he found out how weak she had been? Would he look at her in disgust? Could she handle his rejection? Soon she would find out the answer to all of those questions, and that thought made her stomach clench in pain. Grabbing her stomach, she moaned under her breath.

"Are you okay?" Duncan stopped her, turning her toward him, his golden eyes filled with worry.

Pam could only nod. The large lump in the back of her throat prevented her voicing the lie. She was far from okay.

"Are you in pain?" His concern echoed in the deep rumble of his voice.

Swallowing hard, Pam shook her head.

"Do not lie to me." Duncan frowned, but kept his voice low without anger.

Knowing she had to say something, she cleared her tight throat. "Just a little hungry," she finally answered. It wasn't a total lie. Her stomach felt hollow, and she knew that wasn't good. Even though food was the last thing she wanted, she needed to eat.

Duncan stared at her a second longer before nodding. "Never hesitate to ask me for anything you need." He gently squeezed her arms before grasping her hand. "Let's get you something to eat before we talk to Sloan. I'm sure Sid has something in the kitchen."

Only having been at the VC Headquarters twice, Pam was totally lost in the maze of hallways. She let Duncan lead the way, but stopped cold before he pulled her into a kitchen and dining area where people she lied to could be. Taking a deep breath, she stepped inside to face whatever came her way.

All noise stopped as everyone stared at her. Pam's eyes started to go to the floor, but she spotted Nicole and couldn't look away. Even though she had talked to Nicole briefly over the phone the last three months, so much had been left unsaid. Nicole stood and walked around the table to stand a few feet away from Pam, her eyes taking in her now one golden eye before going straight to her stomach.

"And everyone thought I'd be the first one knocked up." Nicole broke the silence. "Looks like you finally got the boobs you always wanted."

"Yeah, no more training bras for me," Pam replied, a laugh and sob trembling from her lips as a tiny piece of her heart mended.

Nicole took two steps toward her and opened her arms. "If you don't get over here and hug me, I'm going to kick your ass, breed."

Pam rushed into her friend's arms, holding tight. She had been so lonely for so long that she soaked in any type of kindness.

"I'm so sorry," Pam whispered. Knowing she had held the hug too long, Pam reluctantly let go and stepped back.

"You have nothing to be sorry for." Nicole shot a frown at her, but soon was grinning excitedly. "When are you due?"

Again, Pam wanted to hug her friend. So far, her being pregnant wasn't being brought up. It was as if a dirty secret was being revealed.

As if no one said anything, it would go away. She didn't want it to go away. She was having this baby with or without the support of the ones around her. "I'm not sure. I couldn't find a doctor who would see me."

Duncan walked up beside her, placing his hand on her shoulder. "We'll find you a doctor." He nodded as if it was already done.

"I'll make some calls." Nicole winked at her, and then slapped her hands together. "My God, I'm going to be an aunt. Should I go with Auntie Nicole or just Aunt Nicole?"

"Come on. Let's see what Sid has to eat over there." Duncan rolled his eyes as he led Pam over to where Sid stood busy at the stove. She had seen him eyeing her and felt nervous approaching the Warrior she didn't know well.

"What are you craving?" Sid looked down at her, his face emotionless. "If I don't have it, I'll get it. If I don't know how to make it, I'll learn."

"Why? Is Rachael Ray having a segment on Foods Pregnant Women Crave?" Nicole snorted, heading back to her seat at the large kitchen table.

"Excuse me," Sid told Pam before glaring over the top of her head at Nicole. "Shut it, vampira."

A true smile spread across Pam's lips. She had really missed this, missed them all. She couldn't believe they were accepting her after everything. She had expected pointing fingers, not everyone acting like nothing happened.

"Whatever everybody else is having is fine." She looked away, feeling uncomfortable from his stare. Sid was one Warrior she didn't know well, so she still didn't know what to think of him.

"How do you like your steak?" Sid turned to head for the fridge.

Pam licked her lips, her stomach cramping. "Rare?"

Sid frowned with a nod before looking away, grabbing the steak. "Be ready in no time. Have a seat."

Placing her beside Nicole, Duncan stayed near; actually, he hovered.

"Where's Damon?" Tessa asked, surprised the large Warrior was nowhere to be seen.

"Don't know." Nicole shrugged her shoulders. "And don't really care."

"He's at the warehouse taking over for me," Duncan answered. "I took over for him when Tessa and Nicole got arrested for breaking into your apartment."

"Are you serious?" Pam's eyes widened in shock. "Oh my God. I didn't think. I'm sorry."

"It's no big deal." Nicole shook her head. "Well, at least to me it wasn't any big deal because I knew you gave me permission, but hubby got a little upset because I had been talking to you without telling anyone."

"But that was my fault. I made you promise." Pam glared at Duncan. "He shouldn't be mad at her."

Sid stepped up before Duncan could reply. After placing a large rare steak in front of Pam, he stepped back, watching her closely. "Rare enough?"

Looking at the blood streaming from the huge hunk of meat had the saliva in Pam's mouth thick. "Perfect," she replied, her voice hoarse with thirst and her one golden eye black with hunger. Not able to control herself, she picked up the steak with her hands, pushing it into her mouth, sucking the much-needed blood down her throat. A lone blood tear escaped one eye, as a clear tear escaped the other, both shimmering down her cheeks in embarrassment. She was starving and not for food.

"Whoa, slow down, honey." Duncan reached for her hand, but stopped when she growled. He looked at her in surprise. "Pam, slow down. You're going to choke."

"Pretty hard to get the blood you need without fangs." Sid eyed her. "What happened to your fangs, Pam?"

"What the fuck?" Duncan cursed, forcing her hands and steak away from her mouth. Blood colored her full lips. Slowly, he ran his thumb over her upper lip, lifting it slightly. Shocked, he looked into her eyes. "This is the only blood you've had? What happened? Did your fangs not grow out when you changed?"

Staring into his eyes, she wanted to lie. How could she tell him the truth? Would they look at her different? Would they see her as weak? Pulling her face away, she wiped her mouth.

"Yeah, they grew in." She scooted her chair away from him and stood. "But Kenny didn't want anyone to know I had been turned, so he had me wear contacts, and he had my fangs filed down." She didn't mention he'd had it done without any numbing; she kept that to herself.

"That son of a bitch!" Duncan slammed his hand down on the table in anger so quickly Pam jumped, covering her face.

Realizing what she had done, and the look on everyone's face, she knew she couldn't do this. She needed to be alone, away from people until she could get this fear under control.

"I can't do this." Pam walked backward towards the door. "I really can't do this." She turned, running out of the room.

Duncan chased her down, catching her easily. "You are not running from me again." He picked her up carefully, carrying her away from the kitchen up a set of steps.

"I'm too messed up, Duncan." Pam pushed lightly on his chest. "Just let me go."

Looking down at her, he stopped in front of a door. "I will never let you go." Holding her with one hand, he opened the door with the other, kicking it the rest of the way open. "You are not alone in this anymore. You are mine, and I will always be yours."

Chapter 6

Duncan sat her on the bed he had never laid in. This was just a place he stored clean clothes and showered. His home was a few miles away, which he would take her to soon. Leaving her, he went to the bathroom to grab a towel. Laying it over her legs, he knelt down in front of her. Raising his wrist to his mouth, his fangs gleamed in the light as he bit down on his own wrist. He watched the raging war in her eyes. His blood ran down his arm, dripping onto the towel, but he didn't force her to take his blood. He waited patiently for her to make the decision.

Slowly, she reached, her fingertips touching his, her eyes leaving his wrist to meet his. "Thank you."

His other hand palmed her cheek, his thumb brushing back and forth against her softness; still he waited. Finally, her hands gripped his, bringing his bloodied wrist to her mouth. He held back a moan as her tongue snaked out, taking a taste. Her lips latched on his wrist; he felt the pull of her mouth taking his blood and damn, didn't that make him feel more like a man than he ever had. His protectiveness tripled at that moment. No one would ever harm this woman again.

Duncan lost track of time as he watched her take his blood, binding her to him more closely than anyone had ever been. Feeling her pull away, he stopped her. "Take as much as you need."

Grabbing the towel, she wiped her mouth, and then cleaned his wrist, which was already healing. "I'm fine. I don't want to take too much."

"You can have it all." Duncan smiled at her.

"Then you'd be a shriveled-up Warrior." Pam grinned, feeling better than she had in a long time.

Seeing the ragged edges of her fangs where they'd been filed down,

47

made Duncan frown. Pam closed her lips, covering her mouth with her hand. "Don't." He pulled her hand away. "Don't hide anything from me."

"It's ugly." Pam grimaced. "As soon as I get a job and some insurance, I'll get them fixed."

"If you want them fixed, then we will get them fixed." Duncan grabbed the bloodied towel, throwing it toward the bathroom.

Pam shook her head. "I don't expect you to do everything for me, Duncan." She rubbed her full belly. "I am going to get back on my feet."

"I know that, but not alone." Duncan watched her hand run small circles over her belly.

"I'm keeping the baby."

Duncan's eyes shot up from her stomach to her face. "I wouldn't expect anything else." He watched the relief flash across her face.

Pam nodded, taking a deep breath. "I know that, it's just..." Grunting in frustration, her hands balled into fists.

"Listen to me." Duncan grabbed both of her hands, forcing her to look at him. "You are not alone in this anymore. I'm not going to sit here and say I know what you went through, but I have a pretty clear idea. Nothing, and I mean *nothing*, will stand in the way of my support for you and your baby."

"So you don't care that bastard is the father of my baby?" Pam's chin trembled.

Dropping one of her trembling hands to her lap, he placed his larger one on her bulging stomach and felt a warmth he had not felt in such a long time swarm through his body.

"This little miracle you carry is a part of you, so how can I not love the child?" He winked at her with a grin, reaching up with his other hand to cup her chin. "I have seen a lot in my lifetime, Pam Braxton, but I can tell you one thing, I have never seen anyone more beautiful than you carrying your precious child. When I look at your growing stomach, I only see the wonderful mother you will become. Nothing else matters. No one else matters. Do you understand?"

"You make me feel like I can be normal again." Pam smiled sadly. "Thank you."

"There is nothing normal about you, babe." Duncan leaned close, but slow enough not to spook her. He had to take things extremely slowly. "You are everything special." His lips touched the softness of her cheek, and he wanted to shout victory when she didn't flinch from his touch.

Pam did jump, but not because of the kiss to the cheek. "Did you feel that?" She grinned at Duncan, putting her hand on top of his and pressing down.

A large smile spread across Duncan's handsome face. "Think you got a fighter on your hands." Duncan laughed when the baby kicked again. "Doesn't that hurt?"

"No." Pam laughed with him. "It's actually a comfortable feeling. I like feeling him move."

"Him?" Duncan ran his hand all over her stomach, wanting to feel the little fighter kick again.

Her face flushed in embarrassment. "I don't know why I keep calling him, *him*."

God, he loved seeing her like this. "Do you have names picked out?" His voice deepened. He couldn't believe he was talking to her. Hours ago, he was at a loss to where she even was.

"No, not yet. I don't even know when I'm due." She frowned. "I'm pretty big for three months, so I'm a little worried. He gave me a shot of something when he was…."

He watched as she withdrew, horror at what she was about to say hit her. He wasn't going to let her withdraw from him. "When he was what?" As hard as it was, he kept the anger out of his voice. He knew what she had been about to say, and it turned him inside out with rage.

"Raping me." After a few minutes of silence, she finally whispered what she needed to say out loud.

The anguish in her voice and eyes tore him in two. "I'm sorry." He did not look away. "I'm so sorry."

She nodded, quickly looking away. "I need that vial. Can you take me to my old apartment tomorrow?"

"I'll find it," he assured her.

"No, I need to do this. If I don't start facing what happened and dealing with it, I never will."

Duncan nodded, but wanted to protest. His need to protect her was immense, but wanting to help her heal was greater. "I'll take you."

Before Pam could respond, someone pounded on the door. Duncan stood with a reluctant grunt as answer.

"Sloan wants to see us." Jared stepped into the room with Tessa by his side. "Tessa will sit with Pam so they can catch up." Jared winked at Pam.

"But I thought he wanted to talk to me." Pam stood holding her back.

"Just relax." Duncan walked over to the bathroom, disappearing for a second before reappearing. "I put a towel on the sink if you want a bath. The second drawer in the dresser has shirts if you need something to change into."

Duncan wanted to take her in his arms, assuring her that everything would be okay, that she would be okay, but he knew he had to take things slowly. He couldn't crowd her; he couldn't push her away. With one last glance her way, he followed Jared out of the room.

The two Warriors headed down the hall to Sloan's office. Each step away from Pam he took, the more rage he felt.

"You okay, bro?" Jared eyed him.

"No." Duncan's teeth clenched tight. "And I won't be until that son of a bitch is dead."

"Did she tell you what happened?" Jared ventured, but seriously didn't know if he wanted to know.

"She didn't have to. I can see it every time I look into her eyes." Duncan slammed open Sloan's door harder than he intended. Sid and Damon stood behind Sloan, their eyes plastered on the big screen across the room.

Jared and Duncan stopped, also watching as the camera zoomed in on Pam and Duncan, his arm protectively around her, pushing her behind him. "Shit."

"I know." Sid cocked his eyebrow. "The camera adds ten pounds. You look like shit."

Sloan ignored Sid's smartass remark. "Shit? Shit is the only thing you can think to say?" Throwing the remote on his desk, it skidded off, hitting the floor. "Goddammit! Didn't one of you think you should warn me about this?"

"I was a little busy." Duncan replied, more used to Sloan's temper than anyone else in the room.

"Oh, you were a little busy. Well, let me tell you about busy." Sloan tossed one hand up in the air before slamming it down on his desk, rattling the one picture on the wall, his eyes blacker than midnight. "I've been on the fucking phone since I've been back. I've had government officials calling me, shitting themselves thinking we are going to breed like rabbits."

Sid snickered, opening his mouth to respond, but Damon elbowed him hard, shaking his head.

"How in the hell did the media get hold of this so fast?" Sloan asked them all, not picking one individual to ask.

"Detective Ferguson is trying to flush out Kenny Lawrence," Duncan growled, remembering the salute the asshole had tossed his way.

"So he's using Pam being pregnant as bait." Sloan nodded, getting the point real quick. "The fucking bastard."

Someone knocked on the door. Sid, who was standing near, reached over and opened it. "What's up?"

Adam walked in wearing a large frown. "Have you checked the monitors out front lately? There are reporters all over the place setting up camp."

"Let me take care of this." Sid slid his hand through his blonde hair.

Sloan looked around at the group with a long drawn-out sigh.

"Surprisingly, you seem to be my only choice at the moment."

"What the hell does that mean?" Jared stepped forward.

"I mean what I said." Sloan cocked his eyebrow. "I can't chance Damon decapitating anyone who pisses him off at the moment; my hands are full. You, being newly mated, don't have a grasp on your emotions quite yet. And I hope to hell I don't have to explain why I can't send Duncan out there."

"I'm your man." Sid grinned, flashing fang. "I swear I'll make you proud."

Sloan watched him walk out the door fixing his shirt and hair, Adam following behind him. "He drives me fucking nuts." Everyone else nodded their heads in agreement. "Hope that wasn't a mistake."

"Probably the biggest you've ever made," Jared snorted, shaking his head as he glanced at the television waiting to see Sid's ugly mug pop up.

"Where's Pam now?" Sloan dropped the subject of Sid, getting back on track.

"In my room with Tessa." Duncan glanced at Damon. "Where's Nicole?"

"Not sure." Damon glanced away, his frown growing.

"You still haven't talked to her since this afternoon." Jared's attitude got nasty. "What the fuck is wrong with you?"

"Let it go, Jared." Damon growled with a sneer.

"Why are you being such an asshole?" Jared snarled back.

"Fuck you." Damon took a step forward, getting in Jared's face. "You got your own woman to worry about, stop worrying about mine."

"I wouldn't have to worry if you'd step up, man." Jared also took a step.

"Both of you back off!" Sloan's angry voice was enough to stop them from coming to blows. "What the hell is going on? Shit is getting real, and all you guys want to do is tear each other up. I seriously don't need my Warriors fighting like high school pussies with hard-ons."

"My bad." Jared nodded toward Damon who nodded back; both wore frowns still eyeing each other.

"Yeah," Damon replied with a nod back.

Sloan rolled his eyes before looking at Duncan. "I've put a call in to someone who might be able to help Pam. He's a hell of a doctor, and I've asked him to help us out. He is also interested in the half-breeds."

"Good." Duncan felt a little more relief. "Now, if that's all, I'd really like to get back."

"Did the son of a bitch really file her fangs down?" Sloan's eyes darkened as he asked the question then cursed when Duncan's eyes flashed black, which was answer enough. "Has she fed?"

"I took care of her." Duncan headed toward the door, feeling that was enough information on the subject. "Tomorrow I'm taking her to her old apartment. Hopefully, we can find some answers."

"That place has been combed over already," Sloan reminded him.

"She says she knows places he hid stuff. She hasn't been back since she first took off - that we know of - and neither has he." Duncan opened the door. "He gave her a shot of something, and we need to find that vial. It may be what they were going to use on Tessa for breeding. I don't know much about women and pregnancy stuff, but she looks damn big for three months."

"She's one tough woman." Jared added, though there was worry in his golden eyes. "She'll be fine."

"She better be," Duncan growled, walking out. He slammed the door behind him.

Sloan turned to Damon and Jared, but before he could say anything, his eyes landed on the television. "Fuck!" Sloan cursed as he watched Sid physically carrying a reporter off the property.

*****

"Damn, there's more of the bastards." Adam walked out the front door next to Sid. Cameras flashed as video cameras started rolling, reporters falling all over themselves trying to get up close.

Sid's eyes traveled the length of the yard; trucks with large satellite dishes lined the street. The VC Council had always had an open door policy. Anyone needing help could walk right up to their door, but this was ridiculous and it pissed him off.

Forgetting about wanting to look good in front of the cameras, his protective instinct for Pam surged to the surface. *Where the fuck were these douchebags during the height of children being adopted and turned for vampire blood? Now they show interest in Pam being a half-breed and pregnant, which could put her in danger, if it hadn't already.*

"You have exactly five minutes to remove yourselves from this property," Sid called out, his eyes scanning every face.

"Is Pam Braxton here?" One reporter shouted as microphones pressed forward. "Can she give a statement on her condition and who the father is?"

Grinding his teeth, Sid took a step closer. "Don't make me repeat myself." His eyes focused on the asshole who ignored his orders before looking out over the crowd. "I really don't like repeating myself."

"Is the father one of the Warriors?" The man shouted over other reporters asking pretty much the same question, just rephrased.

Sid growled, grabbed the reporter's shirt and picked him up to his face level. "Did I mention I don't like repeating myself, Adam?"

"Yes, I believe you did." Both Adam and Sid grinned, showing large fangs. The reporter Sid held paled, and the rest took a huge step back. "If they don't start leaving, start hauling their asses off the property."

Adam rubbed his hands together, eyeing a few who looked like they wanted to push their luck. "Yes, sir."

With one arm, Sid took the sputtering reporter to the edge of the property, tossing him to the street. "Do not let me catch you anywhere near this place again." With that warning, Sid turned to see Adam walking behind the rest of the group as they all made their way, without help, off the property.

"Did you get that?" The reporter asked his cameraman before turning back to Sid. "You will hear from my lawyer."

"And you will hear from ours for trespassing," Sid shot back without turning around. His eyes were on Sloan, Jared and Damon, who stood a few feet away watching.

"What?" Sid threw his arms out. "I didn't bite, decapitate or kick anyone's ass. I just escorted the asshole off the property. I asked politely for them to leave, but they didn't heed the request, and I don't like repeating myself"

"He really doesn't," Jared agreed with a smirk. Sloan looked ready to kill something.

"Do I need to call in our lawyer?" Sloan growled, looking at all the cameras pointing at them from the street.

"Probably," Sid replied, walking past them.

"Dammit, Sid." Sloan grabbed his arm. "Don't you have any control? I trusted you to take care of the problem."

"And that's what I did. I dealt with the problem. They put one of ours in danger, they deal with me. I'm nice until it's time not to be nice. Those reporters just being here threatens Pam, who Duncan adores, and that just won't do. You know I'm right." Sid snapped his arm away. "And that fucking reporter is still breathing, so that should tell you how much control I had."

"I think our boy is growing up." Jared shook his head, a grin tipping his lips as he watched Sid walk away.

"Shut the fuck up, Kincaid." Sloan slammed his way into the compound, his mood dark.

Chapter 7

Duncan couldn't get back to his room fast enough. The thought of Pam disappearing again played in the back of his mind. He'd just got her back, and his every instinct shouted for him to hurry. Finally making it to the door, he pushed it open so fast Tessa jumped from the chair she was sitting in.

"Where is she?" he demanded, quickly sweeping the room before his darkening eyes landed back on Tessa.

"She's getting a bath." Tessa frowned. "What's wrong?"

"Nothing." Feeling a little foolish, Duncan shut the door glancing at the bathroom. "Is she okay?"

"Well, she was until she saw that." Tessa nodded toward the television.

Duncan looked at the television and saw reporters still surrounding the compound. The camera was going from a reporter back to Sloan, Jared and Damon who stood guard, still as stone. At least the volume was turned down. "Damn," he cursed, grabbing the remote and clicking it off.

"She got upset and wanted to leave so she wouldn't cause any more trouble for us, but I talked her into getting a bath and relaxing." Tessa walked toward the door to leave. "She doesn't have any clothes."

"She wants me to take her to her old apartment tomorrow," Duncan replied taking another glance at the bathroom. "She can pick up some stuff then."

"They aren't going to fit. She needs maternity clothes." Tessa gave him a sympathetic pat on the arm.

Duncan ran his hand down his face. "I should have known that," he sighed.

"Go easy on yourself, Duncan. Finding her was mind blowing enough, but her being pregnant has thrown everyone." Tessa leaned closer. "She needs you more than ever now, so go to her. She's been in there for a while."

Nodding, Duncan watched Tessa close the door softly behind her. His eyes automatically went to the door that separated him from Pam. Two steps and he was standing before it, rubbing his hands together. Raising his hand, he went to knock, but stopped. Cursing silently, he wondered what the hell was wrong with him. He was a fucking Warrior, not some nervous ass kid crushing on his first girl. Rolling his eyes, he knocked quickly and waited. When Pam didn't answer, he frowned and knocked again louder. "Pam?"

Without thought, he grabbed the knob and twisted, opening the door. Pam lay sleeping in the bathtub, her face unlined without stress, turned peacefully toward him. His eyes traveled from her face to the creamy swells of her breast which disappeared in the cooling water. A smile tipped his lips spotting her rounded stomach swelling out of the water. She was absolutely beautiful. Moving toward her, he noticed goose bumps gliding across her arms. Reaching down, he felt her cold soft skin. "Pam." He kept his voice low so not to startle her. "Pam, honey." He shook her arm slightly.

"No." She shrugged him away sloshing water, one creamy breast exposed to his view.

Keeping his eyes averted as best he could, he shook her a little harder. "Pam, wake up." His voice rose trying to get her to wake.

Pam came awake with a vengeance. Her arms slashed out striking out at anything, slapping him across the head. "No! Get away!" Her screams pierced his heart. "Not again, please! No!" She slipped while trying to sit up banging her head against the hard edge of the bathtub.

Doing his best to restrain her without hurting her was harder than he could ever imagine. She was slippery and scared to death. "Pam!" he shouted louder, trying to get her to snap out of the hysteria she was trapped in. He grabbed her face forcing her to look at him, letting her fist fly hitting him wherever they landed. Her eyes were unfocused, and at that second, he knew she wasn't seeing him, but seeing a nightmare happening all over again. If he ever saw that son of a bitch, he would make him suffer and beg for death. "Look at me! It's Duncan! It's me! Stop before you hurt yourself!"

After what seemed like hours, her eyes started to focus and her fists stilled. She searched his eyes, her naked body shaking from cold and fear. Duncan only held her by the upper arms to keep her balanced, so she didn't slip.

"It's me," Duncan repeated more softly. "You're safe."

Her stricken gaze landed on his cheek. A small cry escaped before she could stop it. With one hand covering her mouth, the other hovered over the long scratch mark oozing blood. "I'm so sorry." She dropped her hand without touching him.

"It's fine," Duncan reassured her, but the look in her eyes told him that it wasn't going to be fine. Reaching over, he grabbed a towel.

"It's not fine." She ignored the towel, her face twisted in anguish. "I'm not fine. This isn't fucking fine!"

"Come on, you're freezing." He carefully pulled her up, keeping his eyes on her still stricken gaze. Wrapping the towel around her, he helped her step out of the bathtub.

Pam stood shivering, holding the towel like a lifeline. "I can't do this." Pam shook her head looking panicked. "I'm not going to be able to do this."

"Do what, honey?" Duncan had no clue what she was talking about until her gaze and hand dropped to her stomach.

"Be a good mother." Tears started to flow freely down her pale cheeks. "What if I see him every time I look at the baby? What if my feelings change once the baby is born and I resent..." She couldn't finish.

"Have you ever looked at any of the children you worked with differently because they came from a drug dealing father or a deadbeat mother?" Duncan clipped her chin in his large hand, bringing her face to his. "Have you ever turned your back on a child in need?"

Swiping the tears Pam shook her head. "No."

"You have a heart of gold, Pam. What you have done for children who are not even of your blood, is beyond what a lot of others would do." Duncan's lip curved in a small smile as he placed his hand on her stomach. "This little bundle *is* of your blood, Pam. You are going to love him, or her, like no other, and as for being a good mother, honey, you already are."

"Thank you," Pam whispered still looking down at his hand before placing hers on top.

"Just stating the truth." His other hand touched her cheek; he was pleased she didn't flinch from his touch. "No need to thank me for that."

"I want *me* back." Pam leaned into his hand. "I'm so tired of being afraid, weak and unsure."

"Honey, you never left. You're still here, just a little shaken. I have never met anyone braver." Duncan's voice was strong and true. "Give yourself a little time to work through this. I'm not going anywhere and *will* be by your side."

"You're a good man, Duncan Roark," Pam sighed, feeling a little better.

"Yeah, well, let's keep it between us because if Sid or Jared find out, I'll never get any work out of them." He winked, grabbing the shirt he'd gotten for her to wear. "I'll leave you to get dressed unless you need help."

Cheeks flushed, she shook her head. "I'm fine. I'll be right out." She stopped him before he could leave. Grabbing the wet washcloth she was using, she gently wiped the blood from his cheek.

Duncan stood rigid while she wiped the blood away, her eyes focused on his lips. God knew he wanted to kiss her, but she was going to have to make the first move. As much as it pained him, she was in control. He stood perfectly still as she leaned closer. He watched the war rage in her beautiful mismatched eyes. She was so close, he could feel her raspy breath against his lips. With a feeling of victory, her lips touched his; he had definitely won the war that battled inside her. He was the victor and her lips his prize.

*****

Nicole fought her way through the massive crowd of reporters. If one more reporter shoved a microphone in her face, she was going to shove it up their ass. She was so not in the mood. Finally making it to the front door, she stopped at the sight of Damon leaning against a post, hidden from view of the street.

"Where have you been?" he asked without moving, his golden eyes flicking from her head down her body.

"I'm not in the mood for your protective macho crap, Damon." Nicole cocked her hip.

"I asked you a question," he barked.

"And I gave you an answer," she shot back.

"That wasn't an answer," he snorted. "That was you being a smartass."

"That was me being honest." She took a step toward him tilting her head with attitude. "If you can't take it, that's your problem."

"You're *my* fucking problem," he growled, grabbing her before she could move out of the way. He plastered her against the pole he had been leaning on. His lips mashed down on hers, his hand moving to tangle in her hair pushing her closer. She didn't hesitate, didn't fight. She kissed him just as fiercely. Finally, he pulled away, his eyes black with need. "Do you regret it?"

"Regret what?" Nicole's eyes, cloudy with desire, stared up into his, her chest heaving for breath.

"Marrying me?" For a brief second, his eyes shifted away. It was so fast she wondered if it had actually happened.

"No, Damon. I don't regret marrying you." Her voice was strong and sure. "I do regret that you have no confidence in me. I can take care of myself. I have been, way before you came into my life. I know that's hard for you to understand, but I feel smothered sometimes."

"You drive me crazy." He leaned over kissing her neck. "Absolutely, fucking crazy."

Nicole licked his neck before giving him a sharp bite. "Let's take this inside before we're on the six o'clock news. I'm sure those damn reporters wouldn't pass up a segment on the mating of vampires."

One eyebrow cocked, making him look sexy as hell, he whispered, "Is that what we're going to do?"

"Making up is the best part of fighting." Nicole gave him a sexy smile.

"And you have a lot to make up for."

"Oh, really?" He cupped her intimately over her jeans. "I think you have some making up to do yourself." He rubbed his thumb over her sweet spot, making her moan and squirm.

Swiping her tongue slowly across her lips, she gave him a saucy wink and cupped him, grinning as he swelled in her hand. "Oh, I plan to, Warrior."

Neither one of them heard the click of a camera.

*****

Kenny Lawrence stared at the television, his shoulders heaving. The fucking bitch was pregnant. He didn't know whether to shout in victory or smash his fist through the fucking wall. Leaning closer, he watched Pam stare shocked into the camera. Damn, she looked good, and had always been a terrific lay. Too bad the fucking cunt turned on him. He glanced over at the whore who lay across the well-used bed in the hotel room he rented weekly. It was a rundown shithole in nowhere, Kentucky, with a good supply of whores; he was sick of it. He had worked too hard to be in a place like this, and now because of that bitch, he was on the run, but not for long.

One of the half-breeds Kenny had turned and used at his beck and call, came out of the bathroom naked and ready for another go-around with the whore. Ray was dumb as a stump and would do anything he was told. The nineteen-year-old idolized Kenny and that was good, that was Kenny's plan. He needed the dumbass to trust him because he had big plans, plans that could not fail. He stopped to stare at the television.

"Hey, that's Pam and that Warrior. She looks fuckin' hot." Yeah, Ray Jones was a fry short of a happy meal.

Kenny held his hand back from smacking the little fucker. He needed to keep his cool with the guy. A sly grin tilted his lip "You think she's hot, huh?"

Realizing he had just called Kenny's ex hot, Ray stepped back. "I didn't mean anything by it."

"She is hot." Which she wouldn't be for long, Kenny thought, but he kept that to himself. "How would you like to have a go at her?"

The kid's eyes bugged out of his head. "What?"

"Yeah, I'm done with her and she likes them young." Kenny smirked. "She's a good fuck. Hell, we both might do her. You'd like that, wouldn't you?" He had noticed how Ray would watch as Kenny fucked the whore getting turned on, wanting to join in.

A wicked gleam lit his eyes. "Hell yeah I would." His excitement was showing between his legs. "When?"

Anxious little fuck. "Soon." Kenny looked back at the television. "Go fuck the whore while I make a few phone calls."

Kenny watched Pam and the bastard Warrior on the screen, Ray and the whores moaning in the background drowning out the volume. Grabbing a cell phone, he dialed information. After getting the number he needed, he turned to watch Ray take it to the whore. He unbuckled his pants.

Walking over with the cell phone still to his ear, he stood in front of the whore Ray was taking from behind. Whipping out his hardening cock, he stood still, waiting.

"Yeah, I need to speak with Detective Ferguson." Kenny grabbed the whore's head whipping it up before placing his cock to her lips. He had picked her because she had short dark hair like Pam. "I have important information on the murder of Sheriff Bowman." Kenny's eyes met Ray's and he winked. Ray winked back with a wide grin. Oh, this was too easy. Kenny's grin grew in triumph.

Chapter 8

Pam woke with a start, sitting straight up in bed confused. Her hand went to her stomach as her eyes searched for something familiar. It wasn't until her eyes met Duncan's that she felt at ease. He sat in a chair next to the bed, his legs stretched out with his booted feet propped up, one crossed over the other.

"You okay?" His stare was intense. Actually everything about him was intense.

She nodded then frowned. "Have you sat there all night watching me sleep?" She barely remembered making it to bed after leaving the bath. Her face heated when she remembered she had kissed him. Her eyes went to his lips which curved into a slow smile as if knowing exactly what she was remembering.

"Yes, I sat here all night." He didn't say whether he watched her sleep or not.

She glanced back at the pillow to see if she had drooled. Relief swept through her seeing that the pillow was dry. She knew she snored. To know that Duncan had watched her sleep was unnerving. Kenny used to say she sounded like a freight train when she snored. "Please don't do that anymore." Pam couldn't look at him, too embarrassed to even glance his way. "I mean, don't you need your rest?"

"I don't sleep." Duncan pulled his feet off the bed sitting straight up. "Are you hungry?"

Deciding to drop the 'staring while she slept thing' for now, she nodded. "Starved."

"Then you're in for a treat." Duncan grinned grabbing her clothes. "I had them washed for you. We will go get you some clothes today."

Pam took the clothes hugging them to her chest. "Thank you." Rushing to the bathroom, she hurried and dressed, leaving the zipper down. Just yesterday, she could zip the jeans up almost all the way. Maybe it was because they had been washed and shrunk some. Staring at her growing stomach, she knew that wasn't the case. She was getting noticeably bigger every day, and it worried her. She looked six months pregnant instead of three.

"Let's get something to eat before heading out." Duncan reached out taking her hand when she stepped out of the bathroom.

She took his hand but stopped him. "I really want to get this over with." Pam searched his face, her hunger fading at what was before her today. "Could we just go?"

"You need to eat." He shook his head. "And I need to get you out of here without every reporter in the Cincinnati area following us."

"I forgot about that," Pam moaned, allowing Duncan to lead her out of the room. Nearing the kitchen, she was glad they were stopping to eat. The smells lingering in the hallway smelled delicious.

"It's about time." Sid frowned their way. "I thought you were expecting breakfast in bed, and well, that would've been a long disappointing wait for you."

Duncan grabbed a plate piling everything on it before handing it to Pam. "Here."

"I can't eat all of that." Pam's eyes widened. "I can make my own plate, but thanks anyway." Pam looked at the massive amount of food in front of her face trying not to gag, her stomach dipped, feeling queasy.

"You need to eat."

"And I will, but if I eat all of that I'll get sick." Pam pushed the plate away, grabbing one of her own.

Duncan plopped the plate on the counter with a loud clatter. "Are you okay? Why didn't you tell me you were sick?"

"I'm fine." Pam grinned. "I just have to take it slow in the mornings. Some things make me sick, so I have to be careful what I eat."

Duncan frowned looking around at all the food. "Is there anything here you can eat? If not, I'll take you somewhere else."

"Jesus. Calm the hell down, bro." Sid pushed him out of the way. "Let her breathe and get her own damn food. She's pregnant, not taking her last fucking breath. If there isn't anything she can eat, I'll make her something else."

"But…" Duncan pushed back at Sid to get closer to Pam.

"But…" Sid mocked, then rolled his eyes. "Sit the hell down and eat," Sid ordered.

"Who do you think you're talking to?" Duncan shot back with a deep growl.

"Honestly, it's a fucking mystery to me, 'cause you sure as hell aren't talking like your badass self." Sid snorted shaking his head. "More like Nervous Nellie Nursemaid."

"Fuck you!" Duncan got in Sid's face, his fists clinched.

"Hey guys." Pam held her empty plate to her chest, watching the scene unfold before her.

"No." Sid took a step forward and jabbed a finger in Duncan's chest.

"Fuck you!"

"Guys." Pam tried again, a little louder.

"You got a problem?" Duncan growled.

"Yeah, a big ugly one," Sid growled back.

Pam gave up with a roll of her eyes. Grabbing a slice of toast, she walked to the table and sat down just as Jared walked in.

"What's their problem?" Jared stopped beside her, looking at Duncan and Sid.

"I honestly don't know," she replied with a shrug of her shoulder.

Jared grinned. "Well, just ignore them. It's been pretty intense around here lately." He sat down across from her. "So how you doing, fatty?"

Not in the least offended by Jared calling her fatty, she grinned. She had missed his friendship and sense of humor. "Good." She nibbled on her toast avoiding his gaze. She had been far from good. She was a mess of nerves and emotions she could hardly contain.

"You never could lie worth a damn, Pamster." Jared eyed her with a frown, but let it go when Duncan and Sid broke up their attitude contest.

"Is that all you're eating?" both Sid and Duncan asked at the same time.

"I could use some orange juice if you have any." Pam watched as both men went to get her request.

Sid threw up his hand stopping Duncan. "I got this."

Grabbing the plate he had initially made for Pam, Duncan growled one last time at Sid, before sitting down next to Pam. "You got plans today?" Duncan asked Jared while digging into his food.

"Not really." Jared snatched a piece of bacon off Duncan's plate. "Tessa is spending time with Gramps, and then she has to work. Why? What's up?"

"We're going to Pam's old apartment today and need help getting out of here without a posse of reporters following us." Duncan grunted with a frown.

"You sure she's ready for that?" Jared asked without even looking at Pam.

"Well, since she's sitting right here, why don't you ask her?" Pam replied pushing her plate away clearly irritated.

Jared grinned with a wink her way. "Sorry, but you know how protective we Warriors are."

"And I appreciate it, but I do still have a voice. I may be jumpy here and there, but I'm determined to be back to the smartass Pam you all loved to hate." She also grinned feeling more herself.

"No hate involved, babe." Jared grabbed another piece of bacon from Duncan's plate and almost lost a hand.

"Get your own damn plate, and her name is Pam, not babe," Duncan hissed at Jared before turning his attention to Pam. "No one here hated you, but you were a smartass." A rare grin broke across his face at his own teasing.

"Oh, ho ho." Pam laughed. "The mighty leader does have a sense of humor."

Duncan stopped the coffee cup halfway to his lips, his eyes watching the genuine smile play across her face, her laughter musical. "You are absolutely beautiful."

Pam blushed, Jared cleared his throat, and Sid set down the biggest glass of orange juice Pam had ever seen. "Thank you," she said, but no one knew exactly who she was thanking.

Taking a big gulp of coffee, Duncan avoided eye contact with anyone.

Jared stared at the large glass of orange juice. "Geez, why not bring her a damn bucket, bro."

Pam tried to lift the glass with one hand, but had to use two. She giggled. "It is a little big." When she saw disappointment in Sid's eyes, she quickly put it to her mouth and took a drink. "But perfect. Thank you."

Sid smiled at her then turned and flipped Jared off before walking back to the stove.

Jared shook his head laughing. "Asshole." Then he turned serious as he looked at Duncan. "I got a plan that I think will work. Be back in a few." With that said, he pushed away from the table snatching more bacon off Duncan's plate.

"Dammit." Duncan tried to snatch them back, but was too slow.

"You had a half of a pig on your plate." Pam smirked. "I can't see how missing a few pieces is going to hurt you."

"I'm hungry." Duncan took a huge bite of eggs.

"That's because you didn't eat in three months," Sid replied from the stove. "No matter what I made, he wouldn't eat."

"Shut up, Sid," Duncan growled before taking another drink of coffee.

Pam frowned, feeling awful she had put him through that. "I'm sorry."

Duncan shot Sid a nasty look, but before he could respond, Jared came back in with Damon and Jill following. "What's the plan?" He pushed his empty plate away, his focus on Jared.

Jared pulled Jill in front of him. "From a distance, Jill can pass for Pam." He put a baseball hat on her head and handed her the small pillow he'd been carrying which she put under her large shirt. Damon handed her an oversized coat. "Adam is bringing the car around front. Once he's in front, we will surround her and put her in the car. You guys can leave through the back. We'll follow and meet you at the apartment just in case they catch on and follow."

"Two flaws in that plan, friend." Duncan shook his head. "First, there are reporters surrounding us, and second, the back entrance is for our bikes. She is not riding on the motorcycle."

"As soon as they see Pam, aka Jill, every reporter will rush to the front. They have watchers that will let them know, believe me. And why in the hell can't she ride on the bike?" Jared responded, not liking that his plan was being questioned.

"Because she's not." Duncan's tone was final.

"Why not?" Pam replied. "I would love to ride on the motorcycle."

"Pregnant women should not ride on motorcycles," Duncan replied as if it was law.

Pam frowned. "Who says?"

"Everybody."

"I didn't say that." Jared smirked. "I actually suggested it."

"Yeah, I don't see what the problem is," Sid piped in.

"You're one of the safest riders I know." Damon added his two cents with a shrug.

"It will be fine, Duncan." Pam looked his way. "I really want to…"

"I said no dammit," Duncan yelled.

Pam snapped her head back, her face paling a bit. Her stomach pitched violently, but her eyes were on Duncan. She knew this man would never hurt her, he just yelled. Yelling wouldn't hurt her. Duncan would never hurt her. She repeated that last part to herself.

"Ah, okay. Do you have another plan?" she asked Duncan, surprised her voice held strong.

"Give me a minute." Duncan frowned.

"Why don't you go out front with them, and I'll ride to the apartment with one of these guys," Pam added with a nod toward the other Warriors. Pam did lean back at the look on Duncan's face. His expression scared her more than his yelling.

"Over my dead body." He didn't yell, but his lowered tone of voice warned her she may have pushed a little too far.

"Damon…off with his head." Sid broke the silence with his usual smartass comment. "I've got things to do, and I'm tired of waiting."

"Shut the…"

"Fuck up, Sid," Sid finished for Duncan. "You guys seriously need to come up with something new."

"If anything happens to her, I will kill every single one of you." Duncan grabbed Pam's hand, ignoring everyone as he led her out of the room.

"I don't think he meant you." Jared put his hand on Jill's shoulder. "Then again, if things go bad, I'd hide out for awhile." Jared tapped the front of Jill's cap down over her eyes as he passed her.

*****

Duncan led Pam into the garage that held their bikes. This was a bad idea. He knew it was a bad idea, but yet, here he was, going along with it because the idea of her riding with anyone else drove him absolutely insane. He'd just threatened to kill his fellow Warriors over it. Poor Jill probably thought she was a part of his kill list. God, he had to get a grip.

"This one?" Pam pointed, and when he nodded, she tried to lift her leg over to straddle the seat, but her belly got in the way. "Wait a minute."

Watching her try to figure out how to get her beautiful pregnant body on the back of his bike, did him in. He watched the frustration line her face as she tried hard to prove her point that she could ride.

"This isn't going to work." Pam's eyes shot up to his, full of disappointment. "But I want to ride with you. I've always wanted to ride with you. I was so jealous of Nicole when Damon would take her for rides. Then I would see you pull up to the warehouse on your bike, and I wanted so badly to ask you for a ride, but I couldn't. Now that I can finally ride with you, I'm…I'm too fat!" She threw her arms wide, a disgusted look on her face.

Duncan couldn't help it, he laughed pulling her to him. Her words meant more to him than she would ever know. She had wanted him

75

back then, and that made him soar. "You are not fat. You're gorgeous." He hugged her, placed a kiss on the top of her head. Climbing on the bike, he started it up. After it hummed to life, he crooked his finger at her.

A large excited smile brightened her face. She took a step and stood next to him. "Really?"

"Yeah..." he winked, "really." In truth, he had wanted her on his bike. He had felt the same when he watched Damon and Nicole take off for long rides. He had yearned to do the same with Pam, and even though he was a little nervous and protective over her, he felt the same excitement she had. They didn't have helmets since they never wore them, and it wasn't law in Ohio to wear one, but he would take no chances with this woman, ever. He would ride with care.

Pam clapped her hands and laughed. "How do you want me?"

Duncan moaned at the thoughts that question brought to mind. Instead of answering, he grabbed her hips and turned her around. With ease, he lifted her onto the bike in front of him, sitting her sideways, her legs propped over his. Pulling her into the V of his legs he grabbed her arms wrapping them around him. "Don't let go."

"I won't." She looked deeply into his eyes as if she was not only answering for the bike ride, but for her trust in him also. After a few minutes of just staring at each other, their eyes saying more than words ever could, she laid against him, her head resting where his heart used to beat.

Chapter 9

They arrived at the apartment much too soon for Pam. She knew she wasn't ready, but she was done with the poor me attitude. She had to get her act together before the little one came. She had no choice.

Jared and Sid were already there, sitting on their own bikes. As soon as she and Duncan pulled in next to the Warriors, with a coolness that would make any woman's heart flutter, they stepped off their bikes. Jared waited until Duncan parked before carefully picking her up and setting her down so Duncan could step off.

No one said a word. It was if they all knew something major was about to happen, at least something major to her. Without thinking twice about it, Pam reached out and grasped Duncan's hand tightly. She was scared, scared to death. She was about to step into a past that terrified her.

Walking in the door, she stared straight ahead, swallowing the bile that hit the back of her throat. The smell was the same. She hated the smell of this hallway. It smelled like pain, fear and defeat to her.

Duncan stopped. Immediately, a few steps behind them, Jared and Sid stopped too, waiting for Duncan's signal. "You don't have to do this." He looked down at her, his eyes searching her face for any sign of retreat.

Gratitude filled her, but she shook her head. "I do have to do this, Duncan. I have to take back my life. It's just an apartment...right?" She forced the small smile on her face, but he didn't return it. He just squeezed her hand gently.

They stopped in front of apartment 3. Pam made no move to open the door. Clearing her throat, her eyes steady on the door, she dropped Duncan's hand. "I don't have a key." She was thankful that no one said anything; she would have lost her nerve to speak if they had. She felt their eyes on her. "I wasn't allowed to have a key. If he wasn't here, I waited outside until he got home."

Three different tones of growls filled her ears as Duncan moved her carefully to the side. With one well-placed kick, the door flew open, bouncing off the wall.

"Who needs a key when you have one of us with you?" Duncan winked at her, but didn't walk in, he waited for her to make the first move.

Taking a deep breath, Pam moved one foot in front of the other, feeling Duncan right behind her. Stopping just inside the door, her body froze. Kenny had liked to hide from her after locking the door. He would hide behind the door, and as soon as she walked in, he would either push her into the room or smack her in the back of the head. Her eyes shifted to the door Duncan had just kicked open feeling an unsettling fear that he might be there, ready to pounce.

"No one is here, sweetheart," Duncan said behind her. "You're safe. Nothing and no one will hurt you."

Pam jumped at his voice then slowly looked at him over her shoulder and saw the truth in his eyes. She was safe. Kenny had no power over her anymore. With a slight nod, she stepped the rest of the way into the room and felt a small sizzle of power edge its way back into her mind. She walked into the apartment without Kenny being there. Yeah, she'd take whatever she could; even something as little as that gave her a surge of power. Her eyes searched the small apartment, purposely avoiding the dining table. He had liked to use that table for his sick games. She knew she would have to confront it, but for right now, it was enough that she was inside without breaking out in a cold sweat.

"Where do we need to look?" Sid asked, keeping his voice low, knowing her nerves were on edge and ready to break.

For a second, she didn't say anything. She had to figure out how to keep them out of the bedroom. She knew what was in there waiting for her, but she didn't want them to know. If they had been through it already while she was missing, she didn't know it, and she didn't want to face it with them watching her every move. She could smell the old blood and knew they could too.

"Why don't you start out here?" Pam pointed to the living room area, her voice shaky praying they didn't question her motives. "He liked to hide papers in books. You might find something there. Also under and behind the couch as well as inside the cushion covers."

"Done." Sid nodded glancing at Jared and Duncan with a knowing look. Each Warrior looked toward the closed door at the end of a short hallway where the scent of blood came from.

"Can you look in the kitchen?" she asked Duncan when Jared and Sid started going through their area. "He hides stuff in the freezer at lot. Also, pots and pans." It wasn't like she was lying. Kenny did do all of the things she just said, but she knew where the most important things were hidden, and she had to take care of that...alone.

Duncan stood staring at her, searching her face, but finally nodded. "I'll be right there if you need me."

Feeling her throat close with tears, she could only nod back. He turned first, his gaze landing back on the door at the end of the hall before disappearing into the kitchen. Pam gave a sideways glance at Sid and Jared to find them still searching, but eyeing her. With a deep breath, she focused on her destination, and once again, put one foot in front of the other.

She found herself standing in front of another closed door, this one even scarier than the last. Reaching out, she touched the knob with shaky fingers. Slamming her eyes closed, she gave a twist, swinging the door open with force. When nothing happened, her eyes opened, and just like that, she was taken back, back to the past where every foul word said to her and every foul deed done to her smacked her in the face shocking her with the pain that pierced her chest.

Without warning, she bent to the side, throwing up the toast she had for breakfast.

*****

Duncan stood in the kitchen trying to calm down. His body was buzzing with too many emotions; he felt like he was going to explode. His focus wasn't really on what was in the kitchen because he knew this was a decoy. Pam knew exactly what she was doing and where she needed to look, but she wanted to do it alone. It took everything he had to abide by that because he smelled the blood; though old, he smelled it and knew it was Pam's. That alone sent his protective instincts into overdrive making him shake with rage. Hearing her small footsteps moving down the hall, Duncan stepped out of the kitchen and leaned against the wall where Pam wouldn't see him. He glanced at Jared and Sid, and saw they too had stopped their search, their focus on Pam. They had also seen her ploy and were ready to aid her if needed. It touched him that his fellow Warriors cared for his woman and would protect her if he couldn't.

Pam was one hell of a woman. The more he found out what had happened to her, the more his respect grew for the woman who had stolen his heart, a heart that had felt nothing for hundreds of years. And the more he found out, the more he wanted to find the bastard and send him to hell. Looking around the tiny apartment, he could see her touches here and there, but there was a heaviness…a sadness hanging in the air. The faster he got her out of here, the better. A bitter sound reached his ears. With a quickness, he was down the hall holding her head while she dry heaved, the toast she had this morning already spewed on the floor.

While holding her head, talking softly in her ear, his eyes searched for what had upset her; his rage reached new limits. Chains hung from the headboard posts, the white sheets were spotted with dried darkened blood. His eyes slammed shut, a curse so foul on his lips that he fought to hold back. Turning his focus back on Pam, he picked her up carrying her away from the horror of her past.

"I got you, babe," he whispered gently in her hair, but his eyes were anything but gentle. They were black as midnight, with a hate and rage so deep, Sid and Jared stepped back. He sent them both a silent message which they got loud and clear.

Duncan walked out of the apartment and headed for his bike. Her shaking was scaring him, but her quiet heavy breathing worried him most. Standing next to his bike, he held her, his senses searching out to make sure they were alone.

"Babe, you have got to calm down." Duncan rubbed her back. "Please." He had never said please in his life, but her unresponsiveness was terrifying to him.

She pulled away from his chest, but her hands still fisted his shirt. "I hate him!" she wheezed out, her eyes unfocused. "I hate myself for letting him do…those things."

"You did nothing, Pam." Duncan gripped her chin forcing her eyes to meet his. "Do you understand me? None of this is your fault, and you know it."

For a second, she just stared at him, disgust filling her face. She started to scramble out of his hold. "Let me go!"

It took everything he had not to drop her, her fierceness to get away from him strong. "Stop!" He gripped her as gently as he could to keep her from falling. "You're going to hurt yourself. Think of the baby."

Those words stopped her cold. Disgust left her face in a flash as pure fear and horror replaced it. Her hands flew to her stomach, defeat slumped her shoulders as her head fell forward in shame.

"What am I going to do?" She shook her head. "I was a fool to think I could handle this and be a mother. I'm so screwed up. I can't take care of a baby when I can't even take care of myself."

For the first time in his long life, Duncan was at a loss. He didn't know what to do, what to say. To tell her she was fine would be a lie, and he would never lie to her. Because anyone with eyes could tell she wasn't fine. One thing he did know for a fact was he would be by her side through it all, no matter what.

"I'm not going to stand here and tell you that everything is going to be fine, but I swear to you, I will do everything in my power to help you make it fine." Duncan knelt down slightly so he could be on her level. "I do know that you are one hell of a woman, who will be a wonderful, protective mother. Never doubt that. You have time to work things out, and you have good people behind you ready to help, wanting to help."

Pam sniffed and nodded. "I know that." Her chin crumbled. "I really do. I hate being like this. This is not who I am. I hate him!"

"Then don't let him win," Duncan said, wondering where that Oprah moment came from, but from the look on her face, he knew he'd hit a homerun. "You know I'm right."

Her trembling hand reached up to cup his jaw. "Thank you." A single tear slid down her pale cheek. "For everything."

"Honey, I'm not done yet." Duncan grinned, winking at her. "We *will* get through this. Just take it one step at a time, one battle at a time and you'll be fine. When you're not fine, I'll be here, no matter what."

"I don't deserve you." She leaned up and kissed his cheek.

"If I hear you say that again, I'll take you over my knee and blister that sweet ass," Duncan replied without thinking, the horror of what he said hit him hard. "Jesus...I didn't mean..."

She placed one finger across his lips to silence him. "It's my past that scares me, not you. I know you would never hurt me, Duncan Roark."

Duncan leaned in, placing a light kiss on her lips. "Not one hair on that beautiful head." He winked at her before leaning in for one more kiss.

*****

Jared and Sid quietly worked jerking the chains from the bed and ripping the soiled sheet away, disposing of it all. Standing there they both stared at the stripped bed, a sadness in their gaze.

"I know Duncan has dibs on the son of a bitch, but I swear as I stand here, I will kill the bastard a second time," Sid growled, his eyes still black from what they had just had to do.

"I don't think that's possible," Jared said, regret evident in his voice.

"I don't care," Sid growled. "The motherfucker deserves ten times the pain he inflicted on Pam, and if it's the last thing I do, I'll make sure he is sent to hell where it will feel like a fucking vacation compared to what I put him through."

"As much as your lips flap bullshit, that made perfect sense, and I'm ready to see it happen." Jared nodded, then cleared his throat when Pam and Duncan walked back in the room.

Pam purposely ignored the bed area, but glanced at Sid and Jared. "Thank you." She whispered, embarrassed that they knew what had happened to her and wondered if they would look at her differently.

Neither man spoke, just gave a short nod and took a step back to let her pass.

Walking to the side of the bed, she stopped and looked up. "Can you get me a chair please?"

Sid walked out of the room to get one, but Duncan walked up behind her. "Let me."

Thinking about it for a second, she finally nodded. Deep down she was afraid of what was up there, but if Duncan cared for her as he said, it wouldn't matter what he found. Pam swallowed her pride and fear, and let him take control, which actually felt good. She pointed toward the corner of the ceiling. "It's that tile. Just push up."

Duncan took the chair from Sid. Placing it under the tile, he was tall enough to push it up and over. Fitting his head in, he looked, but stepped down immediately. "There's nothing there."

Disappointment lit her face. "Are you sure? There aren't vials up there? Nothing?"

"No, babe." Duncan hated her disappointment. "Is there anywhere else he might have put them?"

Her eyes flittered back to the ceiling as she shook her head. "No, he wasn't careless. If it's here, that's where it would have been." With a sigh, she shrugged her shoulders. "I guess that's it. Can we get out of here?"

"Do you want to take any of your personal belongings?" Jared asked.

Pam looked around, her eyes landing on Duncan. "No," she replied, grabbing Duncan's hand. "I want nothing from this place."

Jared followed them out, noticing pictures on the small dining table. Stopping, he picked them up, rage choking him. Flipping through the pictures, he stopped at one of Tessa with a red dot on her temple. There were pictures of them all with a red dot from a rifle laser scope on different parts of their heads. Rolling the pictures, he stuck them in his back pocket. If he found out these were legit pictures, Kenny Lawrence wouldn't be able to run far enough from his rage. No one put a target on his mate.

Chapter 10

Jill walked out of the warehouse with her drawing pad in hand. She grinned, thinking about her and Adam's part in getting Pam away from the compound earlier today. That had been a blast. They had pulled it off perfectly. When they had left to come for training, she had dressed as herself without the baby pillow, and no one paid them much attention.

"Hey sissy girl," Steve called out. "We need another player. Come on."

Wrinkling her nose at him, she walked to the other side of the parking lot so she could lean against one of the trees. She wanted to finish her drawing of Pam. Flipping quickly to the page, she stared at it with pride. It was her best work yet, and almost done. Just a bit of shading and it would be perfect. Someone kicked her foot ruining her focus. "What?"

"Come on." Steve kicked dust on her shoes. "We're short one player."

Jill looked at everyone looking at her. "I hate football."

"It's just tag football." Steve rolled his eyes. "We'll take it easy on ya. Come on...stop being such a girl."

"I am a girl," Jill mumbled under her breath, hearing the rest of them calling for her to come on. Standing up, she kicked dust back on his shoes, then shoulder checked him as she ran past, almost knocking him down.

The guys stood around while Adam explained, in quick fashion, the game to Jill who looked bored out of her mind. "You got it?" Adam frowned when she blew a bubble, popping it loudly.

"Run after the guy with the ball and touch him, or catch the ball and run like hell." Jill cocked an eyebrow chomping away on her gum.

Adam nodded looking around at everyone. "Yeah, that's pretty much it."

Walking over, she followed what the other guys on her team were doing, bending over across from someone on the other team putting both hands on her knees. She guessed she was supposed to run in the direction she was facing and catch the football if Adam threw it at her. Seeing everyone else move, she started forward, but found herself on her ass looking up at one of the other half-breeds who bent over, smirking at her.

"You have to dodge, little girl." Jeff, another half-breed, and the one she'd beaten at arm wrestling, laughed as he walked away.

Back in position, she took off and once again found herself ass-planted on the concrete with a smirking Jeff walking away.

"Chill out, Jeff." Adam walked over, holding his hand out to help her up.

"I'm fine." Jill ignored his hand, picking herself up. "Just make sure you throw me the damn ball." Jill walked back to the line and bent down across from Jeff again. She may hate football, but she was competitive and she was catching on...fast.

As soon as Jill saw movement, she thrust kicked Jeff in the stomach, knocking him on his ass. Jumping over him, she turned to look for the ball while running. With a small leap, she caught it and ran where Adam and Steve had told her to go if she got the ball. But before she made it, a heavy weight landed on her back crashing her to the ground. The air left her body with a whoosh. She may be part vampire, but that didn't mean being tackled by a hundred and eighty pound dude was a pleasant experience.

Finally able to suck in a deep breath, she figured Adam and Steve had tugged him off until she heard Jeff's angry tone. "Get the fuck off me."

Jill tried to push herself up, but her body protested. Suddenly Jeff was slammed next to her, his face smashed to the ground. He struggled against the large hand holding his face to the concrete. "Doesn't feel too good, does it, badass?" an unfamiliar, deep gravelly voice growled.

"Damn, girl." Adam leaned down helping her to her knees. "You okay? Jesus, Jeff, what the hell is wrong with you?"

"Get this fucker off me." Jeff still struggled.

Jill held her shoulder, finally getting a look at the owner of the large hand holding Jeff's head to the concrete. He was large, larger than any of the other Warriors. His raven hair was shoulder length and hung in his face as he held Jeff down, his large knee in the half-breed's back. A leather jacket, well worn, hugged his body as did his light faded blue jeans. Wanting to see what his hair covered, she leaned to see his face, but moaned as sharp pain spiked in her shoulder and down her arm straight to her fingertips.

"Are you hurt?" the man asked, pushing Jeff's head harder into the concrete before looking at her.

The breath was sucked right out of her for the second time in less than a minute, she felt light headed. She couldn't have talked if her life depended on it. Could men be beautiful? Because this man was the most gorgeous being she had ever laid eyes on. She opened her mouth to answer, but closed it back when nothing came out. She resorted to nodding like an idiot.

"Hey, dude." Adam stepped next to the man, looking at Jeff. "I think you're breaking his face."

The man looked away from Jill, lifting his knee off Jeff's back. "I'm going to let you up, badass, so I suggest you calm down."

As soon as the man lifted his hand, Jeff jumped up to get in his face. "You son of a bitc-" Jeff's voice squeaked to a stop as soon as he realized he was yelling into the man's chest. His head tilted up to look the man in the face, his throat working in a visibly hard swallow.

"You were saying?" The man frowned down at Jeff, taking a step forward, and then smirked when Jeff took a large step back.

"Jeff, go cool off." Adam gave him a small push. "I think you just bit off more than you can handle."

"Apologize before you run off." The man's deep voice radiated authority.

"She kicked me," Jeff argued. "I'm not apologizing to her."

"And from what I saw, you were supposed to be playing tag football, but the first two hits you gave her didn't look like tag to me," the man growled. "Now apologize."

Jeff frowned looking like he was going to refuse. "I'm sorry, okay?" His tone clearly indicated he wasn't sorry at all.

"She doesn't accept," the man growled. "Now get the fuck out of here before I give you an ass kicking you won't ever forget."

Adam stopped Jeff, whose brain malfunctioned into the stupid level as he took a step toward the man. Giving him a hard push, he waited until Jeff was gone before turning back to the man. "Who are you?"

"Slade Buchanan," he replied, walking over to pick up his backpack and duffle bag. "I'm supposed to meet Sloan Murphy here, but I'm a little early."

"I'm Adam." He stuck out his hand. "This is Dillon, Matt, Steve and Jill."

Slade shook Adam's hand, but nodded at the rest of them until his golden eyes landed on Jill. "Is there anywhere I can look at her shoulder?"

Jill had finally stood. "I'm good," she lied. Her shoulder hurt like hell and didn't feel right.

He cocked an eyebrow at her. "Lift your shoulder," he ordered, grunting when she just stood there proving that she was not fine.

"Yeah, come on in here." Adam led the group back into the warehouse. "Where you from? I haven't seen you around."

"California." Slade held the door open for Jill when the others walked on in ignoring her.

Jill nodded her thanks holding her arm close to her body.

"You need me to text Sloan and let him know you're here?" Adam pulled out his phone.

"No. Like I said, I'm early." Slade stood at the door leading into the workout area which was dark. "Is there somewhere I can look at her arm?"

"It's already feeling better," Jill lied again. She really didn't want this man looking at her; she'd rather look at him if she was being totally honest.

"Dressing rooms and showers are in the back." Adam pointed.

"Really, I'm good."

Slade ignored her, placing his hand on her back, pushing her across the mats to the dressing rooms. Once inside, he flicked on the lights, setting his duffle bag on the floor.

Jill stood still watching every move he made. He was so huge, she suddenly felt frightened. He could do anything he wanted to her and she wouldn't be able to stop him. Hell, she didn't know if Adam, she and others combined could stop him. He could be anyone and they just took him at his word, but who was he really?

Slade reached out to touch her shoulder, but she jumped back. "I need to see that shoulder." His deep voice echoed in the small dressing room off from the showers. "With you being half-vampire, it's healing already, and if it's dislocated, you are going to have a serious problem!"

Holding her arm close to her body she stayed back. "Who are you?" Suspicion colored every word.

"Slade," he sighed. "Buchanan. I think I've already stated that."

"I know what your name is, if that is really your name." Jill's chin came up. She tried to appear in control, but inside she was shaking. "But *who* are you?"

Understanding crossed his face. "Sloan called me in," he explained, crossing his arms and leaning against the wall. "I'm a doctor."

She actually laughed. "Yeah, right." Her eyes traveled over his hair, down to the leather jacket he wore so well, to the faded light blue jeans that hugged his lower body like a second skin. "I'm out of here." She went to pass him out the door, but he stopped her.

"So you're a 'judge a book by the cover' girl." He glared down at her. "I'm a doctor and I'm telling you that shoulder needs to be looked at. I can tell by the way you're holding it it's probably dislocated."

"Let me go." Jill jerked her good arm away from him, but gasped at the pain it sent through her shoulder. "Dammit."

"Take off your hoodie," he demanded, reaching down to help lift it off.

Panic gripped her, making her struggle ignoring the pain. "I swear to God, if you don't let me go right now, I'm going to scream."

Their eyes met, both determined, neither willing to give. As promised, her mouth opened wide and out came a scream that could wake the dead.

Chapter 11

Duncan and Pam pulled up to the warehouse with Sid and Jared following close behind. Duncan waited for Jared to come help Pam off the bike again, but he really didn't want to let her go.

"We can go back." Duncan looked down at the top of her head, her arms were still wrapped tightly around him. "Jared and Sid can handle the classes tonight."

Looking up at him, she shook her head. "I'm okay. I don't want to interfere with your life, Duncan."

"Honey you are my life," he whispered for her ears only as Jared walked over to pull her off the bike with care.

"Do you want to take any of your clothes in for you to change into?" Jared nodded toward his and Sid's bikes that had boxes tied down.

"No, I'll wait." Pam glanced at the boxes. After leaving her apartment, the three men had taken her shopping. They had been so sweet, even Sid, who had demanded to buy some of her clothes for her. That had almost caused a fight between Sid and Duncan, but Jared calmed them down while she tried on clothes.

Duncan grabbed her hand leading her inside. Adam, Dillon, Matt and Steve sat around tossing a football back and forth.

"What the hell are you guys doing?" Sid grabbed the football. "You slackers should already be warmed up. I told you we were running late. Where's Jeff and Jill?"

"Jeff took off, and Jill is in the back with...." Adam's words were drowned out by a scream that had the Warriors running.

"Watch her!" Duncan put Pam in the middle of Adam, Steve and Dillon, before taking off after Jared and Sid.

Sid was the first to take in the sight of a huge man grabbing at Jill and Jill trying to fight him off. Without any thought whatsoever, Sid's instincts took over. With one leap, he grabbed the man around the neck tossing him across the room before jumping on him. What surprised Sid, and everyone else, was how fast he ended up underneath the man. Not liking this position, Sid trapped the man's foot and rolled him. Punches were flying everywhere as they fought for position, neither giving up until the sound of Sloan's voice penetrated their thirst for blood.

"What the fuck is going on in here?" Sloan grabbed Sid, who was currently on top, pulling him off. When Sid went to go back for more, Sloan pushed him against the wall. "Stand down, Warrior!"

Everyone stared as Slade picked himself off the ground, his eyes quickly turning back to the golden hue as he looked to Jill.

"Who is this fucking guy?" Jared snarled putting himself between Slade and Jill.

Sloan gave Sid one last warning look before letting him go. "If you Warriors don't stop fighting amongst each other, I'm sending you all back to the shitholes I pulled you out of before you were Warriors."

"This asshole had his hands on her." Sid pointed to Jill. "I don't give a shit if you send me to hell. He better be explaining why she was screaming and fighting him."

That gave Sloan pause as he looked between Jill and Slade. "Either one of you want to explain?"

Jill looked uncomfortable, but Slade stepped forward. "It was a miscommunication," he answered without pause. "She hurt her shoulder and I was trying to look at it."

"Warrior?" Jared spoke up. "You're a Warrior?"

"Yes, he is. And a damn good one at that," Sloan replied still looking pissed enough to spit. "He is also who I called in to help with Pam."

"He's the doctor?" Sid asked, frowning.

"Yeah, he's the damn doctor." Sloan rubbed his eyes, irritation evident in each word. "He even has a damn degree and everything. Jesus, you guys are going to drive me fucking insane. I have enough shit going on without you all adding to it."

"Well, why in the hell didn't you say something?" Sid pushed away from the wall.

"You didn't give me much of a chance," Slade shot back. "Now, if you all get the hell out of here, I can see if her shoulder needs setting before it heals in the wrong position.

"I'll stay." Duncan, who felt responsible for the half-breeds in their group stepped forward, plus he wanted to get a better feeling about this man who may or not be taking care of Pam. He needed to prove himself before Duncan would let him anywhere near her.

"I don't need help." Slade took off his jacket laying it across a bench in the dressing room.

"I didn't ask." Duncan's tone was final.

Slade looked at him for a few seconds before looking away toward Jill. "We good now?" His voice held some irritation.

Looking a little embarrassed, she nodded. "It's just a lot of weird stuff has been going on around here, and well…you just show up and expect everyone to believe you and…."

Walking up to her, he grabbed her elbow with one hand and as the other gently touched the top of her shoulder. "I'm going to be as gentle as I can, but I'm going to try to move it, okay?"

"Yeah." Jill glanced into his eyes before squeezing hers shut. "Is it going to hurt?"

"Probably." His answer was honest and quickly spoken.

"I really hate pain," she mumbled, missing the grin that crossed his face since her eyes were squeezed tight. "I'm sorry I screamed."

"So am I," he grunted with a grin.

Her eyes did fly open at his response, and this time she didn't miss the smile flashing across his face. Her knees felt weak, and it had nothing to do with pain. If she thought he was gorgeous with a frown, he was breathtaking with a smile. He moved her arm just slightly bringing her out of her dazed state. Grabbing his hand with her good one, she stopped him. "Ouch!"

"We really need to get your shirt off." Slade frowned. "I need to see your shoulder. Do you have anything on under your hoodie?"

Jill glanced at Duncan, who leaned silently against some lockers. "I have a tank top, but I don't think I can get it off."

"Let's start with your good arm sleeve." He helped her get her arm out, but when he started with the side of her injury she couldn't take it. "I'm going to have to cut it off."

Frowning, Jill nodded. "Jeff owes me a new hoodie," she mumbled, watching the Warrior doctor get a pair of scissors from his bag.

"Jeff did this?" Duncan growled.

"Well, not really. I mean he did, but we were playing football," Jill replied, not wanting to get anyone in trouble by telling.

"Tag football." Slade stopped cutting her shirt to frown at Duncan. "Someone needs to teach the little badass the difference. It looks to me like he was purposely out to hurt her."

Duncan grunted, making it a point to find out what the hell was going on with Jeff. He had let a lot of things slide while Pam had been missing. He needed to step it up. Whether he liked it or not, these half-breeds were his responsibility.

Free from her hoodie, Slade looked, poked and prodded at Jill's shoulder, a large frown reaching his eyes the whole time. "I'm going to have to set this."

"Is it going to hurt?" Jill's voice sounded shaky and weak.

"Yes."

"You could have lied and given me some hope," Jill groaned. "What happened with probably?"

Slade laughed. "Sorry, but I never lie to patients. It's bad bedside manners."

"For future reference…lie to me." Jill bit her lower lip. "Because now I don't think I can let you do it. I seriously don't like pain."

"Noted." Slade nodded down at her, but the smile and teasing was wiped off his face. He was totally professional. He reached for her elbow, but she backed up.

"No, I seriously don't think I can stand here and let you do this, knowing it's going to hurt." Jill shook her head. "I think I'll be okay. Just give it a day or two and I'll be good as new. It's actually feeling much better."

"No, it won't, and no, it isn't." Slade called her out on her lie. He glanced to Duncan. "I'm going to need your help."

"Why?" Jill was really getting nervous, her breathing coming in short gasps. "What is he going to do?"

"Jill." Slade tried to calm her down. He leaned down into her line of vision cutting off Duncan walking toward them. "Jill!"

"What?" she whispered.

"It will only take a second," Slade assured her.

"A second of pain is a second too long." She hated acting like a pussy, but when it came to pain, she wasn't acting…she was a pussy.

Slade nodded to Duncan who had stepped behind Jill. Slade placed Duncan's hands where he wanted them. "Just hold her still. Don't move." He didn't continue until Duncan nodded his understanding.

Jill started to shake. "Can't you knock me out or something for this?"

"No." Slade put his hands on her shoulder and arm. "Okay, on the count of three…."

"Wait!" Jill's eyes bugged out. "I have to throw my gum away. I might choke on it."

Slade sighed holding his hand out. Jill leaned her head over spitting her gum into his hand. "Thanks." She watched him toss it into the garbage can across the room. "Nice shot."

"Okay, on the count of three I am going to set your shoulder back in place," Slade told her, then looked at Duncan. "Hold her tight."

Jill brought her head up nodding. She couldn't think of anything else to get her out of this so she might as well take it.

"One…"

Squeezing her eyes tight, she waited for three, but three never came.

"Two…" Slade's hands tightened as he jerked her shoulder back into its socket.

"Son. Of. A. Bitch!" Jill screamed then kicked him hard. "What the hell happened to three?"

Duncan and Slade held her still. Slade ignored the pain in his shin and her cursing as he looked over his handiwork. The shoulder seemed in place. "Move your arm." He demanded.

Slowly, Jill brought her arm up and down, rolling her shoulder.

"How does it feel?" He and Duncan let her go.

"Sore and stiff, but better." Jill frowned. "Seriously, what happened to three?"

"I couldn't have you stiffening up, and I knew once you heard three, you would," Slade explained with a grin.

"Well, that was a mean trick." She wrinkled her nose at him.

"But it works every time." Slade put his scissors back in his bag.

"Take it easy for a day or two, then slowly get back to your normal activities. You're healing time will be a lot faster, and you should be good as new in a few days."

"When can she start training again?" Duncan asked.

"That depends, training for what?" Slade picked up his bag slinging it over his shoulder.

"Warrior training," Jill replied walking out the door first.

Slade just shook his head with a laugh passing her. "No sooner than a week." He glanced at her and laughed again.

"What's so funny?" Jill frowned.

"You can't even get your shoulder set without having a panic attack," Slade replied shaking his head. "And you're going to train to be a Warrior."

Once he turned away, Jill flipped him off quickly before he could turn back around to see her. Glancing at Duncan, she shrugged her uninjured shoulder before walking away. She'd show the asshole she could be a Warrior. She trained harder than any of them and maybe she didn't like pain, but that just made her train even harder so she didn't experience pain often. Yeah, she'd show him.

*****

Duncan followed Slade and Jill out to the workout area. It was pretty funny seeing small quiet Jill flipping off the huge Warrior in front of her. Of course, Slade hadn't seen her. His eyes instantly found Pam sitting while talking with Nicole and Tessa. Sid was leading the half-breeds in training while Sloan, Damon and Jared stood next to the women talking.

"Slade." Duncan stood next to Pam. "This is Pam Braxton."

"Nice to meet you, Pam." Slade set his gear down to shake her hand.

"You're the doctor?" Pam asked, surprised as she looked him up and down.

"Think I'm feeling a little sick." Nicole grinned also giving him a once over.

Tessa covered her mouth giving a fake cough. "I haven't felt very well myself."

"He's not a human doctor," Jared growled. "And you were feeling fine just a few seconds ago."

"Where's your office." Nicole ignored Jared. "And how do I make an appointment?"

Damon growled eyeing Slade as did Jared.

"Ladies, even though I would love to examine each and every one of you…" Slade grinned when the growls got louder. "I think it would be in my best interest if I referred you elsewhere."

"You better fucking believe it would be in your best interest, Doc," Jared sneered putting his arm around Tessa.

Slade gave him a nod, then snuck a wink at Tessa. He turned toward Duncan. "Do you have any problems with me being Pam's doctor?"

"No, because if you so much as harm one hair on her head or do anything to upset her, I will kill you." Duncan's tone was threatening, but calm and to the point.

Slade cocked his eyebrow. "Fair enough." He tried to step out of the way when Jared walked by with Tessa on the other side, but he wasn't fast enough and got shoulder checked. Yeah, he got the message loud and clear. The little human was off limits.

Sloan came over at that moment shaking his head at Jared. He handed Slade a set of keys. "Everything you asked for should be in the office. Anything else you might need just let me know."

Pocketing the keys Slade nodded. "Thanks, but I'm sure it will be fine."

"Since Jill is down, she can help you get set up." Sloan volunteered Jill's services. "Won't you, Jill?"

The look on her face said she would rather have her shoulder set again, but she nodded. "Yes, sir, what time?"

"How about ten?" Slade replied not really needing the help, but didn't want to start out on the wrong foot with Sloan.

"If you need any extra help, I'm sure me and Tessa can assist," Nicole added sweetly.

"You have to work," Damon reminded her. "I doubt Mitch will let you have a day off."

Sloan slapped Slade on the shoulder. "Come on. I'm sure you want to get settled."

"It was nice meeting you all." Jared and Damon growled a goodbye, Tessa and Nicole waved with large smiles. He looked at Pam and Duncan. "Give me a few days to get everything ready, then stop by, unless you have any problems before then."

"Thank you." Pam waved as Duncan shook his hand.

"What an asshole." Jared frowned as soon as Slade and Sloan walked out.

"He is not...he's nice." Tessa smiled, then patted Jared's cheek. "You're just jealous."

Jared frowned down at her looking offended. "The hell I am."

"We just don't like our women slobbering over someone," Damon grunted.

"We were not slobbering," Nicole defended. "And like you guys don't check out hot women."

"No, we don't," Jared answered looking down at Tessa. "The only woman I want is right here."

Tessa leaned her body into Jared's whispering something in his ear. His eyes darkened as he grabbed her hand heading for the door. "See you guys."

Nicole and Damon also had their heads together talking softly to each other.

Duncan glanced at Pam who wore a sad expression on her face. "Hey." He tilted her face to his. "What are you so deep in thought about?"

Pam gave him a small smile that didn't quite reach her eyes. "Nothing really," she lied, but how could she tell him that she may never be able to have a close relationship with him like Damon and Jared had with Nicole and Tessa. She had also seen him watching the couples with a wanting expression. "Just tired I guess."

Duncan helped her off the stool she was sitting on. "Come on. Let's go so you can get some rest."

They both said goodbye to Damon and Nicole who halfheartedly said goodbye. They were too into each other to notice anything else.

Chapter 12

Pam woke with a start. Her head snapped to the chair finding it empty. Relief and panic hit her. Relief that Duncan wasn't sitting there watching her sleep, but panic that she was alone. She woke many times during the night having to go to the bathroom and he had sat with his head leaned back, but his eyes would search hers making sure she was okay. Night also seemed to be the favorite time for the baby to move around. Sleeping, eating, and peeing seemed to be what her life revolved around now.

Coming out of the bathroom, her stomach growled. She was hungry. Biting her lip, she glanced at the door wondering if she could just run and get a light snack. Slipping on a pair of her new maternity pants and shirt, she snuck out of her room barefoot.

Seeing a light on in the kitchen and dining area, Pam thought about going back to her room, but her stomach growled again making her decision for her. Walking in, she saw Tessa sitting at the table eating a bowl of cereal, reading.

"Hey," Pam said quietly not wanting to startle her.

Tessa looked up and smiled putting her book down. "The baby demanding food?"

"Yeah. Care if I join you?" Pam walked further into the room.

"Not at all." Tessa smiled. "I'm bored out of my mind. Jared is helping Duncan with something, so I decided to come in and eat, which is a big no-no for me this late at night."

Grabbing a box of cereal, Pam poured herself a bowl then sat across from Tessa. "What are you reading?"

Tessa snorted. "My Vampire Lover." She waggled her eyebrows. "I'll

105

let you borrow it when I'm finished."

Pam glanced at the book then into her bowl. "Does Jared know you read that stuff?"

"Yes." Tessa giggled. "He thinks it's funny, but let me tell you, he proves to me that the vampires in my books are 'big pussies who wouldn't know how to make a woman scream in pleasure if they tried.'" Tessa's voice lowered copying Jared's tone.

"Good impression," Pam smiled.

"Thanks." Tessa grinned back, and then her eyes turned serious. "How are you doing?"

Now wasn't that a loaded question. "Fine...I think," Pam replied honestly. "One minute I'm fine, and then the next I'm...hell, I don't know what I am." Her appetite gone, she pushed her half-eaten bowl away.

"It takes time, Pam." Tessa's eyes were full of understanding. "Give yourself a break. I honestly think you're doing great, but you're going to have moments."

Pam nodded, having had a few moments already. "Can I ask you something?"

"Anything." Tessa leaned up, ready to listen and help anyway she could.

"Were you able to have...you know?"

Tessa sat for a minute staring at her, trying to understand. "Sex?"

Again, Pam nodded. "Yeah."

"I wasn't sexually abused." Tessa frowned.

"Oh." Feeling uncomfortable, Pam pushed away from the table. "Well, thanks for the cereal. Guess I'll be getting back. I'm feeling really tired."

"Don't go." Tessa reached across the table. "And please don't be embarrassed. I know you don't really have anyone to talk to about this, and I want to help you. Even though I wasn't sexually abused, I was abused. I know the feelings. Being around these Warriors has been a true test for me at times. Their tempers soar and they get so loud that I have to remind myself they would never hurt me. Jared has seen me react sometimes, but he understands that it's something I still have to deal with and probably will for the rest of my life."

"What if I can't do this?" Pam looked toward the door. "What if I can't be woman enough for him?"

Tessa crossed her arms leaning back in her chair. "Have you tried to do anything with Duncan yet?"

"No, not really. I mean we kissed…" Pam frowned, "kind of. It wasn't anything crazy."

"And?" Tessa urged.

"It was nice."

"You didn't freak out?"

"No." Pam smiled. "I didn't freak out."

"Do you find the thought of having sex with Duncan disgusting, terrifying, a total turnoff?" Tessa grinned when Pam's cheeks reddened.

"No." Pam grinned. "I'm very attracted to him." The old Pam would have said she wanted to jump his bones, but the old Pam wouldn't be having this conversation with anyone. She would be going for what she wanted, which would be jumping his sexy ass bones.

"Listen." Tessa got up, and walked around the table and sat beside Pam, taking her hands in hers. "Duncan is totally in love with you. He was walking death while you were missing. Just take things slowly, and one step at a time. Duncan will wait for you. He already has."

"That's not really fair to him." Pam felt her eyes well up at her words.

"What happened to you isn't fair, period, but it happened. Now you have to work through it and don't let that bastard run your life anymore. Take it back." Tessa hugged her. "I did. I'm not saying it was easy, but I was surrounded by people who loved me and helped me through the dark times. Duncan will be by your side. If you're ever in doubt, just look into that Warrior's eyes, because honey, that man would go through hell fire for you."

"Thank you." Pam hugged her tightly.

"Hey now what's this?" Jared and Duncan walked into the kitchen as both women wiped their eyes.

"Just girl talk." Tessa grinned when Jared moaned.

"Oh hell. The last time there was girl talk in the kitchen, you and Nicole ended up in jail." He grabbed Tessa's hand. "Time to leave."

"That was so not our fault," Tessa argued.

Jared rolled his eyes as he bent over to place a kiss on the top of Pam's head. "See ya, fatty."

"Bye." Pam smiled watching them leave before her eyes found

Duncan's.

"I can kick his ass for calling you that." Duncan's tone was serious, but his eyes held a smile.

"He's not far off the mark." Pam rubbed her stomach not taking her eyes off him.

"You are absolutely beautiful." Duncan's eyes roamed from her face down her body then back to her eyes.

A sudden urge to test herself came over her, not to mention how handsome he looked as he leaned casually against the table staring down at her. His stare burned her, but in a good way. Standing, she stepped up to him, both hands going to his t-shirt-covered chest. Her eyes didn't leave his. She didn't want to blink, afraid of losing his image and it being replaced with another that would terrify her. With slow movement, her fingers spread out feeling the power radiating off him; her hands made their way to his shoulders. Going up on her toes, she leaned forward placing a kiss on his neck. The only movement he made was to tilt his head slightly. Feeling braver, she kissed her way up his jawline as her one hand cupped his cheek. Stopping just a breath away from his lips, she moistened hers with her tongue. His groan was what she needed to hear, gave her courage to keep going.

Their lips met slow and sweet, tongues dancing at a slow tempo. Duncan finally moved, wrapping one strong arm around her waist, bringing her closer to him, her belly pressed against him. Feeling excited that she wasn't terrified, Pam grabbed his neck pulling his mouth closer to hers. She couldn't get enough of him. She felt a weird sort of freedom at not being terrified of this man's hands on her, their mouths mashed together. Breaking away for a slight second, she breathed in deeply with a moan before going back for more.

******

Duncan fought to keep his control. All he wanted to do was lay this woman on the table and fuck her, but he wouldn't do that. Not now. If he lost control and did what he wanted to do, he would lose her. She was too raw; it was too soon. Right now, she was testing the waters. He knew what she was doing and respected her for it. He needed to make sure she could trust him to stop if she'd had enough. It was the hardest thing he had ever done. Her sweet mouth played havoc with his as her body rubbed against him. He couldn't hide the hardness between his legs that was totally out of his control.

He felt her hand going south, and as soon as it hit the waistband of his jeans, he caught it bringing it back to his face where he left her lips to kiss her palm then placed it on his shoulder before his lips went back to hers. He could feel her control slipping; to prove that point, her hand traveled the same path, and with a discipline he didn't know he possessed, he stopped her hand again before she grabbed onto his rock hard cock.

Pulling his lips from her, he kissed her cheek his lips close to her ear. "Honey, we need to slow down." He nuzzled her hair.

"No," Pam moaned trying to take his lips again.

"Pam. Honey." He tried to put distance between them, but she held on for dear life.

"You too!" Sid walked in just as Duncan pulled Pam off him. "Did you not read Sid's Kitchen Law? I swear there is more screwing around in this kitchen than there is eating. Maybe I need to start charging by the hour. I can make serious cash flow off you guys."

Duncan completely ignored Sid. His focus was on the different emotions playing across Pam's face. The one of horror was the one he didn't want to see, but it was there, chasing her from the room. "Pam!" he called out to her, but she didn't stop. "Fuck!"

Sid stopped his grumbling. "What did I do now?"

"Nothing," Duncan replied staring at the door wondering what to do. Should he go after her, or give her a minute. Dammit, he was in over his head. He, Duncan Roark, leader of the VC Warriors, was at a loss of what to do. Rubbing his hand down his face, he headed out the door. Even though he didn't know what to do, he wasn't a coward. He was going to face this head on.

******

Whore. The evil voice from her past whispered through her head as she hurried down the hallway looking for her room. *No one is going to love you after I'm done with you.*

Making it to her room, she slammed the door before slapping her hands over her ears. Catching her reflection in the small mirror above the dresser, she hissed at her reflection. "I'm not a whore."

"Who the fuck called you a whore?" Duncan's angry face appeared in the mirror behind her.

Pam jumped spinning around. "He did. He always called me a whore. He said no one would ever love me after he was done with me," She whispered, anger mixed with fear shining from her eyes. "Is it true? Do I disgust you because of what he did to me? Is that why you stopped? You don't want me?"

Surprised by her outburst, Duncan stepped back. "I have never wanted a woman more in my life. You have no idea what I wanted to do to you in that kitchen."

"What did you want to do to me?" Pam stared up at him demanding to know. "I need to know, Duncan."

Dare he tell her point blank? The look on her face told him the answer.

She wanted to know how much he really wanted her. "I wanted to throw you across the table and fuck you," Duncan growled.

Pam's eyes widened as her head tilted.

"I'm sorry." Duncan thought that by her expression, it wasn't what he should have said. *Fuck!* "I shouldn't have…"

"No." Pam shook her head. "That's what I needed to hear. I'm not frightened."

"I don't think I could take it if I ever saw fear in your eyes when you looked at me," Duncan replied his voice deep. "That's why I had to stop, Pam. I want you so much that I don't think I can control myself once I'm with you. Making love to you the first time, may be my undoing, and I can't ever hurt you."

"I want you, Duncan." Pam's lip trembled. "As long as I see your face and hear your voice, I know I'll be fine, but I want you so badly, I need you. Does that make me more messed up than I already am? Shouldn't I not want to have sex with anyone?"

"No, it doesn't." He brushed the hair from her eyes. "It makes me respect you even more. You are a strong woman, Pam. I've always known that."

"I'm so confused." Her voice told him how much she hated the confused emotions she was having. "But wrong or right, I do want you."

"There is nothing but right in that, babe," he replied, and then looked down to touch her stomach. "I don't want to hurt you or the baby. You sure we should?"

"We'll be fine." Pam smiled trying not to show how nervous she was. She wanted this and knew Duncan would help her through it. "Please kiss me."

Duncan groaned smashing his mouth against hers. "If you need to stop, we will stop." He kissed down her neck. "I swear to you, I *will* stop."

If she didn't love this man before, she did now. She felt his hands moving over her body. A few times, she opened her eyes to see his face, and that was all she needed. Soon her thoughts only belonged to him, and again she felt free. Not even when he unbuttoned her shirt and was pulling it down off her shoulders did she feel fear. She felt free...she felt loved...she felt him pulling away.

"No, I'm fine." She reached up to pull him back to her. "Please, don't stop. I didn't say stop."

"Pam." Duncan couldn't help but laugh. "Honey, someone's knocking on the door," he whispered, pulling her shirt up, helping her button it.

"Who is it?" Pam whispered, feeling disappointed.

"I don't know, but I may kill them." He winked at her when she giggled. Duncan double checked to make sure Pam was covered before opening the door. He couldn't resist leaning over and kissing her one more time.

Sid stood on the other side when Duncan opened it. "What the hell do you want?"

"Well, if you checked your damn phone, you'd know that Sloan wants you in his office pronto." Sid frowned. "So since you don't answer your damn phone, I have to be the fucking messenger."

"Tell him I'll talk to him in the morning." Duncan went to close the door, but Sid stuck his foot out stopping him.

"Uhm no." Sid walked into the room. "I'm not telling him that. You tell him that. I'm not your bitch because obviously I'm his. I will keep the pregnant one company while you go see what grump ass wants."

"Go ahead, Duncan." Pam smiled nodding to the door. "I need to get to know Sid better anyway."

"That's what I'm afraid of." Duncan glared at Sid in warning before kissing Pam on the cheek. "I'll be right back."

"So you really like the boss man, huh?" Sid asked when Duncan had left. He sat down in the only chair in the room, grabbing the remote.

"Yeah, I do." Pam sat on the bed. "What about you?"

"He's okay…for an asshole." Sid smiled flipping through channels.

Chapter 13

Duncan walked into Sloan's office without knocking. He wanted to get this over quickly so he could get back to Pam.

"What's so important you needed to see me right away?" Duncan stood in front of Sloan's desk. He didn't even want to get comfortable by taking a seat.

"I just got a call from Pete." Sloan tossed his pen on the desk. "Sheriff Bowman's murderer turned himself in."

A bad feeling crept over Duncan. "I take it that someone is not Kenny Lawrence."

"Bingo," Sloan growled. "You know I always hated that fucking dog, now I know why."

"That is bullshit." Duncan slammed his hands on Sloan's desk. "We know he did it. We watched him do it. Everyone in that fucking bar is a witness."

"It's a done deal, Duncan." Sloan cursed. "Kenny Lawrence turned in a half-breed by the name of Ray Jones."

"How in the hell is that a done deal," Duncan shouted. "He's a lying sack of shit."

"The half-breed confessed to it all."

"Fuck!"

"Detective Ferguson has dropped everything against Kenny. He's a free man. Supposedly, he and Ferguson set up a deal before the bastard turned in the half-breed." Sloan frowned. "That's not all."

"As if that's not bad enough," Duncan growled.

"Kenny has taken out a restraining order against the VC Warriors."

"He's a dead man," Duncan warned Sloan. "I swear to God if he comes close to her, I will kill him."

"And that's exactly what he wants. The more Warriors he can get out of the way, the easier he can get to her and the baby."

"Well that will be hard for him to do once he's dead." Duncan had never felt such rage. To even think of that son of a bitch getting near Pam had Duncan wanting to kill something, and he was usually the calm one.

"He's smarter than that." Sloan rubbed his eyes. "As much as I hate to admit it, he pulled one over on us, but the thing he hasn't counted on, is us being a hell of a lot smarter than him."

"Ferguson has his hand in this," Duncan grunted, his mind going a mile a minute. "Did Pete say what kind of deal they made?"

Sloan just shook his head. "Pete is trying to find out what he can."

"We owe that cop a lot," Duncan replied.

"Keep her close, Duncan. Don't let her out of your sight," Sloan ordered as if he had to give those orders. "He's going to try to do this the legal way and get custody of the baby. I'd bet my ass on it. So we have to be a step ahead. The son of a bitch has bit off way more than he can chew."

"Swear to me if anything happens to me, the bastard never gets close to Pam or the baby." Duncan had never been more serious in his life.

"Nothing is going to happen to you, but yeah, I swear to you they will be taken care of," Sloan swore with a nod sealing the deal.

"Does everyone else know?" Duncan asked, walking away from the desk.

"Not yet. I wanted you to be the first, but I'll take care of them. You take care of Pam." Sloan stared at the door as his friend and fellow Warrior walked out. He hated having his Warriors look the fool. Picking up his desk phone, he slammed it down twice before setting it back down nice and easy. Detective Ferguson had no clue who he was fucking with, but he was about to find out.

*****

Pam decided she really liked the smart mouthed Sid Sinclair. He was charming in a funny, in your face kind of way, and had her laughing nonstop since Duncan had left.

"Okay, not much on TV tonight." Sid kept flicking through the channels.

"It doesn't matter to me." Pam stood to go to the restroom. "I never watch much TV anyway."

"You have got to be kidding me. Airplane Repo? How the hell do you repo an airplane." Hearing Pam moan he flipped to the next channel.

"Okay, I'll find something else. How about When Fish Attack 2?" When Pam moaned louder, Sid glanced over at her ready to hand her the remote. "Here you find something."

Seeing Pam bent over holding her stomach had him throwing the remote as he jumped from the chair. "Pam! What's wrong? What is it?"

Pam bit her lip as she tried to straighten up. "Just had a small pain."

"Small pain, my ass." He looked at her pale face. "Let me get Duncan."

"No, wait." Pam grabbed his arm straightening all the way up. "Don't leave me, please."

Sid looked torn with wanting to go for help, but not wanting to upset her more. "Are you sure?"

"Yeah, just let me go to the bathroom." Pam took two steps before stumbling into the wall with a moan as pain gripped her stomach again.

Sid was there in a flash. Carefully he picked her up and headed for the door. "Where's the doc's new office?"

"I don't know." Pam held onto her stomach, her face pale as she broke into a sweat. "I'm scared, Sid."

By the look on Sid's face, that made two of them, but he didn't say it. Going as fast as he could without jarring her, he went down the end of one hallway kicking doors in. "God damn, where is it?" he cursed. "Who the hell designed this place? Whoever it was needs their ass kicked."

"Try that way." Pam held on trying to stay still, but another pain hit. "Oh, God." She clinched her jaw.

"Fuck! Fuck!" Sid went faster. "Don't you dare have that baby yet!"

"I seriously don't think it's up to me," Pam replied unclenching her jaw as the pain faded.

"Just hold them legs together." Sid kicked another door cursing when it was empty. "And don't sneeze."

"Don't sneeze?" Pam looked up at him confused.

"Yeah, we don't need that thing shooting out." Sid was seriously freaking out. "Where the fuck is it?"

Pam laughed; she couldn't help it. As scared as she was, Sid made her laugh. "It's not a thing, it's a baby and I don't think a sneeze will do that."

"Well, let's just not even find out, okay?" Kicking the last door at the end of another long hallway, Sid walked in where Slade and Jill were putting things away in cabinets. "Where the fuck have you been?" Sid yelled.

"Ah, right here." Slade caught sight of Pam. "What's happened?"

"I'm having small pains," Pam answered, feeling much better that they had found the doctor.

"And I repeat, small pains, my ass. She was bent over." Sid still held her waiting for orders.

"Move that stuff off the table," Slade ordered Jill. "Hurry up."

Jill quickly removed a box before laying a sheet across it. Sid gently laid Pam down as Jill placed a pillow under her head. "Where's Duncan?"

"No, don't bother him." Pam grabbed Sid's arm. "It was just a little pain. It's gone now."

"Oh, I so don't want to get my ass kicked, thank you very much," Sid snorted, pulling out his phone hitting a few numbers. "Where the hell are you? Yeah, well we aren't there. She was having pains, so I brought her to the doctor. I have no fucking clue where."

Jill grabbed the phone from Sid. "We're down the hall by the east side exit." She handed the phone back.

"You need signs." Sid moved out of the way. "This place is a damn maze."

"Where's the pain, Pam?" Slade pulled up her shirt just below her breasts and pulled her pants below her belly.

Pam put her hand on her lower right side. "It starts here, but moves across my stomach."

"Have you had any bleeding or spotting?"

"No."

Slade pulled out a stethoscope putting them in his ears and then on her stomach. He frowned when she jerked. "Another pain?"

"No, that's cold."

"Sorry." Slade grinned, then got serious as he listened intently moving the stethoscope around her stomach. "How far along are you?"

"Three months." Pam watched his face closely trying to read what was going on in his expression, but he was a closed book.

"Do twins run in your family or the father's family?" Slade ask not revealing anything.

"Not in mine, and I'm not sure about...." She couldn't say father. He wasn't a father. He was a monster. "His family. Is the baby okay?"

Slade pulled the stethoscope out of his ears. "How long have you been having pain?"

"Just now. Why?" Pam started to feel panic and suddenly wanted Duncan there.

"When was the last time you felt the baby move?" Slade grabbed his phone.

"This morning." Pam tried to sit up, but he put his hand on her shoulder.

Putting the phone to his ear he waited as he stared into her eyes. "This is Dr. Buchanan. I'm bringing in a patient and need a sonogram room ready STAT."

"Oh, God." Pam closed eyes fear gripping her.

Duncan burst into the room heading straight for Pam. Grabbing her hand, he looked at Sid. "What the hell happened?"

"We need to get her to University Hospital now." Slade went to pick her up, but Duncan was faster.

"I'll get the car out front." Sid took off so fast his last word was said from the hallway.

Slade started grabbing stuff, shoving it in bags before following Duncan out the door. "Dammit." He turned, but ran into Jill.

"What do you need?" Jill asked. "I'll get it. You need to stay with her."

"I need my identification stuff. I haven't been to the hospital yet." Slade patted his pockets to make sure he didn't have them. "They're on the desk."

"Go. I got it." Jill went back into the room.

Slade caught up with Duncan. "Any more pains, Pam?"

"No," Pam replied, her head on Duncan's chest. "Why are we going to the hospital? What's wrong?"

Slade's eyes met Duncan's. "Just a precaution," he told Pam, but he mouthed, *hurry*, to Duncan.

Chapter 14

Duncan followed Slade through the hospital emergency room. As soon as he showed his identification, they were escorted to a room. There was a nurse waiting. Slade said a few words to her before turning his attention back to Pam. "Have you ever had a sonogram?"

"No," Pam replied looking away from the nurse who was staring at her.

"Lay her on the table." Slade pulled the machine close.

Reluctantly, Duncan laid her down, but grasped her cold shaking hand. Looking at Slade, he silently dared him to tell him to leave.

Getting the message loud and clear, Slade smiled. Pulling up her shirt under her breasts, and her pants down exposing her whole belly, he watched her closely. "Any more pain?"

"No." Pam watched him work the machine. "Not feeling the baby move is bad, isn't it?"

"Not always. This is going to be cold, so I apologize." Slade applied gel to her stomach. "Sometimes the little one just takes a long nap giving the momma some down time."

"But you didn't hear anything either did you?" Pam's chin trembled, bringing up what she was afraid to bring up at the compound.

"Using a stethoscope isn't the best way to hear a baby's heartbeat. They can be lying in a different position making it impossible to hear. That's why we use sonogram. It's the best way." Slade took the probe placing it in the gel running it along her stomach. "You're going to feel some pressure, but no pain. If you feel any pain, let me know right away."

Duncan watched Pam who watched the screen of the machine holding her breath. "Breathe," he whispered, placing his lips to her temple, his eyes going to the screen. The whooshing sound of the sonogram filled the room. All eyes were on the screen. As Slade ran the probe around her stomach, a different sound filled their ears. The sound of the baby's heartbeat, faint at first, slowly got louder until it filled the room.

Pam lost it. Tears filled her eyes at the sound. Turning her head, she buried her face in Duncan's neck. "Thank God."

Slade hit buttons on the machine before moving the probe more. "You said you estimate you're three months pregnant?"

"Three months and a week to be exact." Pam still had her face buried in Duncan's neck trying to compose herself.

"That's impossible." Slade hit more buttons, the machine making different noises. Even the nurse had a look of disbelief on her face. "You are in the third trimester. Are you sure about the three months?"

"Yes, I'm sure," Pam replied. It was a day she would never forget. "I was given a shot."

Slade looked up at Duncan who nodded toward the nurse shaking his head. "Okay, we'll talk about that in a few minutes." He turned the machine so she could see it better. "Would you like to meet your baby?"

"Yes." Pam sniffed wiping her eyes smearing blood on her cheek. Duncan wiped it away with a small smile. Turning, she looked at the screen, and there was her baby, nestled in her womb. "Is it okay?"

"Yes, ten fingers and toes with a cute little nose." Slade laughed when the baby yawned.

"Oh, did you see that?" Pam's eyes shot to Duncan.

"Yeah, I did." Duncan watched amazed. Never had he seen anything like it. Looking down at Pam's excited face, he felt such a sense of home, it blew him away. Never did he think he would have a family of his own, but looking from Pam to the baby, he knew without a doubt, his secret hope was finally being fulfilled.

"Do you want to know the sex?" Slade moved the probe around more.

"I don't know." Pam looked at Duncan. "Do we?"

"It's up to you, babe." Duncan felt honored she asked him. Even though he wasn't the father by blood, she made him feel that he was.

Biting her lip, she looked back at the screen nodding, excitement blooming across her face. "Yes. We want to know."

A wide grin spread across Slade's face. "Congratulations. Looks like you are going to have a strapping young man."

"A boy?" Pam put her hand across her mouth. "I knew it. I knew it was going to be a boy."

When Pam smiled up at him, Duncan couldn't resist kissing her.

Slade put the probe up, clicked a few more buttons before cleaning off Pam's stomach, and pulled her shirt down. He turned to the nurse. "Thank you for your help. I need a few minutes with my patient."

"Yes, sir." The nurse replied heading out the door.

Duncan helped her sit up. "Thanks."

Slade picked up a few pictures handing them to Pam. "Here's the little guy's first photos."

"How adorable." Pam stared at the pictures, and then laughed. "It looks like he's smiling in this one." She showed Duncan who laughed.

Slade pulled the stool in front of them. "I need to know what's going on." He broke into Pam's excitement. "If I'm going to keep you and the baby alive, I need to know everything. This is not a regular pregnancy."

Pam's mood turned in an instant. "What do you mean keep us alive? You said he was fine."

"He is, but he is a big boy, and you are a small woman." Slade replied glancing at a printout from the machine. "By what I can tell, your due date is less than two weeks. The pains you were having I believe were Braxton Hicks contractions, which is what doctors like to call practice labor, getting everything ready for the real thing. Also with the baby nesting down, and not moving much, could also mean he's getting ready. I'm concerned because he is not in the right position for delivery yet."

"But you can still do a C-section, right?" Pam put the pictures down before she crimped them in her nervous hands.

"Yes, but..." Slade stopped pinching the bridge of his nose. "As a doctor, what you are telling me, I know is impossible. You're telling me you are only three months pregnant, but the size of the baby indicates you are in your third trimester. What I don't understand is how you can be six months off. What makes you believe you are only three months pregnant?"

"I know exactly when I got pregnant because I was raped." Pam reached back grasping Duncan's hand. "As I was being raped, I was given a shot that supposedly contained a fertility substance."

Slade's eyes darkened at the word raped. "I'm sorry."

"Two days after I was raped, I started having morning sickness. I knew what he wanted and what the vial was for, so when I started throwing up, I got a pregnancy test and it was positive. Actually, I took three of them, all positive," Pam sighed.

"How do you know what was in the vial?" Slade frowned.

"Because it was my ex who raped me. He bragged that he was going to make me a breeder." Pam's eyes became angry.

"Breeder?" Slade looked to Duncan. "A breeder of what?"

"Half-breeds." Duncan answered. "Listen, we can fill you in on the rest of it later. Right now I just want Pam taken care of."

Slade nodded in total understanding. "I guess we don't have a vial of what you were given."

Pam shook her head. "I've tried to find it, but nothing yet."

"Okay, well it is what it is." Slade stood. "We just go from here. With your permission, I would like to examine you. I really need to see if you're dilated at all. The timeline is throwing me way off."

"Okay." Pam didn't sound so sure.

"I can have someone else do it if you're not comfortable with me, Pam." Slade informed her wanting her to be at ease.

Remembering the way the nurse had looked at her, Pam shook her head. "No, I would rather you do it."

"I'm going to have to ask you to step out." Slade told Duncan as he pushed the sonogram machine back out of the way. When Duncan looked ready to argue, Slade held up his hand. "I'm going to have the nurse come back in during the examination, but I have to ask you to leave."

"It's fine, Duncan." Pam squeezed his hand. "It's kind of embarrassing anyway, so I'd rather you not be in here if that's okay?"

"Whatever you want, I'll do." Duncan kissed her before heading for the door. "I'll be right outside."

Slade handed her a hospital gown. "I'm going to get the nurse. Go ahead and put this on and I'll be right back."

"Okay." Pam took the gown staring at it.

Duncan watched Pam who looked so alone and scared sitting on the table he almost went back to her, but Slade stopped him. "I will take good care of her Duncan. I swear it."

With one last look, Duncan let Slade push him out the door.

******

"Is she okay?" Nicole ran up to Duncan.

"Yeah." Duncan replied looking at the anxious faces of Damon, Jared, Tessa, Sid, Jill and Sloan as they waited for word on Pam. "She's fine. Slade is going to do an examination on her right now."

"How about the baby?" Tessa walked up next to Nicole.

"The baby is fine and will probably be here sooner than we thought."

"What? Seriously?" Nicole replied looking panicked. "Crap! We haven't had the baby shower yet."

They stepped away from the door as Slade and the nurse came back. Slade knocked making sure Pam was ready. Everyone heard Pam's voice carry through the door.

"I'll be right out when I'm finished, so you can go back in." Slade told Duncan before disappearing inside.

Duncan nodded without saying anything, but as soon as the door closed, he stepped right next to it so he could hear if she needed him. If she did, it would take an army of men to keep him out.

"Is she going to have to stay here?" Sloan asked. "Because that may be a problem."

Duncan's protective instincts kicked in. "Why would that be a problem?"

"Because we didn't cover our tracks, so this place is crawling with media." Sid answered, tossing back a bag of potato chips. "And it will be hard to keep her safe from Kenny."

"You told them?" Duncan glanced at each of them. The angry frowns on their faces answered that question.

"He comes anywhere near her, we'll know it." Jared growled.

Sid watched a nurse walk by eyeing him. Knocking the crumbs off his shirt, he crumbled the empty bag. "So the pregnant one is good, as well as the little rug rat?"

Rolling his eyes, Duncan nodded. "They're fine."

"Good." Sid grinned as the nurse passed again. "Hey Sloan, we got health insurance through the Council right?"

"What the fuck are you talking about?" Sloan looked up from his phone with a growl.

"I think I need to get my blood pressure checked." Sid wagged his eyebrows as he took off after the nurse, tossing his empty potato chip bag in the trash.

"I think I hate him," Sloan sneered. "I really do."

"Ah, he grows on ya." Jared shook his head laughing at Sid.

"Okay, now that the scare is over with we need to plan a baby shower." Nicole whipped out her phone.

All the Warriors threw up their hands in horror, even Sloan, different mutterings of protest coming from each of them.

"What?" Nicole stared at them.

"Me and Nicole can't do this on our own on such short notice. The baby is coming soon. That doesn't give us much time." Tessa flipped her hands in the air. "Come on, guys."

"Babe, we kill shit." Jared talked to her on a serious level. "We don't do baby showers. Nowhere in the Warrior's oath does it say we do baby showers."

"Oh, and it says you kill shit?" Tessa gave him a disbelieving snort.

"As a matter a fact, it does." Jared tossed back at her.

"I'd like to see that oath." Tessa's glare was suspicious.

"Only Warriors can lay eyes on the oath." Jared smiled knowing he had her.

"Uh, actually I've seen the oath and it doesn't say that." Jill stepped next to Tessa and Nicole. "Count me in girls. We don't need their help. We got this. They'd just get in the way."

Tessa elbowed Jared in the stomach when she walked by him, she and Nicole already making plans.

"You'll pay for that in training," Jared warned Jill with an evil glare.

She just shrugged her shoulders with a grin. "Sorry."

Jared snorted at her as she followed Tessa and Nicole. Glancing around at Damon, Duncan and Sloan, he threw his hands in the air. "Thanks for jumping in and helping out guys." Jared growled.

"Hey, you were doing fine," Sloan replied, leaning against the wall.

"Yeah, until you crashed and burned," Damon added with a rare grin. "Didn't really want to go down with you."

"Yeah, and I'll remember that, pal." Jared walked away, but realized he was heading toward the planning women. With a quick turn, he headed back past the Warriors who were all laughing at him. "Fuck you, guys."

Duncan was paying half attention to what was going on. His focus was on what was going on in the room behind him. He tried to get a read on Slade, but he was closed off tight. He wouldn't try to read Pam, didn't even know if he could. He had tried to get into the nurse's head, but all her thoughts were about how she was going to get the new doctor into her bed and he so wasn't going there.

"How you holding up?" Sloan walked over.

"I'll let you know after the doc comes out." Duncan replied glancing at the door with a frown.

"He's the best, Duncan," Sloan reassured him. "I wouldn't have brought him in if I didn't believe that."

"So is he a doctor or a Warrior?" Damon asked, hearing their conversation.

"He's both, but he's a Warrior first. I've known him for a long time. He will be an asset to the team." Sloan patted Duncan on the back. "She is in the best hands."

The door opened as Slade and the nurse came out. He gave her instructions before turning toward Duncan. "I need to talk to you alone."

"Is she okay?" Duncan didn't budge from his stance by the door.

"She's getting dressed." Slade looked around. "Come on."

Duncan followed him to a private room that wasn't being occupied. "You didn't answer my question."

Slade frowned as he closed the door. "Okay, I need to get this out of the way first. I hope to God you find the bastard who did this to her, and even though my priority is to save lives, there are some lives not worth saving. Kill the bastard or I will."

"No worries there. He's a walking dead man." Duncan tried to remain calm, waiting to hear something he was sure he didn't want to hear.

Slade took a second to compose himself, his black eyes going to gold in a flash. "She has been used, hard." Slade growled knowing he didn't have to explain what he meant. "She has a lot of damage that is not repairable. This birth, if natural, is going to be hard on her."

Duncan looked away his face a mask of stone. "Does she know?"

"Yes." Slade replied. "I told her everything. She asked me to tell you; she wanted you to know. She said that you two haven't been intimate yet, but I advise you to go very slow with her."

"Not a problem." Duncan was having a hard time talking, his words coming between clenched teeth. His rage so raw, he was about to explode.

"Have you thought about the possibility she may never be able to be intimate with a man, with you?" Slade's eyes were clouded with sympathy.

"Yes, I have," Duncan replied. "And it doesn't matter to me."

"But it matters to her."

"What the hell do you mean by that?" Duncan's eyes finally shot to Slade's.

"She's very concerned that she can never be the woman you need," Slade said point blank.

"What the fuck did you say to her?" Duncan growled plowing Slade into the wall.

"I didn't say anything to her. I told her how much damage had been done." Slade understood Duncan's rage and didn't push back. "She was the one asking the questions. She is more concerned about you and the baby than she is about herself. I am just giving you fair warning about where her mind is."

"Fuck!" Relaxing his hold, Duncan cursed again as he let him go. "Sorry."

"Don't be. I would be slamming people if that was my woman," Slade replied. "Just go slow with her. Keep her as calm as possible. I honestly cannot pinpoint a due date with her, but I can tell you it's going to be very soon. She is already dilated, but it's different with different women."

Duncan didn't even act like he knew what he was talking about. He didn't care about other women. All he cared about was Pam and that she stayed safe. Duncan stepped away. "Thank you."

Slade slapped him on the back. "Come on. She should be dressed by now."

Duncan walked out of the room and headed to the room where she was. Hearing her voice, he looked down the hall and saw her sitting in the waiting room with Tessa and Nicole. The Warriors surrounded the women as they sat and talked. Pam smiled at something Nicole said, her eyes lifting to meet his. Her smile started to fade as her eyes went from him to Slade and then back to him again. Duncan gave her a grin with a wink, letting her know that he wasn't running; he was here and wasn't going anywhere.

Chapter 15

A tall, older man in a physician's jacket met the large group as they made their way to the emergency room exit. "Dr. Buchanan?"

Slade stepped up. "Yes."

The man stuck out his hand. "I'm Dr. Krebs, chief physician here at the University and would like to welcome you."

"Thank you, sir." Slade shook the man's hand. "I apologize I haven't introduced myself, but we had a bit of an emergency. I appreciate you and your staff setting things up for me."

"Glad we could help," he replied. "I do want to inform you that the hospital is surrounded by reporters who seem very interested in your patient. They are not allowed inside the hospital, but they have the area covered."

"Where's our decoy?" Jared looked around for Jill.

Jill stepped forward. "I didn't bring a pillow," she grinned.

Dr. Krebs smiled. "I think we can help you with that." He walked to the nurses' station giving a few orders before he walked back. "You can bring a car where the ambulances unload."

Slade smiled. "Thank you."

"No problem at all." Dr. Krebs smiled shaking hands with the rest of the Warriors who thanked him. "Dr. Buchanan, I'm looking forward to working with you."

Nodding, Slade watched the older doctor walk away. A nurse came up with a pillow and coat. Jill walked up and took them.

"Be right back." Jill took off to a restroom.

Sid walked up. "What's going on?" he asked, combing his messy hair with his fingers.

"Reporters. Decoy time." Jared answered. "Go get the car and pick up the doc, Duncan and Jill."

"I'm not leaving Pam." Duncan's tone indicated to everyone that he was not leaving her side.

"Okay, I'll go with them." Jared nodded at Sid to go.

"Ready." Jill walked out with her instant pregnant belly and large coat. "I need a hat."

The nurse who brought the other stuff looked around the nurses' station and came back with a baseball hat. "Here." She handed Jill the hat.

Jill put it on her head and smiled. "Thanks."

"I'll let you know when the car pulls up." She grabbed a wheelchair. "Those reporters know the ropes at the hospital. If you walk out of here, they might figure it out. All pregnant patients brought in, leave in a wheelchair."

Jill sat in the wheelchair pulling the cap lower. Glancing up, she caught Slade staring at her. "Do I look like Pam?" she asked.

"No." His reply was short and to the point.

Jill frowned at him as the nurse walked up.

"Okay, there's the car. We have an ambulance that just pulled in, so please try to stay out of the way of the paramedics." The nurse warned them.

"Okay, let's do this." Jared got behind to push Jill.

Slumping down Jill lowered her head. Just as she started to look up, a sweet smell hit her nose. In an instant, her fangs grew, her mouth flowing with saliva. Passing her on a gurney was a man who was bleeding profusely. A growl erupted from her throat that sounded animal like. Her golden eye turned black as midnight.

"Jill?" Jared leaned down to whisper. "What's…?"

She heard nothing but the heartbeat of the man bleeding as it pumped his lifeblood out his wound. Nothing mattered to her at that moment except to taste the sweet blood. In an instant, she was out of the wheelchair.

"Son of a bitch!" Jared reached for her, but missed.

It took Slade a second to realize that Jill was under an attack of bloodlust. Grabbing her before she could reach the man on the gurney, he held her against him as he rushed through a throng of reporters shouting questions. Jill fought him with everything she had, but he was too strong for her. He could feel Jared at his back pushing reporters back. Sid had jumped out, and was ready with the door open. Slade fell in the back of the car with Jill underneath him.

"Jill!" He tried to get through to her, but he knew she was too far gone. Holding her down with his hand on her chest, he sat up trying to get his jacket off with one hand.

"What the fuck happened?" Jared slammed the door as Sid took off.

"Bloodlust." Slade's eyes didn't leave Jill's vacant ones. "Help me get my jacket off."

"They're following." Sid kept his eyes peeled to the road and rearview mirror. "Where do you want me to go?"

"Just drive around until we get word they have Pam back at the compound." Jared informed him while he tried to help Slade.

"Hasn't she been feeding?" Slade demanded.

"I don't know," Jared replied. "I mean, I thought she was feeding with the others."

"Well, I think it's safe to say you thought wrong," Slade mumbled looking down at Jill who had started to calm down, her eyes focused on his. "You back with us?"

She nodded, her frightened eyes open wide. "What happened?" Her voice was raspy and rough.

"Have you been feeding?" Slade asked her, easing the pressure slightly on her chest.

Her eyes shifted away from his. "They don't like me," she whispered.

"What? Who doesn't like you?" Slade asked, confused.

"Never mind," she replied, not realizing she had actually spoken her thoughts out loud. "I'm fine. Please let me go."

"You're not fine," Slade growled down at her. "You're starving and could have killed an innocent because you decided not to be responsible and feed."

With surprising strength, Jill knocked his hand away from her chest and sat up. "I said *I'm fine*."

"And I said *you're not.*" Slade reached for her, but before anyone in the car knew what was happening, Jill opened the car door, jumped out rolling to her feet taking off. "What the hell!" Slade sat stunned for a second before he was out the door after her.

Sid and Jared looked at each other shocked. "Did that just fucking happen?" Jared turned, staring at the empty backseat. "Yep, it fucking happened."

"Guess the cat's out of the bag, or should we say the vamp's out of the car." Sid shook his head in disbelief. "You better call and let the others know. I'll turn around."

Jill ran hard and fast zipping down side streets and back alleys. She didn't know or care where she was going. Horror at what she had almost done spurred her even faster. She had almost killed an innocent. She would be kicked out of the Warrior program for sure, and what would happen to her then? Her family wanted nothing to do with her. She would be alone, and that terrified her more than anything.

Turning down another alleyway, Jill skidded to a stop. "Crap," Jill whispered. Looked like she picked the wrong alley.

Ten men stood in a circle, engrossed in something until Jill's shoes slid on the gritty concrete. "Hey!" One shouted as the others looked up locking eyes on her.

"Sorry, wrong alley." Jill took a step backwards until she saw a woman kneeling in the middle of the group of men. Glancing back up at the men, she noticed they were a mix of humans and vampires.

The man who spoke was vampire, his golden eyes glowing in the darkness. "You got that right, little girl." He nodded to one of the men who grabbed the woman dragging her toward a car. The woman tried to fight, but the man tossed her around like a rag doll.

The woman's eyes met Jill's briefly; she was human. Jill's attention went back to the other men who started moving toward her as a group, the one who spoke in front.

"Holy shit. Luck is with us tonight, boys. We got us a half-breed." The man laughed clapping his hands together. "And I thought it was going to be a light night. We are going to make bank."

Jill kept quiet, thinking of her options, which were few. She noticed that three of the human men had stopped and were edging away from the vampires who pressed forward. Okay, that left five full-blooded vampires; the other full-blood was busy with the woman. Was she ready for this? Probably not, but she wasn't going down without a fight.

His eyes roamed her body stopping on her stomach, his grin widened. "You're the pregnant half-breed." He looked over at the others slapping one on the back. "She's the one."

Her hand going automatically to the pillow still securely tucked in her shirt, Jill frowned, not knowing if that was going to help or hurt her. By the look of glee on the vampires' faces, she didn't think it was a plus.

"Listen, I need help." Jill searched for a solution to her current situation while repeatedly cursing herself for jumping out of the car. What the hell had she been thinking? "I'm running from reporters and need to find the VC Warriors. We got split up."

Fear flashed in a few golden eyes at the mention of the Warriors, but the obvious leader snorted. "Honey, just stick with us." He stepped closer making Jill step back. He cocked his head at her action, a not so nice smile curving his lips. "We can keep you safe and get you out of the city. Don't seem the Warriors are doing a very good job. Heard they were a bunch of pussies."

If they only knew, Jill thought with a snort. "I appreciate that, but they're looking for me now. I'll just head back the way I came. I'm sure they're close."

"I don't think that's her." The vampire on the end had stepped closer looking at Jill.

"What the fuck you mean, that's not her." The main vampire pointed to her stomach. "She's fucking pregnant, isn't she?"

Knowing it was about to get nasty, Jill turned to take off, but wasn't quick enough.

"Where do you think you're going?" He grabbed her arm with one hand as the other reached out to touch her stomach. Jill tried to avoid contact, but his grip was strong, and her not feeding had made her weaker than she should be. His hand sunk into the pillow she had hidden under her shirt. His golden eyes turned dark as he reached under her shirt pulling out the hospital pillow she had used.

"I knew it," the other one growled. "I told you it wasn't her."

The one holding Jill leaned down holding the pillow up. "What the fuck is this?" he growled so close she felt his breath on her face. "What kind of game are you playing?"

Jill knew it was do or die time. Words from the Warriors came back to her in a rush of instructions, but Sid's words rang true in her current situation, 'When all else fails, fight dirty'. Leaning her head back, she thrust it forward with all her might head butting the vampire. Before she could take off, another vampire stopped her. Struggling to get away, she kicked, scratched and punched anything that got in her way.

"You bitch." The vampire she head-butted grabbed her by the shirt throwing her across the alley by the car.

Doing her best to land and roll out of the fall, Jill grunted when her sore shoulder made contact with the hard concrete. Okay, pain sucked. Pushing herself off the ground, she caught sight of Slade standing in the shadows. Shaking her head in warning, she missed the booted foot that kicked her hard in the leg.

"Get up, bitch." The leader picked up his leg to kick her again.

"I wouldn't suggest you doing that." Slade stepped out of the shadows, taking in the situation as he walked right up to the vampire standing over Jill.

"Who the hell are you?" The vampire who she had head-butted turned around. "You're asking for trouble. I suggest you leave and save yourself a lot of trouble."

"Step away from the woman or die." Slade's black eyes narrowed in warning.

The vampire shifted nervously, and then snorted. "I think you're way out numbered to be giving orders, asshole."

Slade cocked his head. "I'm not talking to them. I'm talking to you. Step away from her or die."

"Fuck you." The leader leaned closer to Slade to say those words, stepping on Jill's leg.

Slade spun, his leg kicking out so fast the vampire never knew what hit him as Slade's size 14 met the side of his neck, cracking it instantly. "No, fuck you," Slade spat.

"Watch out!" Jill warned. Another vampire came toward his left, but

Slade stuck his hand out grabbing him around the throat without looking.

"You guys sure you want to play?" Slade said to the others as the vampire in his hold made gasping gurgling sounds. Slade squeezed even harder.

Car lights lit up the alley. Jared jumped out of the car before it even stopped, Sid not far behind.

Looking down at the vampire, who wasn't quite dead jerking on the ground, his neck at an odd angle, Jared toed him with his boot. "This one piss you off, doc?"

Catching sight of another getting ready to take off, snapped Sid to attention, his eyes glowing. "Go ahead, run. Bet I catch ya."

The vampire stopped. "We didn't touch her."

"Get on your knees with your hands behind your head," Jared ordered opening his phone. "Now!" he shouted when only one did as he was told.

Slade tossed the one he held next to the rest of them.

"There's a woman in the car." Jill stood limping her way over to check on the woman.

Out of the shadows, the vampire who had taken the other woman grabbed Jill wrapping his arm around her neck dragging her a few steps back. Jill struggled, but he was too strong.

"Back the fuck up or I'll rip her throat out," he snarled, his fangs gleaming. He looked at the others on their knees. "Get up and get in the car!"

"Let her go or-"

"Or what...die?" The vampire mocked Slade as he leaned down licking the side of Jill's face, a crazy look in his eyes.

As soon as the vampire leaned back up, a hole appeared in the center of his forehead, his body weight falling on Jill, taking them both to the ground. Slade put the gun back in the waistband of his jeans under his jacket, as the echo of the gunshot faded.

The other vampires who had started toward the car dropped once again to their knees, hands behind their heads.

"That was fucking awesome." Sid grinned then mocked the now dead vampire. "*Or die?* Then BAM the bitch is dead! God, I love this shit."

Jill kicked and pushed trying to get the dead weight of the vampire off her. Slade reached down lifting him off her without a grunt, tossing him to the side. "Check the woman in the car," Jill told Slade.

"Sid," Slade called out. "Check on the woman."

Jared stood guard over the other vampires, still talking on the phone.

Slade knelt down in front of Jill. "Where are you hurt?"

"I'm not," Jill replied not looking into his eyes. "There were three human men here also."

"Stop playing Warrior for a minute, and tell me where you're hurt?" Slade growled helping her to her feet.

"I'm not hurt." She grimaced, putting weight on her leg. "I'll be fine in a minute."

"No, you won't." Slade's eyes narrowed. "And do you know why?"

"I don't want to talk about this right now." Jill turned to check on the woman Sid was talking to.

Slade spun her back around. He scooped her up. "I just killed two men. You are going to talk about it, and it's going to be right now."

Flashes went off making the alleyway look like a disco dance floor with strobe lights. Reporters swarmed the place taking pictures of everything.

"Is it really against the law for us to kill reporters?" Sid growled as he stood in front of the woman he had been interviewing.

"Sloan is going to be pissed." Jared frowned.

"What's new?" Sid flipped off one cameraman with a smile. "Just another day at the office."

Chapter 16

Pam, Duncan and the others had pulled into the compound when the call came in. Damon gave Nicole a quick kiss before running out the door.

Sloan passed them on his way out, glaring at Duncan. "You coming?" His tone and glare indicated that he expected him to get his ass in gear and in the van.

"No." His tone was final.

Sloan growled before slamming open the door. "You're lucky I don't put you on report."

"Duncan, please go." Pam urged him seeing the indecision in his eyes. "I'm fine. They need you. This is your job. It's what you do."

Adam had walked out to see what was going on. "Go ahead, man. Me and the others are here. We'll lock up tight and watch some movies or something."

"They've got this," Duncan replied, his stubbornness stamped across his face.

Pam let go of his hand. "If you don't go, I'm leaving."

"No, you're not." He reached for her hand again, but she pulled it away.

"I will not come between your job, and the other Warriors," Pam replied, just as stubborn. "I'm fine, and if anything happens, someone will call you. Now, go."

Duncan shot everyone an evil glare as if it was their fault. "Don't leave the compound." His eyes softened when they came back around to her.

"Not even a toe out the door." Pam nodded. "Now go before Sloan does put you on report, whatever that means."

In front of everyone, he gently grabbed her face, pulling her to him. "I'll be back soon." He kissed her softly, his thumbs caressing her cheeks.

"I'll be here," she replied when his lips left hers. "Be careful."

Duncan looked like he wanted to say more, but nodded before he turned running after Sloan and Damon. Stopping, he looked at Adam. "Lock this door. No one comes in."

"Got it." Adam followed locking the door behind him.

Pam watched Duncan jump in the van, which took off before he even had the door closed.

"Come on." Nicole put her arm around her. "You get used to them running off like that. Let's go find a movie or something. You hungry?"

"No, I'm good," Pam sighed. "Just want to sit down for a while."

"Hey, Adam," Nicole shouted. "Get some popcorn flowing."

"On it." Adam grinned. "Come on, Tess. Help me with some drinks." Tessa and Adam headed toward the kitchen.

"You guys don't have to babysit me." Pam rolled her eyes. "I'm a big girl."

"Honey, we aren't babysitting you. This is an every night occurrence when our men go out on the job. We stick together until they come home safe." Nicole ushered her into the game room. "Welcome to the life of being in love with a VC Warrior."

*****

Slade parked outside the exit door by his new office. Jared had him take the car since Damon, Sloan and Duncan were bringing the van. Walking around, he opened the passenger side door.

"I can walk," Jill grumbled when he opened the door to pull her out. Slade's face was stone cold as he reached in plucking her from the car.

Once at the door, he held her with one arm while getting his key card out of his pocket. Sliding it, the door clicked. Holding the door open with his leg, he put the key card back in his pocket then headed inside to his office.

Jill held on to his neck trying not to look at him. She hated when people were mad at her. It had always been that way. It drove her crazy. With her family, they weren't mad at her for being a half-breed; they were scared of her and didn't want to be anywhere near her, but Slade was mad. He set her gently on the table, but his touch left her abruptly.

"Listen, I'm sorry." Jill scooted further back on the table wincing when pain radiated up her leg. "I shouldn't have run off like that."

Slade didn't say a word, not even a grunt as he pulled off his leather jacket tossing it on a chair.

Knowing without a doubt that he wasn't going to take her apology, she frowned getting ready to hop off the table and leave. She had caused him enough problems since she met him; she was done causing him anymore. Just like her family. They didn't want her around, so she disappeared. She would do the same with him.

"If you get off that table, I'm going to blister your ass." Slade's back was still to her, but his voice stopped her cold.

"Excuse me?"

"You heard me." Slade finally turned around, his face still set in stone, beautiful carved stone. "Move off that table and your leg will be the least of your worries."

"You wouldn't," Jill replied, but the look in his eyes said he would.

"Don't test me, Jill." Slade reached out to touch her shoulder. "Did you damage your shoulder?"

"No." Jill jumped when he hit a sore spot proving she was a liar.

His eyes narrowed. "What about your leg?" He ran his hand down her leg with pressure and frowned when she jerked. "I guess that's fine also." His tone was sarcastic.

"You know what?" Jill pushed him away before sliding off the table. "The good thing about being a half-breed, actually the only good thing about it is I heal fast."

"Not if you don't feed." Slade shot back blocking her way to the door. "You're strength is compromised by your choice to not feed when you need to."

"You know that's none of your business." Jill side stepped, but he side stepped with her.

"None of my business?" Slade's eyes darkened slightly making Jill step back. Slade pressed forward. "You almost killed an innocent. When confronted about why you haven't been feeding, you put everyone, including yourself, in danger by jumping out of a moving vehicle, and if that's not bad enough, you find yourself in the middle of God knows what, where I have to kill two men. So yeah, this is my fucking business."

"I said I was sorry." Jill knew without a doubt her time with the Warriors was over. "I'll go pack and be out of here."

"What the hell are you talking about?" Slade yelled finally losing his cool.

"I screwed up, okay," Jill yelled back. "I put everyone in danger, you said so yourself. I can't be trusted, so I'm taking myself out of the program before I'm put out."

"You need to feed, Jill," Slade demanded.

Frustrated beyond belief, Jill felt all the rage of being turned and losing everything come bubbling to the surface. "I know that, dammit. Don't you think I fucking know that?" She threw her good arm in the air. "But who the hell do I have to feed from? The other half-breeds have those bitches they feed from. All those women want is to mate with a Warrior; they want nothing to do with me, and believe me, the feeling is mutual. I got the message loud and clear when I went to them the first time to feed."

"But that's their job. They get paid by the council to take care of…"

"Male Warriors and half-breeds, not some chick that's trying to keep up with the boys," Jill shot back.

"Then they need to be fired," Slade replied with an angry sneer.

"Oh, yeah. That will make me popular with the unmated males around here," Jill snorted. "Get rid of the hot, sexy blood banks because the poor little half-breed girl is whining about it. No, I don't think so."

She missed the grin that tipped his lips. "But that *is* their job, to supply blood," Slade added again.

"Why can't they have hot, sexy male blood banks walking around for the women? Huh? I mean how would you feel latching your lips on Sid or Jared?" Her eyes finally shot to his in time to see him shiver with revulsion. "Yeah, that's what I thought."

"You should have gone to Duncan with this." Some of Slade's irritation had left his tone.

"For three months, Duncan has not been here. Even when he was sitting behind his desk, he wasn't here. Pam's disappearance was more than enough for him to handle, not my little problem." When he started to open his mouth, she shook her head knowing what he was going to stay next.

"This is not a little problem," Slade argued staring into her mismatched eyes.

"I learned a hard lesson after I was turned. Once you become a problem, you're put out. When I was turned, I went home, but it was too much for my family, so I left. They were afraid of me, but I was still me. If I become a problem here, I have nowhere else to go." She looked away from his eyes, feeling uncertain. "If I leave now, I can still keep the friends I've made here. I wasn't that lucky with my family."

Slade was quiet for what seemed like forever. With a sigh, he took off his shirt. "You can feed from me tonight." He tossed his shirt on his jacket. "I will find someone male you can count on to feed from in the future."

Her eyes traveled the expansion of his chest down to the fine hairs that disappeared into the waistband of his jeans. His body was carved to perfection making Jill swallow hard.

"Uhm, that's okay." Jill pulled her eyes away from his body feeling like a sex fiend teenager that had never seen a man's bare chest. She had seen plenty of bare chests, but none like Slade Buchanan's. "I'm good."

"Oh, really? If you're fine, why did you almost attack an innocent at the hospital?" He walked toward her putting his hands on both sides of her legs caging her on the table. He cocked his eyebrow at her before tilting his neck. "Feed. Make sure you hit the vein."

Jill took a deep breath closing her eyes wondering how she got herself into these messes. Nervously, she opened her mouth and eyes at the same time, but just stared at the vein in his muscular neck.

"Jill?" Slade's voice broke the silence.

"Huh?" She still stared at the vein, her mouth and eyes wide open.

"Is there a problem?"

"Na uh."

Before he could move to see what she was doing, her sharp fangs broke his skin sinking into his vein. A hiss escaped him, but he stopped her when she started to pull away, putting his hand on the back of her head. "Don't stop."

She honestly didn't know if she could stop if she wanted to. His blood was warm with a hint of spice. She'd had a small amount of blood before, but never had it tasted like this. Her hand went to the other side of his neck, her fingers splayed apart, her thumb slowly moving back and forth across his skin. Never had she taken blood from someone's neck. It had always been the wrist. Her body was coming alive with feelings that were new to her and she was liking it…a lot. She felt lost in the moment, her body pressed closer to his as she took her fill.

Not having any idea the effect she was having on Slade, her body pressed closer as the tug of her mouth seductively took pulls of his skin. Moans reached her ears, but she didn't know if they were her own. She didn't care. Not really knowing how much she should take, she reluctantly pulled her mouth from his, licking the two puncture wounds taking the rest of his weeping blood.

"Is that enough?" Slade's voice was rough and low.

"I was going to ask you the same thing?" Jill replied into his neck, afraid to make eye contact with him yet. Her emotions and feelings were raw.

Slade leaned back away from her. "You probably don't want to take too much. My blood is going to be more potent than others." He looked down at her legs which were wrapped around his lower body.

Her eyes followed the path his had taken. A blush bloomed across her face. "Oh, I'm sorry." She unwrapped her legs, scooting further back on the table.

He only nodded as he reached to grab his shirt. "You should heal quicker now." He tugged his shirt over his head. "I'm having appointments with all the half-breeds next week, so I'll see how you're doing by then. If you need anything sooner, just let me know."

Hopping from the table, Jill was totally shocked when her leg held and didn't hurt at all. She moved her shoulder not feeling a twinge of pain. Hell he was a walking cure for aches and pains. Feeling dumb and inadequate just standing there, Jill headed for the door figuring she was dismissed.

"Thank you," Jill replied, finally able to make eye contact with him.

"It's my job, Jill." He nodded. "I'll find someone to take care of your needs, but for now you should be fine."

Okay, that hurt a little, but what did she expect? For him to fall to his knees announcing his undying love for her and swearing that he would be her hot, sexy blood bank? Yeah, in her dreams. Taking one last long look at him she savored the moment, because she was sure she would never have her lips or anything else on this man again. Men like him didn't go for girls like her, and at that moment that's what he made her feel like, a little girl.

"Well, I appreciate it, Dr. Buchanan." She added his title, because the sooner she realized he was way out of her league, the more protected her heart would stay. This was a man she could fall for…hard. Jill moved too fast once she was out the door, missing the cursing and loud bang of a fist going through the wall of the room she had just left.

Chapter 17

Duncan watched Pam pack her things. Tonight, Nicole and Tessa were throwing her a surprise baby shower at his place. It was time he took her to his private domain.

"What time did you get in last night?" Pam asked, folding a shirt and placing it in the small suitcase Nicole let her borrow.

"It was late." He smiled. "You don't remember me carrying you to bed?"

Pam laughed. "I actually thought it was a dream until I woke up in bed. Then I knew you had carried me here."

By the time they had come back from taking in the vampires, questioning and processing, not to mention cleaning up the mess Slade had made, everyone at the compound had been fast asleep, except for Nicole and Adam.

"You talk in your sleep," Duncan teased as he closed her suitcase for her, setting it by the door.

"No, I don't," Pam argued then frowned. "Do I?"

He grinned, wrapping her in his arms. "You do." He kissed the tip of her nose.

"What did I say?" She put her head on his chest liking the feel of his hands rubbing her aching back.

"Well, it was kind of hard to make out because some of it was mumbled, but I did hear my name a few times." He liked her soft sighs when he rubbed her back. "Does that feel good?"

"Yes, it does," Pam replied nodding into his chest. "Do you think it will always be like this?"

"Like what?" Duncan had closed his eyes, resting his chin on the top of her head.

"Nice, like this," Pam whispered. "Not fighting or hating each other."

Duncan pulled away, forcing her to look at him. "We're going to fight, Pam, but never would I hate you."

Before Pam could answer, someone knocked on the door. With a long sigh, Duncan let her go to answer it.

Slade stood on the other side. "Hope I'm not interrupting, but I wanted to see how Pam was doing before the meeting."

"Come on in." Duncan opened the door wide. "Is it five already?"

"Almost," Slade replied looking at Pam. "You look much better today."

Pam smiled. "I feel much better, thanks."

"No pain?" Slade's turn from Warrior to doctor was instant.

"None." Pam rubbed her stomach with a motherly smile; she absolutely glowed. Both men stared at her. "What?" Pam laughed nervously.

Slade cleared his throat. "You're beautiful." Slade slid a glance at Duncan. "Sorry."

Duncan glared at Slade.

"I'm just saying she makes a very beautiful pregnant woman." Slade tried to explain, but when Duncan continued to glare, Slade chuckled. "Listen, I don't want your woman. Just a compliment. I swear it."

Pam walked up to Duncan wrapping her arm around his. "Thank you...Dr. Buchanan." She grinned when Duncan's frown slipped into a half smile.

"He's right. You are gorgeous." Duncan looked down at her, his true feelings there for everyone to see.

"So I'm not a dead man for complimenting your beautiful lady?" Slade teased heading for the door.

"Guess I need to get used to that, or I'm going to have to take out most of the male population." Duncan winked at Pam. "So today, you live."

"Much appreciated." Slade laughed. "See you at the meeting."

As soon as the door shut, Duncan kissed Pam, pulling her close. "I have to go."

"You sure you have to?" Pam nuzzled his neck.

"Yes," he whispered in her ear, making her shiver. "Or you will probably be witness to one of Sloan's temper freak outs."

"Then go, because I don't think I want to see that." Pam pushed him toward the door.

"It's pretty ugly. Scared the shit out of me the first time I saw him having one," he teased. Leaning down, he kissed her goodbye. "As soon as I'm done, we'll take off to my place."

"Can't wait," Pam replied, feeling excited to actually be looking forward to something. It felt great for a change. "Duncan, thank you."

"For what?" He stopped right outside the door.

"Everything." Pam smiled, feeling radiant by the look he gave her. With a nod and wink, he was gone. Walking to the mirror, Pam looked at her reflection. She hardly recognized her happy face. "Welcome back." She grinned into her own reflection.

******

Duncan walked into Sloan's office, and by the look on Sloan's face, Duncan was ready to walk back out. "Happy you decided to join us," Sloan growled tossing him a look.

Knowing that keeping his mouth shut was the best thing to do, Duncan took an empty place against the wall.

"Good, now that we're all here..." He glared at Duncan who just stared without any facial expression at all. "I'll just start this little meeting with these." He slammed pictures on his desk, spreading them out with his hand. Everyone's eyes fell on the pictures.

"Oh snap!" Sid grabbed one of Nicole and Damon at the front door of the compound, Nicole's hand clearly cupping Damon. "Shit, I can't even think of anything to stay," Sid snorted, shaking his head and practically wheezing with laughter.

"Well how about this one?" Sloan grabbed one of Sid throwing the reporter off the property onto the street. "You got anything to say about this?"

"Photoshop." Sid tossed Sloan an innocent look.

"Then I'm sure this one is also Photoshop?" Sloan picked up one from last night with Sid flipping off the camera.

"Damn, that was fast." Sid glanced from the picture to Sloan's angry scowl. "Isn't it amazing what they can do now with computers?"

"That's actually a good picture of you." Jared observed tilting his head. "You should get that one framed."

"Thank you." Sid grabbed it looking it over. "I think I may just do that."

"Dammit!" Sloan shouted. "Do you take anything seriously?"

"Now, boss…" Sid began, but stopped at Sloan's sneer. "You were saying?"

"There are more pictures of Duncan, Jared, Slade, me, your mates, the half-breeds and this one is my favorite." He handed one to Jared. "Hope you have a good excuse for this one."

Jared's eyes darkened as he looked at the picture of him and Vicky, one of the female vampires the Warriors fed from standing close together looking as if they were having a secret meeting. Both wore smiles as they stared at each other their heads bent toward one another. She was excited because she was finally getting out of working for the Council, and was opening her own candle shop with a friend, but the picture made it look like they were having a secret lover's meeting.

"Not so funny now, is it?" Sloan glared watching the expressions cross Jared's face. "We are under the microscope more than ever now, and I don't think I need to tell you how important it is to watch yourselves, and your actions, because it doesn't seem like their interest concerns just Pam."

Duncan looked through the pictures finding at least ten of Pam, but the one that froze him was of her staring out the window. If a photographer got this close, so could Kenny.

159

"Next on the list." Sloan sat down running his hand through his hair. "Our girl Jill stumbled on something last night. After interviewing the vampires we took into custody, we didn't get much out of them, but the girl had plenty to say. Sid, fill us in since you interviewed her."

"Her name is Janie Sandfoss. Three of her human male friends were looking to make some good money by selling her to the vampires last night, who are part of a human trafficking ring, here in Cincinnati. She was to be sold to the vampires last night, who would then take her to an undisclosed location to be sold at auction to the highest bidder. Seems overnight, the need for human women has become highly profitable. Once sold to the highest bidder, they will be turned into half-breeds to breed. Pam's pregnancy has started this new trend."

"And she knew all of this?" Duncan asked.

"Yeah, she said that her three friends, who she named - we have our people, plus local law enforcement looking for them - were starting a new business and everything was discussed in front of her during the trade."

"Had the money traded hands yet?" Duncan asked.

"Yes." Sid frowned looking at each of them. "Ten thousand."

"Shit, that's enough for them to hide out for a while," Jared cursed. "And enough for a father to turn over a daughter, or a husband a wife. Does it ever end?"

"No, it doesn't," Sloan sighed. "Not only are we fighting the blood trade, we are now fighting human trafficking. We need to get those half-breeds trained fast. We are drowning here boys. We need all the help we can get."

"The last thing I have is this bullshit with Kenny Lawrence." Sloan shuffled some papers around until he found a folder. "Everyone in this room, except for Slade, knows that Kenny Lawrence killed Sheriff Bowman. Most of you witnessed it. Tomorrow, I have an unscheduled appointment with Detective Ferguson."

"Unscheduled?" Slade asked.

"Yeah, means he won't have time to figure out a lie," Sloan replied. "Have you talked to Pam about the charges being dropped and him being a free man?"

Duncan looked at Slade before answering. "Not yet."

"Well you need to, soon," Sloan ordered. "I'm going to raise all kinds of hell and stir up shit Ferguson thinks is buried. If I can get the charges reversed and put back on Kenny, she may have to testify."

"I don't want to do anything that could upset her until after the baby," Duncan replied again looking to Slade.

"I agree." Slade nodded. "She really shouldn't be put under any stress right now."

Sloan sighed nodding in agreement. "Okay, one more thing. What about Jill?" He looked around at the group. "Did anyone talk to her about what she heard last night?"

All eyes went to Slade. "I took care of her injuries, that's all."

"Sid, go get her." Sloan ordered.

"Isn't she with Nicole and Tessa getting everything ready for the baby shower?" Damon spoke up.

"I just saw her on my way in here." Sid headed out the door. "I'll get her."

Everyone was quiet as they waited. Sloan broke the silence. "California seeing any of these problems?"

Slade nodded. "Crimson Rush is the main drug on the streets. Actually, I had heard of Nicole before coming here. She's well known for her work in trying to put a stop to the blood trade with children."

"I'm not surprised." Damon's smile was full of pride.

Sid walked in with Jill following. She slowed when she saw everyone, her eyes avoiding contact with Slade.

"Jill is there anything that happened last night that you can fill us in on?" Sloan didn't beat around the bush. "The woman was being sold by her friends to the vampires."

Jill frowned. "Why?"

"From what she said and heard, she was going to be sold at an auction to the highest bidder."

Jill thought for a minute. "The one who seemed to be the leader was pretty excited that I was a half-breed, and said something like he thought it was going to be a light night, but they were going to make bank with me, which I guess is a lot of money," Jill replied, then her eyes widened. "They were going to auction me off?"

Sloan looked at Duncan and the others. "That's what it sounds like. If they don't have to turn you, they can go ahead and auction you off. Faster payday for them." Sloan frowned thinking out loud. "I don't want you leaving the compound alone until we figure out if this was just these idiots trying to make a fast buck, or if this is widespread."

"But…" Jill started to argue.

"That's an order." His tone left no room for argument.

"Yes, sir." She nodded. "Guess I need a ride to the party then."

"You can ride with me squirt." Sid nudged her, sending her a few steps forward.

"Do I have to?" She teased wrinkling her nose at him.

"Watch it or I might auction you off myself." Sid's eyebrow cocked at the thought. "Maybe with her being a half-breed, she'd go for more than ten thousand. I could use ten thousand."

"Ten thousand?" Jill sucked in her breath. "As in dollars?"

"Nice chunk of change, huh?" Sid grinned. "You better be nice to me, breed."

Jill rolled her eyes. "Is that all you needed me for?" she asked Sloan.

"Yes, you can go." Sloan gave her a rare smile. "Thanks, Jill."

"No problem. If I happen to remember anything else, I'll let you know." Jill turned to leave still keeping her eyes averted from Slade.

"How you doing today?" Slade asked as she passed.

"Good, thanks." Jill obviously rushed her steps as she went by him.

Everyone was staring at her retreating back, and as she disappeared, they all looked at Slade. "Is that all?" He looked at Sloan ignoring the inquiring stares. He was a doctor asking a patient how she was doing, that was all.

Sloan grabbed a few more pictures. "Actually, no."

"Please tell me those aren't of any of us naked." Sid grabbed them, but his humor was quickly replaced with anger as he shuffled through them.

"Jared found those in Pam's old apartment." Sloan plucked one of Damon with a red laser dot on his temple. "We had them analyzed. They're fake. Kenny was using them to control Pam. We needed to make sure there wasn't an assassin out there waiting for the go ahead to take anyone out."

"Good to know." Jared frowned, but his eyes were locked on the picture lying on Sloan's desk of him and Vicky.

"Okay, get out of here." Sloan stood. "I'll see you guys later tonight."

"You coming?" Duncan asked as he passed.

"Wouldn't miss it." Sloan nodded picking up the phone. "Need to make a few phone calls, then I'll be on my way. I'll make sure I'm there before you and Pam."

Jared hung back letting everyone leave. "How did this picture get here?" He pointed to the one of him and Vicky.

Sloan frowned. "It was mailed today." There was also an envelope exactly like this addressed to Tessa. "I saw her leaving with Nicole so I gave it to her."

"Dammit." Jared cursed. "That picture makes it look like something it wasn't."

"I know that." Sloan's voice rang true. "And I'm sure Tessa will know it also."

"Are we being set up?" Jared rubbed the bridge of his nose.

"It looks that way, but just not sure by who and why." Sloan slapped his back. "But we'll find out,"

"Yeah, we will." Jared walked out of the room, a look of dread on his face.

Chapter 18

Duncan's house went from manly bachelor pad to festive baby décor. Everywhere you looked there were white and blue balloons, congratulations banners and beautiful wrapped gifts. Tessa watched Adam and Angelina hanging blue and white balloons. She was happy to see them together. She knew they had hit a rough spot in their relationship and were trying to work it out.

Looking away, she continued cutting the vegetables for the veggie tray, but her focus was elsewhere. The mail Sloan had given her on their way out had thrown her world upside down. She knew she had to give Jared a chance to explain, but in all honesty, the picture in the envelope said it all. All her past insecurities weighed her down, and she hated it, hated feeling less than.

Vicky was a beautiful woman, and she was a vampire. Tessa was not. She couldn't even give Jared what he needed. Her blood wasn't enough for him. He had to go elsewhere. It hadn't really bothered her before. No that was a lie. It had bothered her, that he was taking blood from a woman whose beauty put hers to shame. The real sad part about it was Tessa actually liked Vicky. Her personality matched her beauty. Tessa should hate her, but she didn't or at least she hadn't.

"I think you killed the cauliflower, sis." Adam teased, grabbing another bag of balloons.

Tessa looked down at the mess she had made. The cauliflower would be better suited snorted than eaten. Without saying anything, Tessa wiped it off the cutting board into the trash grabbing more to cut.

"What's wrong?" Adam was at her side. As brother and sister, they had always been in tune with each other's moods.

"Just tired." Looking at their grandfather, Tessa tried to throw the attention off her. "Does gramps need anything?"

"Yeah, for you to tell me what's wrong." Adam tossed Steve and Angelina the balloons, and then leaned on the counter staring at his sister.

"Nothing's wrong, Adam." Tessa sighed chopping away on another head of cauliflower. The knife slipped slicing down straight across her index and middle fingers.

"Dammit, Tessa." Adam grabbed the knife from her. "Watch what you're doing."

They both looked at the clean cut that didn't start bleeding until seconds later, and then the blood gushed. Grabbing her, he led her to the sink sticking her hand under the faucet. Glancing at her face as he held her hand under the water, her face paled. "We need to get you to the hospital."

"No." Tessa replied through clenched teeth. "I'm not going to ruin Pam's party. Just get me a band-aid."

"A band-aid?" Adam snorted. "You're going to need stitches. You can see the bone, which is really gross by the way."

Tessa also saw the bone. "Don't pass out. Don't pass out," she repeated to herself. "Get me a towel."

"What happened?" Nicole walked over, glancing into the sink to see what they were doing. "Oh crap. Tessa, what did you do?"

"She about cut her damn fingers off." Adam came back with a towel.

With a shaky hand, Tessa turned off the water then grabbed the towel. "Stop cussing so much, Adam," Tessa mumbled, wrapping her hand as tight as she could. If she was a vampire, she would be healed by now. Shaking that thought away, she used her good hand to apply pressure.

"Tessa, honey, you need to get to the hospital." Nicole frowned watching the blood seep through the white towel.

"I will after Pam gets here. I don't want to miss her surprise. Just get me another towel please." Turning back to the sink, Tessa unwrapped her hand sticking it back under the water missing the glances shooting back and forth between Nicole and Adam.

"Who the hell is bleeding?" Sid said as soon as he and Jill walked in the door followed by Jared, Damon and Slade.

Jared knew as soon as he smelled the blood. He was at Tessa's side in an instant. "Are you okay? What happened?"

When he tried to look at her hand, she pulled it away to wrap it in a clean towel. "It's fine. Just a little cut."

"You can see bone, Tessa." Adam glared at her. "That's not a little cut. And for you not to be screaming in pain or passed out is a miracle."

Because I'm numb, she thought, but kept that to herself. "Just because I'm human, doesn't mean I'm a pussy," she shot back. "I said I'm fine."

No one said a word, but looked at her a little shocked.

Slade walked over staring at the towel wrapped around her hand. Again, blood was seeping through. "Is that a sterile towel?"

"I seriously doubt it." Tessa shrugged her shoulder. "It's okay for now."

"May I?" Slade reached for the towel, but Tessa pulled away. "I don't want to ruin Pam's party for a little cut."

"Let him look at it, Tessa," Jared said, his eyes on her trying to read her.

"Adam, can you please clean this up for me before Pam gets here?" Tessa asked walking away from Jared looking at Sloan. "We need to do this in the bathroom?"

"Can you get my bag out of Jared's car?" Slade asked Jill as he followed Tessa to the bathroom watching her closely. She swayed slightly but caught herself.

Duncan's bathroom was bigger than average, but Tessa felt claustrophobic with Slade and Jared looming over her as she sat on the toilet.

Slade washed his hands before kneeling down to gently unwrap her hand. "Find me a towel to put over her legs," he instructed Jared, who immediately went to find one.

Jill knocked, then walked in carrying Slade's bag.

"Just put it here." When she started to leave, he stopped her. "Can you wait, just in case I need something?"

"Sure." Jill stood back out of the way.

"What were you doing?" Slade asked as he looked her hand over.

"Chopping cauliflower," Tessa replied, looking at the ground instead of her hand. She was feeling a little woozy and light headed. "With an axe?"

Tessa snorted. "Was that doctor humor?"

"Pretty lame, huh?" Slade's lips curved. "You need stitches. I don't think you hit any nerves, which is a miracle, but you definitely need stitches."

"Okay, can you do that now?" Tessa adjusted the towel Jared had placed across her lap.

"I could, but I don't have anything to numb you up with." Slade rummaged through his bag.

"I don't care." Tessa avoided Jared's gaze. "Just do it."

Slade looked up at her then to Jared. "I don't advise that. You need to be numbed up and in a sterile environment. I don't think a bathroom constitutes a very sterile environment."

"Come on." Jared went to grab the towel. "Let's go."

Tessa grabbed the towel keeping it on her lap. "Can you put something on it until later? I'm staying for the party."

Looking uncomfortable with the obvious tension between Jared and Tessa, Slade nodded, going back into his bag. "I can put some steri-strips across it with some antibiotic cream, but you need to have this looked at in the next hour or so."

"Can you stitch me up in your office?" Tessa asked after he cleaned up her hand and closed the wound together with steri-strips before wrapping her whole hand in gauze.

"Well, yeah I could ..." Slade started, but Jared's frown stopped him.

"He said you needed to be seen at the hospital." Jared stared down at her. "We're going to the hospital."

"I'll stop by after the party if that's okay?" Tessa held her hand against her stomach.

"Can you guys excuse us for a minute?" Jared didn't even look at Slade or Jill, his eyes were focused on Tessa.

Slade and Jill couldn't leave the bathroom fast enough. As soon as the door shut, Jared knelt down in front of Tessa. "You saw the picture." It wasn't a question.

Tessa stared at her lap silently, telling herself she wouldn't cry. Not trusting her voice, she just nodded.

"It was nothing, Tessa." Jared reached down to cup her face, but she flinched away from his touch to look at him.

"They say a picture says a thousand words." Tessa looked at him, her eyes searching his. "I saw the look you were giving her, Jared."

"I know what it looked like, but I'm telling you it meant nothing." Jared caught her face with his hand this time. "I love you. I would never do anything to hurt you."

"Why?" Tessa felt her eyes welling up, dammit.

"She was telling me about the shop she was…."

"No, Jared. I don't care what she was telling you." Pulling her face away from his hand, she stood up. "Why did you have to look at her like you look at me?"

"I could never look at another woman like I look at you. You are my world." Jared carefully, without jarring her arm, took her by the shoulders forcing her to look at him. "Do you trust me so little that a picture could tear us apart?"

Tessa knew it was only a picture; she wanted to believe him and she did believe him somewhat, but that didn't mean it hurt any less. Her own insecurities were playing havoc with her emotions. The seed of doubt had been planted and she really didn't know if she could overcome it because she always wondered how he could love her, an overweight human, when a beautiful vampire - who had everything he needed - was right underneath his nose.

A knock sounded on the door before Nicole's head appeared. "Sorry, but they're here. He's parking now." Nicole looked between the two of them then at her hand. "You okay?"

"Yeah, I'm coming." Tessa waited until the door shut. "I don't blame you, Jared. I know having a human as a mate is not the way it's supposed to be. You need someone like …like her."

"So that's it?" Jared shook his head in disbelief. "Because of a damn picture?"

Tessa walked to the door opening it. "Yeah, that's it."

"The fuck it is." His voice followed her out. "I love you, Tessa, and one of these Goddamn days you're going to believe that."

Chapter 19

With the mess cleaned up from the party and the last person out the door, Duncan clicked the lock closed. Crossing the room to where Pam sat going through her gifts, he smiled. She belonged here, in his home…their home.

"Aren't these adorable?" She picked up a pair of tiny shoes.

"They're so tiny." He laughed taking them from her. Setting the shoes down, he reached out his hand. "I have a gift for you."

"Duncan, this is more than enough. You didn't have to get anything." Pam took his hand as she followed him up the stairs. Her eyes taking in everything since she hadn't been up there yet.

Stopping at a closed door, he turned the knob pushing the door open. Stepping back, he let her look inside.

Pam took a step inside, her head moving back and forth not knowing where to look first, her eyes trying to take everything in at once. The room was decorated in rainbow colors with animals painted on each wall. A tree with full-leaved limbs was painted in one corner with little monkeys hanging from the limbs. Anything and everything a baby would need was in the room - from the beautiful crib, down to a diaper pail. Pam walked further into the room taking it all in. Making her way to the tree with the monkeys, she reached out to touch one.

Glancing back at Duncan, she shook her head. "Why?" She didn't want to sound ungrateful, but no one had ever done anything like this for her before, and even if they had, there was a price to pay.

"You don't like it?" He frowned looking around the room. He should have waited and let her pick out everything she would need. "I can have anything changed that you don't like or replace it all. I just wanted to surprise you. Jill painted all the animals. Everyone chipped in to have it ready for today," Duncan's deep voice, with a hint of disappointment, rumbled through the room.

"No!" Pam turned back toward him. "No, please. I love it."

"Pam, you look anything but happy." Duncan walked toward her. "Never lie to me. If you don't like it, we can change it."

"Don't you dare change a thing in this room! It's just no one has ever done anything like this for me before. I'm a little overwhelmed with the party and now this." Pam laughed, shaking her head in disbelief.

Duncan nodded feeling relieved, but if this overwhelmed her, then the next two gifts he had for her would blow her mind.

"I have more for you." He walked toward her reaching into his pocket pulling out a small box. "This is just for you."

"Duncan please, you didn't have-" She stopped, seeing his frown. "Thank you." She took the box glancing at him then back down at the small box in her hand. Lifting the top off, Pam stared at the key lying in the soft cotton.

"You will always have a key here, Pam." Duncan lifted her face to his. "Forever if you want it."

The significance of this small gift hit her hard. The day Kenny took her key away from her was the day she totally lost herself. To have to wait, embarrassed and humiliated until he got home to go inside when neighbors in the apartment building would come home, had hit her hard. At first, she would leave to drive around, but Kenny started checking her speedometer, allowing her a certain amount of miles a day, so she had to wait. It had become a running joke with the neighbors... 'Lost your key again?' they would tease. She would just nod with a shrug as she sat by the door waiting. Sometimes he would be inside, but would make her wait in the small hallway until she heard the click of the lock. Only then was she allowed to enter what had once been her apartment

Slowly, her eyes left the key to stare up at the man she had sacrificed herself for, to keep him and the others that were here tonight, safe from a maniac. Had it been worth it? Seeing the love in Duncan's intent stare and the room done in love by friends was answer enough. It has been worth it; it had led her back to where her heart belonged.

"I've never been given a gift that meant so much to me," Pam whispered.

"Then I'm glad it came from me," Duncan replied proudly.

Pam took the key out of the box, holding it to her heart.

Watching her stare at the key as if it was the best gift she had ever received, told Duncan more than any words could have about what she endured at the hands of that bastard. Reaching into his pocket, his hand grasped something small. In that one moment, he knew without a doubt that he wanted her forever, if only she would have him. He had kept the ring close, waiting for the perfect time. Not knowing if this *was* the perfect time or not, he decided he didn't care. All he cared about was making her his.

His unconditional love for this woman gave him the courage to pull his hand out of his pocket. His fist was holding tight a future he wanted, more than anything he had ever wanted, in his long life.

Grasping her chin with his other hand, he brought her eyes up to his. He searched so deeply he felt lost until the smile that spread across her face reached her eyes. "I want you to know that I have loved you for a long time." Duncan's voice was deep with his own emotions.

"Duncan, I-"

He put a finger over her lips shaking his head. Slowly, without breaking eye contact, he bent to one knee. "Pamela Cecilia Braxton." He could tell by the look in her eyes she knew what was coming next, yet his determination was strong even though for the first time in his existence he feared rejection. He cursed himself as his gaze shifted away from her for a second, but knowing that this is what he wanted, he looked back into her beautiful mismatched eyes. "Would you become my wife, so I can be a husband to the woman I love and a father to the little guy?" He placed his hand on her belly.

Pam eyes widened. "You want to marry me?"

"Why does that surprise you?" Duncan watched the emotions play across her face.

"I don't know if I..." Pam stopped speaking to search his eyes. She wanted more than anything in the world to say yes, but was terrified that he would regret it.

"If you what?" His tone was level, not raised. Deciding then and there she would make it work, her heartbeat picked up speed as a wave of fierce resolve filled her. She wanted to be his wife. She would do anything to be whole again, and her first step would be to marry this incredible man.

"Yes."

"Yes?" Duncan looked surprised but hid it quickly.

"Yes," she whispered again, then watched as he quickly slipped a beautiful princess-cut engagement ring on her finger. Her hand shook as she held it up looking at it. Biting her trembling lip, she shook her head.

"What?" Duncan could tell she was upset by the way she bit her bottom lip. Tears had welled up in her eyes, but not a single tear had fallen...yet.

"I don't want to let you down." One tear finally escaped, sliding from the corner of her eye. "I don't know if I can be who you want me to be, Duncan."

"You will always be who I want you to be." Duncan's voice was firm, his eyes gentle.

"I do love you, Duncan." Pam reached up to touch his face. "I will make you proud. I promise."

"You have already made me proud." Duncan leaned down to kiss her. "You have made me complete.

*****

Jeff stood in the compound entryway when everyone walked in. Flashes of lights followed them in.

"Don't they realize the pregnant one isn't with us?" Sid mumbled, aggravation lining his face. "These reporters suck if you ask me!"

Adam snorted then noticed Jeff standing there. "Where the hell have you been?" Adam walked straight up to him. "You've been gone for almost a week."

Jeff looked around nervously at all the attention, his eyes landing on Slade then Jill. "I know." He shifted nervously. "I had a lot of thinking to do."

"Still man, you got to check in." Adam frowned. "Duncan is going to chew you out big time on this one."

"Yeah." Jeff looked away clearing his throat. "I know."

Adam tapped his shoulder hard. "What's wrong with you?"

"Nothing's wrong," Jeff growled noticing everyone going their separate ways, his eyes watched Jill head off with Jared, Tessa and the asshole who made him look like a fool. "Where's Duncan and Pam?"

"Why?" Adam asked with suspicion.

Jeff's eyes darkened when they shot back to Adam. "Because I need to see if I can come back," he spat out. "Why the hell else would I want to know where he was?"

"He and Pam are staying at his place." Adam glanced at his phone. Angel had driven separately because she came straight from work. She was supposed let him know when she got home.

"Guess I'll talk to him tomorrow." Jeff glanced once more down the hall where Jill and the others disappeared.

Adam's phone rang. "Yeah, make sure you do." He walked away answering his phone. "Hey babe."

Jeff glared at Adam's back. He had always hated him; even in high school he had hated him. Pulling out his phone, he dialed, putting it to his ear, looking around. "Yeah, it's me," he whispered walking in the opposite direction of Adam.

*****

Tessa and the rest stopped at the door of Slade's office as he unlocked it. She tensed when Jared put his hand on her shoulder. "Jared you don't have to be here for this."

"You don't want me here?" Jared asked, his eyes darkening.

Not able to look into his eyes, she looked away. "No, not really."

Jared stared at her, his eyes narrowed. He stopped her from following Jill and Slade through the doorway. "This has gone far enough."

"I agree." She shrugged her arm out of his hold.

He watched as she disappeared into the room, shutting him out. He knew this had to be about the way her ex, Sheriff Bowman had treated her, and it pissed him the hell off. Even dead, that asshole was causing problems with his relationship with Tessa, and to be put in the category of a cheater with the dead asshole, pissed him the fuck off.

Knowing what he had to do, he turned and started down the hallway with determined steps. With any other woman, he would have said fuck it, but not Tessa. Never with Tessa. He would fight the devil to keep her.

Tessa closed her eyes as soon as she heard Jared's heavy footsteps fade down the hall. God she felt horrible. Her hand hurt, but her heart hurt more. She wondered suddenly if she was doing the right thing.

"You okay?" Jill whispered as Slade prepared to stitch Tessa's fingers.

"No, not really." Tessa walked over to sit in a chair, feeling weak and shaky.

Slade rolled a low stool over and started unwrapping her hand, but blood had dried some of the towel to her hand. "Jill, can you get me a large bowl of water?"

"Are you going to be his assistant?" Tessa watched as Jill did what he asked quickly and efficiently.

Jill set the water down in front of Tessa. "Sloan wants me to help out until I can start training again." When Slade pulled out a shot with a long needle, Jill grimaced. "I really don't think this is my thing."

"Not big on needles, huh?" Slade tossed her a teasing grin.

"Not in the least." Jill turned and busied herself with anything except watching that needle go into her skin.

"Okay, this is going to sting a little." Slade swabbed her hand with cold alcohol.

"Don't listen to him," Jill said over her shoulder. "And if he says he's going to count to three, he's lying. It's two."

The first smile all night appeared on Tessa's face. "Sounds like you have exprience with his bedside manner."

"Oh, yeah." Jill frowned.

"Needles don't bother me." Tessa glanced up at Slade who waited. "Give it your best shot...pun intended." Tessa welcomed the pain in her finger as the needle found its mark. At least it made her forgot about the pain deep in her soul.

"I'll give it a few minutes to get good and numb, and then we'll get these cuts cleaned and stitched up." Slade stood to dispose of the needle.

Tessa nodded staring down at her hand. "Sounds good."

"Where did Jared go?" Slade asked after a few minutes of waiting for the numbness to set in., sitting back down in front of her using a long Q-tip dipped in a dark liquid to clean her wounds. When she didn't answer, he looked up at her. "Sorry. None of my business."

Tessa didn't even acknowledge she'd heard him. She just sat watching each stitch he made. Growing up and taking care of Adam, she had seen her fair share of blood and gore; it didn't bother her. Never did. She probably would have made a great veterinarian, even a nurse. Instead, she worked in a rundown bar serving drinks. Shaking those thoughts away, she frowned, knowing feeling sorry for herself wasn't going to do anything. She had gotten over Otis; she would get over Jared. Deep down, she knew without a doubt she was lying to herself.

"Okay, looks good." Slade lifted her hand closer to check his work. "Let me bandage it, and then you can get out of here. If the pain gets too bad for over-the-counter stuff, just let me know, and I'll get you something stronger."

"I'll be fine," Tessa replied. When Slade went into the other room, she looked at Jill who had finally turned around. "How much do I owe you? I don't have insurance."

"The Council will take care of it," Slade replied, not in the least worried about payment.

"But I'm not part of the Council and I'm human." Tessa frowned. "Just give me a bill."

Slade watched her for a few seconds, and knew by the look on her face that she wasn't going to let this go.

"I'll write something up and give it to you next time I see you." Slade played along. He wasn't going to take her money.

A sad expression colored her face. "You can't write it out now?"

"We haven't unpacked the paper stuff yet," Slade answered, shooting Jill a look when she started to open her mouth.

"Oh, well okay." Tessa frowned. "Nicole knows my address if I don't see you, so make sure you send it."

"Will do." Slade walked into the other room carrying the surgical supplies he had used.

Tessa sighed then looked at Jill. "What are you doing tonight, Jill?"

"You're looking at it." She smiled, tossing bloody towels into a bag closing it up.

"Would you like to go to my place with me tonight?" Tessa asked, hoping she said yes; she didn't want to go home alone.

Jill hesitated for a second, catching herself from asking why she wasn't going with Jared. "I'd like that." Jill smiled, figuring if Tessa wanted to talk, the least she could do was be there for her. Tessa had been so nice to her - always making her feel welcome. "Let me finish up here real quick, and we'll go."

Tessa nodded, trying to keep the tears from flowing. She prayed she could make it through this first night without Jared. Wiping the tear she felt slipping down her cheek, she looked up and found Slade staring at her.

"Are you in pain?" He frowned.

If he only knew, she thought. Shaking her head, she pushed her shoulders back. "Nope. Just a delayed reaction from the shot. I seriously hate shots," she lied terribly, and then lifted her hand up. "I could cut them off and not feel a thing."

"Let's keep all knifes away from her," Slade teased, but the smile didn't reach his eyes.

Chapter 20

They had left the baby room making their way to his bedroom, the room they would share. Pam looked around and felt a sense of belonging that she hadn't felt for quite a while, and it warmed her. Rubbing her belly, she walked over to the bed and sat down.

"You feeling okay?" Duncan frowned.

"The baby is moving a lot tonight." Pam grinned then grimaced. "And very strong."

Duncan sat down on the bed, leaning against the headboard. "Come here." When she walked up to him, he pulled her onto the bed between his legs with her back against his chest. Both of his large hands rested on her stomach and began to gently massage in soft, tender strokes.

Lying back against him, she enjoyed the gentle motions of his hands. The baby gave one solid kick, stilling his hands. "Did you feel that?" She laughed.

"Doesn't that hurt?" Duncan continued to massage.

"Yeah, sometimes." Pam leaned deeper into him. "But it's a good hurt."

"Do you need to feed, babe?" Duncan rested his chin on the top of her head.

She tensed momentarily before taking a calming breath. "If you don't mind." Pam still had a hard time with her need for blood. "I think the baby is taking a lot out of me. I feel weak and shaky a lot."

"Turn around." With his help, Pam turned, sitting on her knees.

"Should I get a towel? I don't want to get blood on your bed."

"Our bed," his deep voice rumbled.

"Our bed," she repeated with a whisper, her golden eye glowing dark.

With an approving nod, he lifted his wrist to his mouth but stopped at her frown. "What?"

"I want to take it from your neck, but I can't." She looked away from him, swallowing a nervous lump that had filled her throat. Her first test at wanting to be close to him was a total fail, what she feared most.

Duncan growled low as he reached into his back pocket. Flipping a knife open with one hand, he raised it to his neck. "There is nothing I would love more than you taking from my neck."

"Really?" She looked back at him, and immediately screamed, grabbing for the knife. "What are you doing?"

He caught her hand with his free one. "Be careful. This knife will cut you to the bone."

"Don't you dare cut yourself!" Pam looked at him in horror. "Your wrist is fine. I can take from your wrist."

"Honey, I know knives better than I know anything else." With no hesitation, he made two large, expert nicks in his neck. Closing the knife, he set it on the table next to the bed close enough to reach if he needed it. Grasping the back of her neck, he pulled her to him.

Pam looked at his strong-corded neck where two puncture wounds slowly leaked blood. "I can't believe you cut yourself."

"For you I would do anything." He adjusted himself to make it more comfortable for her.

With a sigh, Pam placed her lips on his neck. The taste of his blood was addicting. Soon she was taking long pulls. Her body reacted with an intense need, her breasts feeling more heavy and sensitive. She became wet instantly and wanted nothing more than to feel him between her legs. The thought and feelings shocked her, but made her glow in excitement that the feelings were there.

Taking a chance and letting her rush of need lead her, her hand ran down his heavily muscled arm to grasp his hand. Slowly, she placed his hand on her leg bringing it slowly up her body, placing it on her aching breast. When she felt him hesitate, she pulled her lips from her neck.

"Please, Duncan," she whispered. "I want you."

Another growl rumbled in his chest as his hand cupped her soft breast on its own. He rubbed her nipples over her shirt making them pucker for more. Running his hand down her body, he slipped under her shirt pulling her bra away, giving him what he sought. He was in heaven, her soft moans of pleasure urging him on. He couldn't wait to taste the sweet bud poking his hand, begging for more. With twists and tugs, he felt her body buzzing with want. His buzzed along with hers as his cock hardened painfully pressing against his jeans, wanting to be free.

Pulling away from his neck, she licked his wound. Her mouth found his as she kissed him frantically, straddling his body. Breaking the kiss, she looked down into his face as she lifted her shirt off tossing it to the floor. His eyes roamed her body with hot desire instead of disgust making her soar.

"Fuck," he growled, desire thick in his voice. Placing his large hand on her back, he pulled her back down, his lips finding the sweet nipple his fingers had brought to peak. His tongue swirled as his mouth sucked, moving from one breast to the other.

Wanting to see him, she reached under her to pull his shirt up, helping him pull it over his head. Her hands slowly ran down from his shoulders to his chest, her thumbs stopping and circling his nipples. Her fingers lightly played over his hard stomach.

Duncan noticed her eyes kept flying to his face as if to assure herself who was here with her. It didn't bother him that she did it for her own state of mind, but he wanted to kill the bastard who put that fear in her. He swore then and there that he would make her forget Kenny Lawrence ever existed.

"Make love to me, Duncan," she whispered.

"You know we can't until after the baby." Duncan hated the disappointment and embarrassment that flashed across her face.

"I just know I can now and I…" He shushed her with a finger to her lips.

"You don't have to explain anything to me, babe." Duncan pushed her hair out of her eyes. "But I won't put you or the baby at risk. I'm sorry."

"I know," Pam sighed. "It's just I'm not afraid like I thought I would be, and I want to make sure I can be with you. I mean, I did agree to become your wife, but was afraid that I wouldn't be able to….you know. And now that I know I can, I can't. It's frustrating." She knew she was rambling, and it irritated her. She hated to ramble. With a sigh, she flopped down hard making him hiss.

"Easy." He grabbed her hips to hold her still. "As you can obviously feel, I want you really bad and believe me…frustration is not what I'm feeling at the moment." She looked beautiful and sexy as hell straddling him, wearing only her skirt.

A grin played across her lips. She wiggled a little, surprised by her own actions. Was this the old Pam coming out? Was Duncan bringing her back to herself again?

His eyebrow cocked at her teasing as his hand went up her leg under her skirt. His fingers worked their way to her sweet spot. "You want to tease me, do you?"

Her eyes rolled as they closed. Her moan echoed in the room. "Oh God."

"No, Duncan." He grinned when her eyes shot open, looking down at him. "And I'm going to make you scream." His fingers worked magic.

Before long, Duncan made good on his promise as Pam's screams of pleasure filled his home.

*****

Jared rushed down the hall with Adam hot on his heels. The door to Slade's office was wide open. "Where is she?"

Slade looked up from a small desk in the corner. "Tessa? She left about fifteen minutes ago."

"Where the hell did she go?" Jared demanded, looking pissed.

"That, I don't know." Slade frowned. "Is everything okay?"

Jared just growled, turned and walked out.

"Thanks." Adam nodded to Slade before he followed Jared.

"Can you get a read on her?" Jared asked over his shoulder as he rushed back down the hall.

"No, I've tried. Check your room and I'll check Gramps," Adam said as he split down another hall. "Text me if she's there or meet me back here."

Jared knew she wasn't there, but opened the door, walking into the room and checking the bathroom. Heading back, he met Adam. "She's not with Gramps?"

"No." Adam stood thinking. "Is her car still here?"

Jared didn't answer, just headed toward the garage where her car was usually parked. The spot was empty. "Fuck!" Taking out his phone, he hit her number. It went straight to voice mail. "Dammit!"

"Where else would she be?" Adam looked at his phone to make sure he hadn't missed a call from her.

"Think she would have gone back to the house?" Jared glanced at Adam.

"That's the only place I can think she would have gone." Adam followed, jumping in Jared's car. "Was the picture that bad?"

"It was nothing." Jared growled as he started the car.

"I know my sister, Jared. It must have been something for her to disappear like this. I warned you not to hurt my sister." Adam glared over at him. "You know I'm on her side, no matter what."

"I wouldn't expect anything else, Adam." Jared pulled out of the garage, coming too close to a few reporters who still sat outside of the compound. "There is *nothing*, and I mean absolutely *nothing*, going on between me and Vicky."

"You better hope not," Adam warned. "After everything Tessa has been through, she deserves happiness, not another loser who's going to break her heart."

Jared didn't answer. He just needed to find Tessa and put this whole thing behind them. He would not accept it was over between them. She was his life, and without her, he was nothing.

*****

Waking up next to Duncan had been wonderful. The way he had woken her was mind blowing. Turning the bacon that was frying and popping, Pam smiled. After last night, she knew she was going to be okay. Duncan's touches had brought her so much pleasure, making her yearn for more, so much more. Not once was she disgusted or humiliated. Kenny had been so far from her mind that she had felt liberated, so much so that she had been brought to tears.

"Smells good," Duncan said, warning her that it was him behind her before he wrapped his arms around her bulging stomach.

Just the little things like the warnings that he was coming up behind her showed her how lucky she was to have someone like Duncan in her life. He understood her more than she understood herself sometimes. She hated how she acted yesterday with the baby room and wanted to make it right.

"Listen, about yesterday." Not facing him at the moment gave her more courage to speak her mind. "I'm sorry that I didn't act like I appreciate everything everyone has done. I truly am, but I'm just not used to it."

"I know that," was Duncan's only reply.

"I'm going to be okay." Pam nodded, smiling down at the bacon.

"I know that also." Duncan grinned.

Pam snorted, turning to look at him over her shoulder. "Is there anything you don't know?"

His face turned serious. "Yeah, can you cook?"

"Actually, I can cook very well," she informed him. "You hungry?"

"Starved." He leaned down kissing her neck, his hands roaming to her breasts.

Pam smiled happily. She loved the feel of his hands on her body. She leaned back into him, savoring the feelings that rushed through her body. She felt him hardening against her lower back. Turning, she went for the waistband of his jeans. "Let me take care of you."

"Honey, you have done more than take care of me. I'm a patient man, and you are *so* worth the wait." He turned her back around. "*And* the bacon is burning."

"Oh!" Pam grabbed the fork she had been using, saving the burning bacon from the skillet just as someone pounded on the door.

"Stay here." Duncan turned Warrior in an instant, heading out of the kitchen. A few seconds later, Sid walked in behind Duncan.

"Hey Sid," Pam smiled. "You hungry? Just don't critique my cooking please."

"I would never." He smirked. "I'll just have some coffee."

"There's plenty." Pam poured him a cup, pushing the sugar and cream toward him.

"Thanks." He added a little sugar, but no cream. "Have you guys heard from Jared or Tessa?"

"No," Duncan replied, sitting down resting his elbows on the counter. "She saw the picture I take it?"

Sid nodded. "She left last night after Slade stitched up her fingers. Adam said they tracked her and Jill to her place. She won't talk to anyone or answer her phone."

"What picture?" Pam sat the plate of food in front of Duncan and picked up his coffee cup refilling it.

"You didn't tell her?" Sid glanced at Duncan.

"No. Didn't really have a chance to." Duncan winked his thanks for the food and coffee.

"Well you do now, so tell me." Pam grabbed some toast and orange juice, sitting down next to Duncan.

"Someone is taking pictures of us all, and one of the pictures was of Jared talking with Vicky." Duncan took a long drink of coffee. "It looked like more than it was. It's kind of hard to explain, but Tessa saw it and obviously thought the worse."

"Is there anything between Jared and this Vicky, or has there ever been?" Pam took a bite of bacon not really feeling hungry.

"There was, but it was actually kind of over before Tessa came on the scene," Sid replied when Duncan kept quiet.

"Didn't her ex treat her pretty crappy?" Pam glanced between the two men. "He cheated on her, didn't he?"

"Yeah, he was a real asshole," Sid hissed. "Almost got us killed."

"Listen, I don't know Tessa real well, but I don't think it's Jared."

Figuring they had no clue what she meant since they were staring at her with vacant eyes, she tried to explain a woman's thought process. "A few times she's mentioned her weight in different ways. I've seen her pulling her shirts down or pulling them out from her body. I also noticed she dresses down, wearing large shirts and things to hide herself."

"But she's a gorgeous woman," Sid replied looking confused.

Pam pushed her half-eaten piece of toast away. "We women are more self-conscious than men. It's a fact, and it sucks, but that's the way it is. We will never be happy with our looks. We will either be too large, too thin, too short...you get the picture?"

"None of that matters to us." Duncan rolled his eyes. "Maybe human men, but not Warriors. We see what we want, and we go after it. It doesn't matter what size or shape the woman is if we love her."

"But it matters to her." Pam sighed. "I haven't seen the picture, but if I had, and it was me, I would probably be upset, just like any of you would if there was a picture of your woman and another man."

Both their eyes narrowed. "Good thing there would be a picture," Duncan replied with a growl.

"Yeah, need something to remember the dead son of a bitch by," Sid finished with a sneer.

Pam rolled her eyes at their macho mumbling. "What other pictures were there?" Pam asked, even knowing there were probably tons of her with her big belly.

Sid and Duncan shared a glance. "Sloan had the pictures Kenny had of us analyzed." Duncan looked at her. "They were faked."

Pam's forehead wrinkled in confusion until her eyes narrowed in anger. "Fake?" Her expression changed to anger as soon as what that meant sunk in. She stood up knocking her stool over. "You mean I went through hell to keep you safe over *fake* pictures."

"Calm down, babe." Duncan stood, picking up the stool so she wouldn't fall over it.

"That son of a bitch." Pam didn't hear anything, just kept stomping around cursing. "That goddamn bastard son of a bitch." Pam grabbed a knife throwing it.

Both Sid and Duncan watched as the knife stuck in the wall, the handle vibrating.

"Damn." Sid glanced at Pam then back to the knife. "Impressive."

"Pam." Duncan walked toward her still looking at the knife, also impressed as hell and actually turned on. How fucked up was that.

She reached for another knife, but Duncan stopped her. Her eyes flared up at him. "How could I have been so stupid?"

"You had no way of knowing they were fake." Duncan reassured her.

Sid walked over pulling the knife out of the wall. "The pictures were of high quality. We couldn't even tell. That's why we sent them out to have them analyzed."

Pam pulled away from Duncan, walking to the hole the knife left. "Oh my God," she cringed. "I'm sorry." She put her finger in the hole.

"Actually, I'm pretty damn impressed." Duncan smiled. "A little putty and paint will fix that right up."

Pam looked from the hole back to Duncan. "I can't believe I did that."

She took two steps back toward the island but stopped suddenly. Grabbing her stomach, her eyes widened, and a splashing noise on tile filled the room. "I think my water just broke."

Chapter 21

"You think your *what* just broke?" Sid eyed her funny.

"My water." Pam looked down with a grimace, still holding her stomach. "It just broke all over your floor."

"Our floor." Duncan automatically corrected her then snapped out of his stunned state. "Shit!" He ran up to her, slipping in the wetness on the floor.

"Get me something to clean this up." Pam looked at the mess horrified. "I'm here for a day, and I'm already tearing your house up."

Sid went for the paper towels, but stopped when Duncan yelled.

"Fuck the floor," Duncan growled. "We need to get her to the hospital," he yelled at Sid.

"We can't leave this on the floor." Pam looked a little panicky. "I'm fine. Get something, Sid."

Sid started to go for the paper towels again, but stopped when he heard a God awful moan.

"Oh shit. Not again," Sid moaned right along with her. "I'm having flashbacks from before."

Feeling an uncomfortable ache start in her lower back, Pam frowned. Within seconds, the ache radiated into a full-blown pain, spreading around to her stomach. A surprised scream poured from her mouth.

"Sid, come here, dammit," Duncan yelled. Picking up Pam, he rushed to the living room and put her on the couch. "I have to call Slade. *Do not* leave her side."

Running over, Sid stood next to Pam, who held her stomach. "Okay, we've been through this before," Sid assured her, but his eyes were wide with panic. "Just hold that thing in until help arrives. Aren't you supposed to be breathing funny or something to help with the pain?" Sid started breathing like he had seen in a movie of a woman giving birth.

Pam glanced at him and started breathing along with him. Then after a few minutes, stopped. "Okay, I think I'm hyperventilating," Pam panted, sweat beading her face. Her eyes finding Duncan, who only stood a few feet away from her on the phone, talking frantically, but his eyes never left her.

"She's okay," Sid yelled over to Duncan. "I don't know about me, but she's okay. Dammit, why am I always around you when that thing is getting ready to pop out."

"It's not a thing, and he isn't going to pop..." Feeling the dull ache start again, Pam gritted her teeth. "Oh, God."

"Again?" Sid sounded panicked. "Are you serious?"

"No." Pam glared at him. "I'm fucking with you, just for the hell of it." The old smart-ass Pam was back in the flesh. This contraction was worse. She grabbed Sid's arm squeezing with everything she had.

"Damn." He looked down at where her hand was about to break his arm. "Come on, breathe like before; it helps and it may keep you from breaking my damn arm."

"Let me pull your balls..." Pam stopped to grit her teeth, trying to ride the wave of pain, "out through your throat, and tell me if breathing helps." She glared at him.

Sid's head snapped back in surprise, but he moved his lower body a little further away from her. "You don't have to be vicious."

196

Pam raised her head when the pain eased, letting go of Sid's arm which he started rubbing vigorously.

Duncan came over kneeling beside her. "Slade will be here any minute."

"Why not the hospital?" Sid and Pam said at the same time.

"The contractions are too close, and he doesn't think we'll make it." Duncan had grabbed a cold washcloth and dabbed it across her forehead. "He wants to be here just in case we didn't make it to the hospital, and I think that's smart. He's close."

"Does he have drugs?" Pam whispered, her voice raspy. "Please tell me he has drugs."

"I wish I could take your pain." Duncan frowned, still running the cool washcloth across her face.

"So do I." Pam gave a weak grin. Her eyes shot open as the pain hit again. She gritted her teeth as a low moan began building in the back of her throat.

"Watch your balls, man," Sid warned Duncan. "Trust me on that one."

Duncan ignored him, his focus on Pam. "Come on, babe. Hold on just a few more minutes."

"Hold on?" Pam yelled in the peak of her pain, sitting up with on hand on the back of the couch and the other on Duncan's leg. "You have a seven-pound baby come out of your penis and then tell me about holding on. I have to get him out."

"Is she pushing?" Sid leaned back in horror. "She can't push. Pam, don't you fucking push."

"Sid, shut the hell up and go wait for Slade." Duncan held on to Pam. "Come on, babe, just a few more minutes and he'll be here."

Sid jumped up from the couch running for the door. He could face the biggest fuckers in hand-to-hand combat, but this shit sent him running like a little bitch, and he wasn't ashamed of it.

"You're doing great. I know it hurts, but just think of the little guy," Duncan whispered calmly. "You are going to be such a great mom."

Pam's breathing slowed as the pain once again subsided. "Do you really think I'm going to be a good mom?" She turned her head to look at him.

"The best." He kissed her softly. "You have a name picked out?"

She shook her head. "What's your middle name?"

"Daniel." Duncan replied.

Pam raised her hand to touch his cheek. She started to say something, but the pain started again, but this time it felt different. *"Duncan!"* she cried out. "I feel a lot of pressure," she panted, her breathing coming in fast hard gasps.

"He's here!" Sid yelled from the door.

"Tell him to hurry the fuck up," Duncan yelled back. "Come on, babe, hold on."

Sid practically tossed Slade into the room. Slade was taking in the situation in one quick glance. "How far apart are the contractions?"

"Pretty much back-to-back," Duncan answered, his eyes never leaving Pam's face. "She says she feels pressure."

"Call an ambulance," Slade ordered not caring who did it. "We need to get her to a bed. I need sheets and towels."

Duncan picked Pam up as carefully as possible, heading for the steps.

"Did you bring drugs?" Pam gritted through her teeth.

"Honey, you are too far along for that." Slade followed them up. "This little guy is ready to come now."

Hurrying to the bed, Duncan started to lay her down.

"No, I need her toward the end." Slade ran to the bathroom to wash his hands. "Is Sid getting the sheets and towels?"

"Yeah, I got them." Sid ran in. "The ambulance is on the way."

Slade came out putting on gloves. "Duncan, I need you behind her to support and help her push." He looked at Sid. "I need you on my right next to Duncan."

"Fuck that." Sid started to head out to wait for the ambulance. "There's only one reason I look between a woman's legs, and this is definitely not it."

"I might need your help Sid. You need to stay." Slade glared at him before turning back to Pam.

Sid stopped and sighed long and loud. "What do you want me to do?" Sid asked, looking nervous for once.

"Just be ready," Slade said, not really paying attention. His focus was totally on Pam.

"Ah…okay," Sid sighed with a roll of his eyes. "Just be ready, he says…."

Once everyone was in position, Slade pushed up her skirt. Taking the scissors, he cut her soaked panties off. "Well I have good news." Slade glanced up at Pam. "The baby is in position and I can see the head."

Sid made a gagging face, then frowned when Duncan punched him in the leg.

Pam nodded, her eyes closed. "So he's okay?"

"He's more than okay. He's ready to meet the world," Slade replied. "You having any pain right now?"

"No, I feel it building though," she sighed, preparing herself for the pain that would seize her tired body.

"You are going to want to push, but you need to wait until I tell you to." Slade looked up when she didn't answer. "Pam, this is important. Do you understand me? Do not push until I tell you to push."

Pam nodded with a moan. "It hurts so badly!" she cried out, biting her lower lip.

"I know, but you're doing great," Slade reassured. "Just hold on for a few more seconds."

"I love you." Duncan whispered, but his eyes watched Slade's reaction to everything. "It won't be long now."

Pam's moans turned into screeches of pain.

"Now Pam." Slade looked up. "Push."

Duncan grabbed her hands, so she could hold onto something and squeeze. He used his upper body to push her forward. "That's it."

"Okay, good. Relax," Slade instructed as he checked. "Next time, I need you to push a little harder." Slade didn't have the luxury of a monitor. He had to guess at the right time for her to push. Seeing her face scrunch in pain, he waited for a few seconds.

"The ambulance is here," Sid announced in relief, even though everyone in the room could hear the sirens.

"Pam this is it." Slade's voice took a totally different tone. "You have to push like you've never pushed before, and keep pushing."

"I'll try." Pam's voice sounded weak with exhaustion.

"Listen to me." Slade's face was stern. "You have *got* to do this. There is no *trying* to it. Do you understand?"

"Pam?" Duncan shook her.

The paramedics entered the room assessing the situation, and then stood at the head of the bed ready if needed. Slade acknowledged them quickly. "Be ready for transport."

"We're ready," one of the paramedics answered. "Do you need assistance?"

Slade shook his head at the paramedic. He put his hand on her stomach and felt another contraction building. "Pam you need to start pushing." When she didn't respond, Slade yelled. "Push!"

"Okay, dammit!" she hissed, using Duncan's chest to push herself forward. "Anyone with a penis needs to die."

Sid took a side step with a frown. "What is it with her wanting to rip balls out the throat and kill anything with a penis?"

"Because…" Pam panted, "a penis…." she grunted, "is what's…." she made a guttural sound, "causing this pain, and *you all need to die.*" The word die was drawn out in a scream that seemed to last forever.

Sid glanced back at the EMT's. "Guess she has a point."

One of them snickered while the other one elbowed him.

"That's it." Slade didn't grin or laugh. "Now push."

Pam grunted, groaned, screamed and cursed as she pushed. Running out of breath, she flopped back against Duncan.

"Push, Pam." When she didn't respond, Slade looked up at Duncan. "She needs to push. If she doesn't push, we are going to lose the baby."

Hearing Slade, Pam stirred and sat up, her eyes determined. "I'm not losing him," she grunted crying out. "Don't you dare let anything happen to him!"

"Come on. You're doing great. His head's out." Slade watched as Pam took a small break, before leaning forward again with determination on her face. "One more big push, Pam. You can do this."

"Come on, Pam," Duncan urged her. "One more time, babe. I've got you."

Those words gave her the extra strength she needed. He was there for her, and he wasn't going to let her fail. She gave everything she had with a long drawn out yell. Total exhaustion and fatigue shoved her back against Duncan. Not hearing anything from anyone, her eyes opened to slits when she heard a tiny whimper that soon turned into a full-fledged cry from a baby, her baby.

"You have a healthy boy with strong lungs." Slade grinned, holding the crying baby up so she could see.

"No fangs?" Sid teased with a big grin.

"No fangs." Slade rolled his eyes at Sid then glanced at Pam and Duncan. "Who wants to cut the cord?"

Pam looked up at Duncan. "Please."

Looking down into her eyes, he was choked with emotion. Shifting himself, Duncan took hold of the surgical scissors from Slade with a forced steady hand, listening to the instructions of what to do. Placing the scissor where Slade's fingers were, he cut the cord of life between mother and baby.

Slade took the baby into the bathroom and quickly returned with the little one bundled up, placing him into Pam's arms. "So what's his name?"

Pam looked down, running her finger along her child's soft cheek. "Daniel Duncan Roark."

Chapter 22

Pam stared down at her baby, smiling when his little lips puckered. Duncan sat on the hospital bed watching them both.

Slade stood writing notes. "How you feeling, Pam?"

"Great," she replied without looking up.

"Any pain?" He scribbled more notes.

"Nope." Pam grinned when Daniel yawned. "Never felt better."

"Doctor Buchanan?" An older nurse walked in with a smile at Pam and the baby. "We need to take little Daniel down for prints and pictures."

"Can I go with him?" Pam asked, looking worried.

"You need to get some rest." The nurse came next to the bed looking down at Daniel. "Boy, he sure is a cutie."

"I'm fine. I want to be with him." She felt uneasy and didn't want to be away from him.

"I can go." Duncan stood. "You really need to rest." He kissed her forehead.

"I'm sorry, sir, but only the father is permitted." The nurse frowned. "I assure you he will be safe. Ms. Braxton, you and the baby have matching wristbands for safety reasons. This little guy will be absolutely fine, plus all the nurses want to hold him."

"He is the father," Pam replied after the nurse finished.

The nurse immediately looked flustered and nervous.

Duncan picked up Daniel smiling down at him. "Let's go flirt with some nurses, buddy."

"Hey." Pam frowned. "No flirting until he's...twenty-one."

"Can I speak with you, Dr. Buchanan?" The nurse was staring at Duncan then at Slade.

"What is it?" Slade looked up from his paperwork.

"This isn't the man who's saying he's the father," the nurse whispered, not realizing that Duncan and Pam could hear her perfectly.

"What?" Pam paled. "Who's saying they're the father."

"It's all over the news," the nurse replied, embarrassed that she had been heard. She pointed to the television up near the ceiling. "He's been talking to all the reporters saying he's the father of the half-breed's baby."

Pam scrambled to grab the remote. Aiming it at the television, she clicked it on, changing the channels quickly.

Duncan and Slade glanced at each other, which Pam saw. "What's going on, Duncan?" Pam frowned still clicking through to find the news channels.

A voice from her past filled the room chilling her to the bone.

"Well, of course I'm excited." Kenny told the news reporter holding the microphone. *"I've been away on business and just got the news. Didn't even have a chance to get cigars or flowers for the beautiful Momma."* Kenny stared into the camera, his smile portraying a happy

new father, but his eyes said much more and only Pam could read the message they sent.

Pam clicked off the television, throwing the remote as if it was cursed. "Is he here?" Pam asked, staring at the television. "Is he here?" she yelled, panicked, her eyes searching.

"That was the front of the hospital where media are allowed to report from," the nurse replied, looking surprised and a little shocked at Pam's reaction.

"Jesus." Pam started to scramble out of the bed ripping off monitor prongs. "Where's my clothes. Where's my fucking clothes? Give me Daniel. We have got to get out of here."

Duncan handed Daniel to the nurse. "Don't move from that spot," he warned her, then turned to Pam. "You need to calm down."

"Are you crazy?" Pam smacked at his hands. "He's here for the baby. He's not touching him."

"Pam, I will not let him near you or the baby." Duncan invaded her space, forcing her to stop and see him. "Do you hear me? I *will not* let anything happen to you."

"Did you know he was out?" Pam shook. "Why isn't he arrested and in jail? He killed that Sheriff."

"I'll explain later." Duncan kept glancing at the door. "Right now we have..."

"You knew?" Pam's whole body slumped. "And didn't tell me?"

The look of betrayal on her face was more than he could take. "Do not leave this room," he ordered her, but before he could move, the door opened.

"Pam, honey. I got here as fast as I could." Kenny Lawrence walked in like he belonged, two uniformed officers behind him. His eyes landed on Pam and then on the baby in the nurse's arms.

Duncan was in front of Kenny, blocking him from Pam before anyone could stop him. Slade had one hand on Duncan's arm. "I suggest you get the fuck out of this room." Duncan stared down at him, his eyes blacker than midnight.

"Is that so?" Kenny smirked. "I have more right than you to be here. As a matter of fact, I've got a restraining order against you, so I suggest you get the fuck out of this room before I have you arrested."

"Try it," Duncan hissed. "Give me one reason not to kill you on the spot. If they even try to arrest me, I will kill you before they take a step. You know it, and I know it. You may have gotten away with killing Sheriff Bowman, for now, but you will not lay one hand on Pam or the baby."

"Who do you think you are?" Kenny spat. "I'm that baby's father and I will be in their life. There is nothing that you can do about that."

"I'm going to tell you one more time." Duncan stepped forward making Kenny and the officers step back. "Get the fuck out of here. I don't care if I go to jail for killing a worthless piece of shit like you. If I do, I'll go with a smile because that means you will never hurt her again."

Kenny just stood there, red faced, his anger overflowing, but he wasn't a stupid man. "You'll pay for this," Kenny swore before his eyes swung to Pam. "You are making a big mistake. You'll see me in court. That is my child, and I *will* get custody."

Pam had taken the baby from the nurse, holding him close. Her fear of Kenny left as anger and protectiveness for Daniel fired her blood. "You will never get custody. I will fight you with everything I have. I know you killed that sheriff, and I *will* find the proof to put you away. Stay away from me and *my* son."

"Looks like you grew some balls since the last time I saw you," Kenny snorted, then spit on the floor as his eyes narrowed not caring that he was showing his true colors. "We'll see how brave you are when this fucker isn't standing between us. I will definitely be seeing you soon." He stabbed his finger at her.

Duncan went for him then, but Jared, Sid and Damon just walked in when all hell started to break loose. Sid and Slade took care of Duncan as Jared and Damon took care of Kenny.

"Whoa there, big guy." Sid had Duncan pushed against the wall.

"Get the fuck off me!" Duncan fought, breaking free, knocking Sid against the other wall then flipped Slade on top of him. Pam's voice broke through his rage stopping him.

"Duncan!" Pam shouted again. Daniel began screaming with all the noise. The nurse stood plastered against the wall, pale and shaking. When his eyes met Pam's, she shook her head. "Don't."

"I *will not* let him hurt you again, Pam." Duncan's rage swirled in his eyes. "Never again."

"He won't." Pam lifted her head in determination. "I need to see whoever handles crimes against half-breeds. I don't care if it's the council or local law enforcement. I'm pressing formal charges for rape and domestic abuse." She watched Duncan fight for control, and she understood it, but this was going to end and she was the only one who could end it. It was time she took control back.

In two steps, Duncan had her in his arms, careful of the baby. "I still want to kill him," he whispered into her hair. "And if he ever comes near you again, I make no promises that I won't kill the bastard."

Slade picked himself off the floor glancing at the nurse who looked to be in shock. Walking over, he touched her shoulder. "You okay?"

Her eyes focused, looking around. Then, she looked up at him. "You're not a normal doctor are you?"

His golden eyes glowed with a smile. "No," he chuckled, and then frowned, rolling his sore shoulder. "No, I'm not."

She nodded, and seemed to shake off the drama that had unfolded, resuming her professional air. "Well that doesn't matter. We still need to get the baby's picture and prints." Looking at Pam, then Duncan, she nodded. "You both can come."

Pam held Duncan back until everyone had cleared the room. "Why didn't you tell me?"

"Because, I didn't want to upset you," Duncan replied without hesitation. "You were safe."

"I know I was safe, and I appreciate you didn't want to upset me, but please don't keep something like that from me again." Pam frowned. "I needed to be prepared, and I definitely wasn't. And he used to keep things from me. I don't like it."

"I'm sorry." Duncan frowned. "I was just trying to protect you."

"I know, but I have to hit this head on, and I need to see what's in front of me." Pam touched his face. "I can't be blindsided like I just was. Please understand that."

"I will always protect you, but I won't keep anything from you again." Duncan rubbed her cheek with his thumb. "I swear it."

"Thank you," Pam replied, glancing at the door Kenny had left through. Her body shook from the inside out at seeing Kenny again, but she had held it together. She saw one thing that she had never seen before, and it gave her hope; it gave her courage. Kenny Lawrence was afraid of something; she had seen it in his eyes, and that something was the man standing so protectively in front of her.

"Are you okay?" Duncan watched her closely.

Looking away from the door, she nodded. "Yeah, I'm okay."

Pam lifted the baby to Duncan and watched him take the baby in his arms, love and protectiveness shining in his eyes as he looked at him. Knowing that if anything happened to her, Daniel would be taken care of and loved made her heart soar.

*****

Adam jumped up on the porch slamming into the old house. Walking into the kitchen, he looked around. Hearing voices out on the back porch, he headed that way.

"Hey, Jill." Adam nodded toward her. "Can I talk to Tessa for a minute?"

"Sure." Jill glanced at Tessa leaving the box of Christmas decorations she was going through.

"What the hell are you doing?" Adam waited until Jill was back in the house before he spoke.

"I'm getting the Christmas stuff out," Tessa replied without turning around, digging with her good hand through a box. She knew exactly what he was talking about, but talking about it with him wasn't something she wanted to do.

Adam grabbed the box throwing it to the side. "That's not what I'm talking about, and you know it." He grabbed her turning her around, being careful of her bandaged hand. Dark circles shadowed her eyes. "Jesus, sis."

"Stay out of this, Adam." Tessa jerked away from him.

"No, I'm not going to stay out of it." Adam kicked a box out of his way so he could sit down on an old bench. "I stayed out of it with the Sheriff, but I'm not going to stay out of it this time."

"Why is my personal life so important to you?" Tessa threw up her uninjured hand in frustration.

Adam frowned. "Because you're my sister, and I can't stand to sit by and watch you make the biggest mistake of your life."

"It's not a mistake," Tessa replied, her tone angry because she honestly didn't know if she was making a mistake or not. She was torn with what to do. Her head said one thing while her heart said another. "I know what I'm doing." She totally lied and hoped her voice didn't give her away.

Adam stared at her for a long moment. "You're afraid." His eyes widened realizing the truth. "You're afraid that Jared is going to do the same thing that bastard did to you."

"Otis is dead, Adam." Tessa frowned. Damn her brother for knowing her so well, for being able to see right through her.

"Is he?" Adam cocked his eyebrow looking much older than his age. "Not in your mind he isn't. Jared isn't Otis, Tessa. You're afraid. Admit it."

She just shook her head at him, turning back to the box she was working in. "I'm busy, Adam."

"You're afraid and running." Adam stood. "Admit it."

"Okay, dammit. I'm afraid. You happy?" Tessa turned so fast, her head spun. "Just a picture tore my heart out. I don't know what I would do if I found them...together. So yeah, I'm afraid....scared to death that I won't be able to get over it this time."

"Jared isn't Otis, Tessa." Adam reached out grabbing her hand. "Do you think I'd be here on his side if I even had a hint that he would treat you that way?"

"No, but..."

"No, I wouldn't." Adam finished for her. "I would be kicking his ass as best I could for just the picture."

"You don't understand," she replied, staring off at nothing. Wanting to forget it all, forget she ever met Jared Kincaid, but just the thought of forgetting him sent her heart to her stomach. It hurt. It was an actual pain in her chest that wouldn't go away. She wondered absently if someone really could die from a broken heart.

"He let me read him." Adam ignored her last statement.

Her eyes shot to his surprised.

"I saw the picture, and I even doubted. I told him so." Adam never looked more serious in his life than he did at that moment. "Without thought, he held his arm out and told me to read him. Surprised the shit out of me let me tell you. As secretive as those guys were, he opened everything up to me just to prove himself. He has no feelings for Vicky. None. We even looked everywhere to find you. Called constantly so I could read him in front of you."

Tessa looked away, wiping a single tear that leaked from her right eye. "Why are you doing this, Adam?" Tessa hissed. "Why can't you just leave it alone?"

"Because I've never seen a love like he has for you, Tessa, and I probably never will. Honestly, it was a little embarrassing for me, but he just stood there as I read every thought." Adam turned toward the door to leave. "When I touch people, they can't hide their thoughts from me, they can't change them. Do you love him, Tess?"

Still, Tessa didn't say anything, but more tears fell. 'Yes!' She wanted to scream, but she was afraid to say it out loud, fear of more pain stopping her.

"I know you do, so I hope you make the right decision." Adam stopped before walking back into the house. "I hope you're the person I always thought you were."

"Adam?" Tessa turned to look at her brother, her face full of pain.

Three steps, he was hugging her. "I love you, Tess. I love you enough to tell you when you're wrong, and..." he looked deep into her eyes, "you are *so* wrong." With a kiss to her forehead, he was gone.

Tessa stood, staring at the door long after Adam left. She wanted to believe Adam, but even knowing that Jared cared for her, she had doubts always in the back of her head. How could such a handsome man like him go for someone like her? She had seen the looks people had given them, heard whispers from strangers, mostly women.

Finally looking away from the door, she looked around at all the Christmas decorations scattered around her and felt such a loss and loneliness, it doubled her over. Dropping to her knees, the room blurred as deep racking sobs rocked her body.

Blinking and wiping tears away, she spotted her phone. Reaching out, she grabbed it and looked at the screen. Just one push of a button and she could see him. But was she too late? Was she willing to face her own fears of having what was left of her heart broken? Slowly, her fingers began to move, typing out a message, but before she could hit the send button, her hand dropped to her lap. Adam was right; she was afraid, and running seemed to be the only way she could protect herself.

Chapter 23

Pam was filled with excitement on the day of their release from the hospital. A warm buzz of contentment filled her chest every time she thought of the possibility of her life with her son and Duncan. Slade had insisted on one final test that needed to be carried out on Daniel, and then they would be home free. She smiled at the thought, waiting impatiently to finally be given the all clear.

She was completely healed, which was one plus of being a half-breed. Having a baby one day, up and running the next. She felt stronger than she had ever felt.

Slade finally walked in, smiling at Duncan who sat holding the baby. "Have you even gotten to hold him yet?" He grinned at Pam.

"Hardly," Pam teased. "Can we get out of here yet?"

"You both are officially released." Slade laid out some papers. "Daniel seems healthy as any newborn. We did do the jaundice test which came back normal, but what wasn't normal was the little prick marks on his feet healed within seconds. Usually they bruise and you can see where the needles go in, but his are all gone."

"What does that mean?" Pam glanced at Duncan, who was staring back to her.

"Well, that he's a fast healer for one, but until he grows and gets older, we're not going to know," Slade replied. "I would like to see him every two weeks to weigh and measure, check his motor functions and to answer any question either of you might have."

"I appreciate that, thank you." Pam nodded.

"Also, I had a friend of mine look into what you could have possibly been given when you became pregnant. If it was some kind of fertility drug, it may have not only gotten you pregnant right away, but affected how fast the little guy grew during pregnancy." Slade handed Pam her release papers. "That's another reason I want to check him frequently. I want to see if his growth spurts are going to continue."

"And if it does?" Pam asked, looking worried.

"Then we will deal with that then," Slade replied with a reassuring smile. "I have good people working on this, but without knowing exactly what we are dealing with makes it hard."

"I appreciate everything you've done, Slade." Pam actually walked up and hugged him.

"It's been my pleasure." He shook Duncan's hand. "Now, get out of here."

Walking out, they were met by Nicole, Damon and Sid. "Give me that adorable little Warrior." Nicole took Daniel from Duncan. "Come to Aunt Nicole." She kissed his plump cheek.

"We parked by the emergency room." Sid hit the elevator button. "The reporters are swarming, expecting her to leave out the front."

"Did you get the car seat in?" Pam asked, stepping in the elevator.

"Could they make that thing any more complicated? Took most of the damn morning." Sid frowned down at Daniel. "You sure that thing is going to fit?"

"That thing," Nicole growled, "is a baby, and if I hear you call Daniel a thing again, I'm going to tell every woman I see what you watch on a daily basis."

"You know that's getting old," Sid hissed at her. "Get something new, vampira."

"Your Uncle Sid watches chick shows," Nicole cooed at Daniel. "Yes, he does."

Sid rolled his eyes, but a small grin tilted his lips. Sid held the door when it opened, letting them all out. "Okay, Dunk, my man, you and Pam ride with them."

"Dunk?" Duncan's eyes narrowed as he passed him.

"Yeah, I'm giving everyone nicknames." Sid grinned. "I'll wait for a minute and go get your car and meet you back at your place."

"Thanks." Duncan still eyed him.

"No problem, Dunk." Sid went to follow them, but stopped when Duncan stepped in front of him.

"If you call me that one more time, I'm going to beat your ass." Duncan tilted his head, his eyebrow raised in warning.

"What? You don't like..." Sid tilted his head to match Duncan. "Dunk."

Duncan just growled.

"Okay, I'll come up with something new." Sid sighed.

"Are you bored or something?" Duncan frowned at him.

"You don't even know, bro." Sid shook his head walking away. "You don't even know."

"You need a woman," Duncan called after him.

Sid flipped him off without turning around, making Duncan grin. A blind date may be in order.

Once everyone was in the car, they took off without any reporters following them. Damon glanced at Pam in the rearview mirror. "Kenny has been charged with rape and domestic abuse. I have papers here that you have to sign to make it official. There is also a restraining order for you to sign. Sloan pulled some strings on that, so you didn't have to go to the police station."

Pam nodded, grasping Duncan's hand. "Thank you."

Nicole turned to look at her with an understanding smile. "He deserves this, Pam. He shouldn't get away with what he did to you."

Squeezing Duncan's hand, Pam nodded. "I don't want him to do it to anyone else. I wanted to do this for a while, but was too scared." She glanced at Duncan. "But I'm not anymore, and I feel I have a responsibility to stop him."

"Sloan has turned it over to another local Warrior charter who will be handling it since we are too close to you," Damon added. "Also local law enforcement is involved, and there is an active search for him."

Nicole handed her the papers with a pen. Pam looked them over, and then handed them to Duncan to read.

Duncan read the papers, his eyes darkening. He handed them back to her with a nod, putting his arm around her. "Everything looks fine, and I'm sure Sloan has already been through them." He voice was deep with anger, but there was no trace of anger in his eyes.

With shaking fingers, she signed her name, a feeling of empowerment shooting through her veins. Handing them back to Nicole, she leaned back into Duncan, her hand reaching for Daniel's little hand. It was time to start over, leaving the past in the past.

"I'm proud of you." Duncan leaned close, talking low. "I will be with you every step of the way."

Turning her head, she looked up at him. "I know you will."

As soon as Damon pulled up to the front door, Duncan helped Pam out, and then walked around to get Daniel out of the car seat, handing him to Pam.

Once inside, Damon nodded toward the door giving Duncan 'a look'.

"I'm going to help Damon with the car seat and get the rest of the stuff." He smiled as their eyes met. He kissed her long and hard. He couldn't help it. She looked so beautiful holding Daniel.

Once the men were outside, Duncan leaned against the SUV. "Who's in charge of Pam's case?"

"Roger Parks." Damon opened the back pulling out a few bags. "He and his guys are good. They'll find him. They're staying in close contact with Sloan so we'll know what's going on."

Duncan nodded deep in thought.

"We can't get involved, Duncan," Damon warned. "We need to do this right, or Pam may suffer for it."

"Yeah, I know," Duncan cursed, opening the door to get the car seat. "I just have a bad feeling about it."

"Just keep her near until he's caught and charged," Damon grunted. "We both know the restraining order isn't going to mean shit to the bastard."

"Yeah, just like the restraining order he has on us means nothing."

Duncan carried the car seat up the steps to the front door. "If he even breathes in her direction, he's a dead man. Next time, he doesn't walk away, and I have a feeling he's not going down in a courtroom."

"I got that same feeling." Damon smacked him on the back as they headed up to the house.

*****

Jill walked out on the back porch after Adam left. Tessa was kneeling on the floor looking at her phone. Rushing over, Jill helped her up.

"I want so badly to text him." Tessa looked up from the phone. "I have it all typed out, but can't hit the send button."

"Hit the button, Tessa," Jill urged. "You're miserable and I know he is."

"Was I stupid to feel this way?" Tessa looked at her searching for answers, but before Jill could answer, Tessa kept going. "It just hurt so badly, to see him with her like that, but..." Tears fell down her cheeks.

"But what?" Jill felt so badly for her, but didn't know what to do. She had limited knowledge of relationships. Jill knew that Pam or Nicole should be the ones here talking to her, but unfortunately, they weren't. It was just her, the chick who couldn't get a date if she paid a guy.

"I can't give him what he needs." Tessa's voice turned hopeless. "He will always have to feed from someone else, and I can't keep putting us through this every time."

"Did it bother you that he fed from Vicky before the picture?" Jill asked, trying to understand.

"Yeah, it did because it wasn't me." Tessa flipped her uninjured hand in the air. "Even though Jared made sure I was always present when he fed, I still hated it. How selfish is that?"

"I don't think it's selfish at all. I mean if you love someone, I would think you'd want to be the one giving your partner everything they needed." Jill shrugged. "I think it's totally normal to feel the way you feel."

"You do?" Tessa looked at her with hope. "I don't sound like a selfish bitch?"

Jill laughed. "No. You sound like you want to give your man everything he needs and there isn't anything wrong with that, actually that's the way it should be."

"Are you happy being a half-breed?" Tessa asked, then cringed. "I'm sorry I shouldn't have asked that."

"No, it's okay." Jill was quiet for a few moments deep in thought. "It's kind of cool, but lonely. My family pretty much wrote me off as you already know. All I have is you guys and the Warriors; to everyone else I'm a freak of nature."

"No, you're not." Tessa hugged her. "You're a good friend, Jill. Thank you."

"Why did you ask me that, Tessa?" Jill hugged her back before leaning away looking at her.

"I want to be the one he comes to so I can give him what he needs to survive. Isn't that what how it's supposed to be?" Tessa looked away, her shoulders slumping in defeat.

"Then today is your lucky day." A male voice came out of the doorway.

Jill and Tessa turned toward the voice. "What are you doing here?" Jill asked surprised. Knowing something wasn't right, she stood slowly.

"Answering her prayers." He raised a gun, aiming it at Jill. "And teaching you a lesson."

The sound of a gunshot echoed through the small house, along with a woman's scream.

Chapter 24

Pam stood over the crib watching Daniel sleep. With a belly full of formula and a dry diaper, she knew he would be sleeping peacefully for a couple of hours. She frowned as she thought of the formula milk. She couldn't breastfeed. She had wanted to, had been desperate to, but her milk never came in. Slade hadn't known why; the likelihood was it was because of her half-breed make-up. She pushed her frown away. While she had been saddened by not being able to breastfeed, she knew that his tummy was still full. That was all that really mattered. Leaning down with a smile on her face, she kissed Daniel on the cheek.

Hearing Duncan's deep voice down the hall in his office, Pam grinned. Walking to the small mirror in Daniel's nursery, she fluffed her hair, unbuttoned two buttons and ran her teeth over her bottom lip making it puffy and red. Turning on the baby monitor, she grabbed the remote and walked down the hall, leaving Daniel's door half closed.

Leaning against the door, she watched Duncan as he talked on the phone, writing a few notes. Finally, his eyes looked up, running up and down her body. His eyes stopped on her breasts, which were full and pressed against her shirt. Even though she hadn't produced any milk, her boobs hadn't cared and filled out nicely.

"Listen, I'll have to get back to you on that," he said distracted, into the phone, his eyes hot and intense staring her down. "Yeah, sure will." He hung up the phone without saying a word. He didn't have to, his eyes said it all. He wanted her, and she wanted him.

"Where's Daniel?" His voice had deepened.

"Sleeping." She set the baby monitor on his desk. Her hands went to the buttons on her shirt.

"Are you sure you're ready for this?" Duncan frowned, but his eyes remained on her fingers as they undid each button on her shirt.

"Yes." She sounded out of breath.

"Slade gave his okay? You're not too sore?" His questions were a low growl as his eyes remained on the tops of her breasts that overflowed her bra.

"Shut up, Duncan." Pam gave him a half grin when he growled louder. Dropping her shirt at her feet, she waited for a second, loving the feel of his eyes on her. There was nothing but desire and love in his caressing look. She had never felt more female than she did at that moment.

When she reached for the button on her jeans, he cursed, stood, grabbed the baby monitor and picked her up as his lips crashed down on hers. "The first time I take you is going to be in our bed." He looked down at her, his eyes black with desire. "Then, we will make our way into my office where I have dreamed of making love to you on my desk."

"You have?" Pam moaned, her stomach flipping in excitement.

"Baby, when I first laid eyes on you, my first thought was where I was going to take that sweet body of yours first. I will make love to you everywhere in this house." Duncan held her close as he strode into their bedroom. "But the first time will be in our bed."

Pam was glad he'd had Nicole order them a new mattress, which was already in place. Old, bloody baby goop would have put a big dampener on the moment.

He set her on her feet, kissing down her neck, between her breasts, trailing down her stomach to the button of her jeans. Her stomach still pooched some but was already almost back to normal. Boy, if she could bottle up her healing after having a baby, she'd be a rich woman,

Pam thought, though she still sucked her stomach in, self-conscious as only a woman would be.

Running her fingers through his hair, she let him gently remove her jeans. Standing up, he went for her mouth, his hands running around to unhook her bra. But she stopped him.

"It's my turn now." She smiled, running her hands down his chest to the bottom of his shirt. Once the shirt was off, her eyes and hands roamed freely, loving the feel of the hardness. Her hands reached his jeans, and as quickly as she could without injuring him, she had them off. She almost purred when she realized he was commando, and what his jeans hid made her body quiver.

A wide, manly grin spread across his face at her reaction to him. As quickly as she had taken off his jeans, he had her standing bare in front of him. "I have never seen a more beautiful woman in my life." He kissed her left shoulder. "So soft."

Excited by the surge of desire pumping through her, she cupped him, feeling devilish and free, finally free. "So hard." She giggled when he growled, picked her up and laid her on the bed. He reached back grabbing the baby monitor, setting it on the small table next to the bed.

When he started tasting her with his mouth and tongue, she stopped him. "No." She rolled him, so she was on top and over him. "You've already touched me. I want to touch you now." She licked her lips in anticipation.

Duncan's eyes shot to her mouth, his eyes darkened in lust. "I don't know how much I can take, but have at it." He groaned when she leaned down licking his nipple. "Not much. I won't be able to take much."

Pam chuckled again, but soon her laughter died as she tasted and touched every inch of him. As she made her way back up his body, his hand caught in her hair, pulling a little. Her body stiffened. Her mind shut off.

"Hey." Duncan sat up. "Pam, look at me."

His voice broke through, and she slowly looked up; his understanding eyes looked deeply into hers. "What did I do?"

She shook her head refusing to let this moment be ruined. "Nothing."

"Don't lie to me." Duncan clipped her chin making her look at him. "What did I do, Pam? I have to know, so I don't do it again."

"You didn't do it on purpose." Pam looked away when he wouldn't let it go. "I don't like my hair being pulled."

Glancing at her shorter hair, he now knew the reason she had cut it. She did it as a sign of defiance, and he loved her all the more for it. Grasping her arm gently, he pulled her up his body then rolled on top of her. "I'll be more careful." His words were sincere and gentle. Immediately, her body relaxed. "Do you want to stop?"

"No, I don't." Wiggling underneath him, she loved the feel of his hands on her body. They were big, hard and rough, yet gentle in a way she knew he wouldn't hurt her. She felt safe with him. "Please, Duncan."

"I will try my best to go easy and be gentle," Duncan whispered as he raised one of her legs for a better angle. "Just say the word if you need me to stop."

"If you stop, I may kill you." Pam grinned when his eyes shot to hers. "I'm not going to stop, Duncan. I want you as much as you want me."

With those words, he pushed into her, his size filling her with pain and pleasure. It was a mind-blowing sensation, and she was more than ready for it. He started to move slowly, pulling all the way out to the tip then slowly pushing his way back in stretching her with his size.

"Open your eyes," Duncan growled. "I want you to see exactly who is making love to you."

Pam pulled up her other leg wrapping them both around his back. "I know exactly who is making love to me, Duncan Roark." Pam arched her back with a moan as he hit her sweet spot. "The only man I've ever made love to."

He hissed as she tightened around him. "You keep doing that, and this is going to be over real quick." She did it again making him groan in pleasure, his hips moving a little faster and deeper. "Damn, woman. You're gonna kill me."

"I love you, Duncan," Pam moaned. "Now stop making love to me and fuck me like you wanted to in the kitchen at the compound."

He looked at her shocked, then a pure sexy grin spread across his lips. "I promised you I would never let you down," his deep voice rumbled. "Not about to start now." He slammed into her, but his eyes stayed glued on her, making sure she was still with him and not sinking into a nightmare from the past.

"I'm not the innocent timid thing you thought, huh? I refuse to let my past break me and run my life. I am stronger than that. It just took you to show me who I once was." She met his thrusts with determination. "Know this, Warrior, now that I know I can have you without fear, you will never get any rest. Shocked?"

"No," his voice rumbled. "I'm one happy son of a bitch." And he meant it. He didn't think he'd ever been happier in his long life. She was everything he had ever wanted. He knew the Pam before all of this, and even though he was surprised how she took to his touch after what he could only imagine she had been through, he knew without a doubt that she was a survivor. The way she came in to save them the night Sheriff Bowman had been killed and Tessa and Nicole had been taken. Yeah, his girl was a survivor and Warrior in her own right.

"Please," she whispered, her eyes shining bright with emotion.

Putting his hand on each side of her head, he stared down into her eyes. "Don't take your eyes off me." He began moving in a gentle rhythm, bringing her back slowly. Then his movements got faster and harder, to the point where she had to hold onto his strong forearms. Her moans and whimpers urged him on until she arched finding sweet release, their eyes never breaking. His neck corded, his teeth clenched as he joined her in a release so strong he could swear he felt his heartbeat.

"I love you, Pam." He took her in his arms holding her tight. Feeling wetness on his chest, he pulled back concern etched in every part of his face. "Jesus, did I hurt you?"

Pam shook her head. "No." She sniffed, hugging him tight. "I'm just so happy. Thank you."

Duncan grinned. "Honey, you are more than welcome, and it was definitely my pleasure."

They lay together entwined in arms and legs. Pam's human side was seeking sleep. Just as her mind settled, a small sound came from the baby monitor, so she started to get up, but Duncan stopped her. "Rest." He kissed her cheek. "Let me get him."

He grabbed his jeans putting them on without buttoning them, and hurried out of the room. Daniel was making noises, but not full out crying. Duncan looked down and smiled.

"What's wrong, buddy?" Duncan picked him up then wrinkled his nose. "Oh damn, son What did you eat?"

Standing there holding him, he looked around knowing he was way out of his element. "Okay, we can do this." Walking over to the bag the hospital had sent with them, he grabbed a diaper out of it along with some wipes. Spotting what he heard Pam call the changing table, he headed that way and set everything down. Carefully, he laid Daniel on his back then unbuttoned his little sleeper he was dressed in.

Down to nothing but his soiled diaper, Daniel started to fuss with a little more attitude. Peeling the diaper away, the smell hit Duncan full in the face.

"Boy, you'd put Sid to shame." Spotting the nastiness in the diaper, Duncan tried not to gag. Having no clue what he was doing, he carefully held Daniel's two little legs up with one hand, and the other, he held the dirty diaper. Reaching with his foot, he hit the pedal and tossed the dirty diaper in what he hoped was the diaper pail. Grabbing a wipe, he gently wiped Daniel's little butt. "You sure did a number. You've got shit everywhere, buddy. We are definitely teaching you how to sit on a toilet early."

Once Daniel was clean, he lay wiggling, naked and making little noises. "Ah, I guess you are happy now," Duncan chuckled, but his grin faded as he stared down at the little guy who carried his name. Never did he think he would have a son to carry his name, but here he lay. He may not be of his blood, but Duncan didn't care. It didn't matter whom Daniel's father was, it would be him to teach him alongside Pam. As his eyes connected with Daniel's, he felt a connection that shook him to his very core, bringing moisture to his eyes.

Taking a step back, Duncan fisted his hand. Crossing his right arm placing his fist over his heart, he bowed his head to the child, chanting in the old language. Finally, his head raised to find the child quietly watching him intently. "I, Duncan Daniel Roark, vow to keep you,

Daniel Duncan Roark and your mother, Pamela Cecilia Braxton, safe forever and always." His eyes moistened with joy and love for the boy. Duncan's voice rang loud and true throughout the room until Daniel let out a loud squeal.

Duncan laughed. "So you liked that did you?" Grabbing a clean diaper, he went to put it on him, but before he could, a straight stream of Daniel's pee hit him in the chest. "Why you little…you just peed on me."

Pam stood watching from the shadows, tears streaming quietly down her face. Nothing had ever touched her more than watching Duncan vow to her son to keep them both safe. Seeing him jump back, Pam watched as Daniel peed on him. Throwing a hand over her mouth, she quietly took off running down the hall jumping on the bed. Burying her face in the pillows, she laughed and cried so hard, she couldn't breathe. Hearing Duncan coming down the hall, she tried to get a grip. Sitting up, she choked back her giggles and sobs.

"There's your mommy." Duncan grinned down at Daniel

"Everything okay?" Pam took Daniel keeping her head down so he couldn't see that she had been crying.

"Perfect," Duncan replied walking away. "I'm going to take a quick shower."

Pam watched him walk into the bathroom. Holding back laughter, she looked down and noticed Daniel was in a little shirt and diaper. Picking him up to pull the shirt down, the diaper fell off. Her heart constricted, and then melted even more. If there was ever a man worthy of her love, she was absolutely sure that Duncan Daniel Roark was that man.

With a smile, she quickly jumped off the bed, and headed to Daniel's room to put a new diaper on him before Duncan got out of the shower.

"Not a word about this, Daniel," she cooed down at him. "We don't want to hurt your daddy's pride. He is a Warrior you know."

Daniel made a little squeal in agreement.

Chapter 25

Jill opened her eyes slowly. Her chest felt like it was on fire. Glancing down, she frowned. There was blood everywhere. That bastard shot her. She was lying in the boxes she and Pam had been going through; the gunshot blast had taken her off her feet.

She could hear voices coming from inside the house. Moving her head slowly, she didn't see Tessa anywhere, didn't hear her voice. Reaching slowly to her chest, she felt the bullet wound, but didn't feel any fresh blood coming out. She was healing already, but she didn't know if that was a good thing. She was having a hard time breathing, and that scared her.

As quietly as she could, she sat up listening closely for the voices to stop, but they didn't. She couldn't really make out what they were saying. There was a slight buzzing in her ears, and she prayed she didn't pass out. Getting out of the boxes quietly was a feat, but she did it. She struggled to her knees, and then to her stomach as the Warriors had shown them to do, slithering along the ground. She bit her lip keeping in the cry of pain. She had to ignore it. She had to find Tessa.

Making it to the doorway, Jill inched her way until she could look in. Sitting at the table was Kenny Lawrence, across from him was Tessa tied up, her eye swollen and red as blood ran from her nose. And there leaning against the counter was the bastard that shot her, that betrayed the Warriors.

"I don't care what you do with her after I get what I want." Kenny spat slamming his hand on the table.

"We'll get a lot of money for her at auction." Jeff's grin was full of greed. "She said she wanted to be changed."

"Well if you hadn't killed the breed in there, you could have gotten a lot more." Kenny pointed over his shoulder.

"Yeah, well, I just couldn't help myself," Jeff snorted. "The stupid bitch deserved it "

Jill scooted back looking around frantically. She was way too weak to take on not only one, but two of them. Something caught her eye and she shimmied her way toward Tessa's phone. Her own phone was in her bag in the kitchen. She stretched using her fingers to grab it, but could barely reach it. Clinching her teeth, she slid sideways finally able to grab it. Sliding the side button, she silenced the phone. Thank God, it was just like hers. Going to the messages, she saw Tessa's message to Jared. Tessa hadn't hit the send button.

Taking a quick glance at the door, she finished the message to Jared.

AT TESSA'S NEED HELP NOW KENNY JEFF HERE.

Jill hit send, hoping it made sense, and then cringed when she heard heavy footsteps.

"What the hell was that light?" Jeff walked in spotting Jill trying to get up. "Are you fucking serious?" He walked over grabbing her by her shirt, dragging her into the kitchen.

"I thought you killed her?" Kenny shook his head. "Damn, can't you do anything right?"

"She texted someone." Jeff looked up at Kenny. "You better get out of here. I'll finish her off and then be there."

Kenny tossed a paper with writing on the kitchen table before grabbing Tessa who tried to fight. He smacked her, almost knocking her out. "Don't tempt me, bitch. I don't need you alive that badly."

As soon as Kenny was gone, Jeff pulled out his gun again, his grin spreading.

"What the hell are you doing with Kenny Lawrence, Jeff?" Jill had managed to get to her feet. "The Warriors were trying to help you, and you turn on them. Why?"

"Because he wants to bring the Warriors down and so do I. I never fit in there," Jeff hissed, pointing the gun at her. "They all walk around like they're perfect, even that fuck Adam. I'm sick of them looking at me like I'm a piece of shit. They even picked you over me. A fucking weak-ass girl."

"Kenny just wants Pam and the baby. He doesn't care about you." Jill shook her head. "And he's too much of a coward to face the Warriors, just like you. Kenny is using you, dumbass."

"Shut up." Jeff screamed shaking with rage.

"What? Are you going to shoot me again?" Jill knew she couldn't take another bullet, especially at this close range, but her mouth wouldn't stop; she was so mad and she needed to get him a little closer. "You afraid of me? You have to use a gun on a weak-ass girl?" She tossed his words back at him.

He reached out and backhanded her across the face. "I always hated you," he spat.

Jill tried to block the pain. "Why? Because I beat you in arm wrestling? Grow up, you pussy." She actually felt her face swell making it hard for her to talk. Remembering the lessons on gun defense, as quick as lightning, she used both hands in a slapping motion toward each other knocking the gun out of his hand. Then she punched his surprised face.

"Guess you missed that lesson, asshole." Jill swung again, but he blocked hitting her in the stomach.

"I didn't miss that one though, did I?" He went for the gun again.

As if one of the Warriors were standing right in front of her giving lessons, she saw her opportunity. Calm and determination spread through her body. Falling to one knee, she spun in a complete circle swinging her other leg out, hitting Jeff in the kneecap. A sickening crunch echoed in the room as both Jeff and Jill fell to the ground. As he screamed in pain, Jill tried to crawl her way out of the room, but her own pain made her slow.

Jeff caught her foot pulling her back. "You broke my fucking leg."

Kicking out with her other foot, she heard another crunch and scream, the hold on her foot gone. As fast as she could, she crawled, trying to scramble to her feet. The click of a gun stopped her cold. This was it, and the only thing she could think of was she had never gotten to kiss Slade - how sad and messed up was that! Not going down like a coward, Jill stood and turned to face her fate.

"You can kill me, but your problems will double. The Warriors will hunt you down for killing one of their own." Jill's voice was strong and true.

"You're not a Warrior." Jeff aimed the gun straight at her heart. "You're just a half-breed bitch nobody will remember."

"I'm more of a Warrior than you could have ever been." Jill stood straight, her chin tilted proudly. If she was going to die, she was going to die on her terms. "Pull the trigger, *pussy*."

The room erupted in total chaos as Warriors came through every opening. Jill was knocked off her feet as the sound of gunshots echoed throughout the house.

"Don't kill him!" Jared shouted.

"Jill!" Slade was leaning over her. "Talk to me."

Jill's eyes slit open. "I got shot." She frowned. "And my face hurts."

"Goddammit!" Slade ripped her shirt to find the bullet wound; it was already closing. Carefully, he lifted her up to see if there was an exit wound. There wasn't.

"I have to talk to Jared," Jill's voice cracked as Slade laid her back down. "Jared!" she called out.

Jared was there kneeling beside her. "Is she going to be okay?"

"I have to get that bullet out." Slade frowned looking around, his eyes narrowing as they fell on Jeff.

"Kenny has Tessa." Jill grabbed the bottom of Jared's jeans. He reached down and grabbed her hand. "I'm so sorry. I tried to stop him."

"I know you did, honey." Jared squeezed her hand. "Do you know where he took her or why?"

"No, but he threw that paper on the table." As Jill's eyes slid past Jared, her eyes met Jeff's. "He knows."

Jared hurried to the table; Sid knelt in his place. "You *are* right. You are more of a Warrior than he will ever be." Sid nodded toward Jeff. "And who in the hell taught you to say, 'pull the trigger, pussy'?"

"You did." Jill grinned, but hissed at the pain it caused. "You heard that?"

"We had to wait to make our move, but then you broke badass, and we had to move a little faster." Sid grinned down at her. "I'm having a proud moment here."

Jill hissed again when Slade moved her upper body. "Stop moving me. That hurts,"

"My moving you isn't what's hurting you," Slade growled, worry etched across his face. "You got shot. That's what's hurting you."

Adam stood over Jill, anger making his golden eye black. Hearing Jeff running his mouth, he was over there in a flash. "Where's my sister, asshole?" He grabbed the front of Jeff's shirt, shaking him.

"Fuck you, Adam." Jeff turned his head spitting blood. Slowly, his eyes rose to meet his. "Your sister isn't who you should be worrying about."

"Don't let him get to you, Adam," Sid warned.

Adam ignored Sid. He had always known Jeff hated him, but he didn't realize just how much. "What are you talking about?"

"You sister is safe, well sort of, for now." A wide, bloody grin spread across his face. "Angelina, on the other hand, well, let's just say, she's probably long gone by now."

"What did you do to Angelina?" Adam's voice was surprisingly calm.

"You know I've hated you since high school." Jeff ignored his question. "Adam, the football star, always getting what he wants. Well this time, I got what I wanted."

Adam lost it, grabbing Jeff, letting loose. Sid stood by watching for a few minutes, allowing Adam his release, before stepping in.

"If you kill him, you'll never know what happened to her." Sid pulled Adam off.

Jeff rolled around on the ground moaning. His eyes found Adam. "Oh, I'll tell you what I did to her because I want to see you suffer." Jeff rolled back up to a sitting position groaning in pain. "She's heading to auction. It was a good payday for me. With her looks and body, she's going to bring a good price."

"Auction?" Adam's face was blank, trying to grasp what Jeff was saying.

"Yeah, you stupid fuck," Jeff hissed. "She will be sold to the highest bidder. By this time next week, she should be a half-breed, pregnant and someone's whore."

Adam roared as he charged toward Jeff, but Sid stopped him.

"Get him the fuck out of here." Jared rushed over as Sid dragged Adam out. "What the fuck does this mean?" Jared shoved the paper in Jeff's face.

"It means a switch." Jeff's laugh was demented. "Your precious Tessa for Pam."

Jared stood still as stone, staring at Jeff. "Where?"

"Now that I don't know, but Pam does." Jeff tried to sit up, but cried out grabbing his leg. "Fucking bitch broke my leg."

Damon, who had quietly stood watch over everything, kneeled down behind Jeff. "Are we finished with him?"

Jeff jumped, looking over his shoulder. He knew what Damon DeMasters was capable of and didn't want any part of it. "Get the fuck away from me, you maniac."

Damon grinned, standing back up when something caught his eye. Walking out onto the back porch, he reached down and picked up a phone. "Hey Jared." When Jared looked his way, he tossed the phone. "Tessa's phone."

Jared caught it staring down at it. Clicking it on, he stared at her background pic of them both laughing, with her giving him rabbit ears.

The whites of Jared's eyes turned black as he turned to look at Jeff. "If anything happens to her, I will make you suffer."

"What are you going to do? Make the maniac decapitate me?" Jeff rolled his eyes trying to appear tough.

Jared took two steps to stand in front of him. "No." He kneeled down getting in his face. "*I* will keep you alive, and every day, *I* will make you suffer in ways unimaginable."

"You can't do that," Jeff snorted, doubt flashing through his eyes. "I have rights. And you have to follow the law."

Jared stood back up. "Damon, did you see that Jeff kid anywhere near Tessa's?"

"No, sure didn't," Damon replied, looking bored as hell. "I don't think he was involved. Last I heard, he met some girl and took off to start a family. Nice kid."

"How about you, Slade? You seen Jeff?" Jared stared down at Jeff, his voice not matching the anger on his face. "We sure could use him around here. He was a great asset."

"I think Damon's right. Last I heard, he went to Florida or was it California?" Slade didn't even look away from working on Jill. "I got some connections in California; I can make some calls and see if we can talk him into coming back."

"But you're a doctor," Jeff shouted, terror evident on his face. "You can't do that."

Slade didn't answer him.

Jeff's eyes shot to Jill's. "This is all your fucking fault. I swear I'll make you pay, bitch." He pointed his finger at her. "You're all lying."

"Yes, we are, and very well I might add," Jared growled. Sid walked in without Adam. "Hey Sid, you seen that kid Jeff?"

Sid stopped and thought for a minute. "Nope, as a matter of fact I haven't." Sid's eyes swung to Jeff. "Last I heard, he up and married some ugly-ass chick he knocked up after a heavy night of drinking. Heard they moved out west to raise them a litter of rug rats. Think he took up ranching since the little lady didn't want him being a Warrior. You know with all the danger and killing. Sure hope he sends a Christmas card this year."

"I fucking hate you," Jeff spat, his eyes narrowed. "I hate you all. And will make you all pay."

"Shut up, you little bitch." Sid glared at him. "You know, I've been so fucking bored lately I think I might pay Jared so I can torture your ass. That's the plan, isn't it?" He asked Jared, but looked directly at Jeff, his eyes unwavering.

"You can have a few days no charge. I'll need a few days rest," Jared replied, heading toward the door. "Sloan's here. Let's go."

Jeff's eyes landed on Jill, who even though in pain, had a knowing half grin on her face. "You think this is funny, cunt?" Jeff growled. "Next time I will shoot you in the fucking head."

Before anyone could stop him, Slade was up, his gun already pulled from the waistband of his jeans. Picking Jeff up, like he was nothing but a child, he placed the barrel of the gun against his forehead. "You just don't know when to stop do you, Badass?" He removed the barrel from Jeff's forehead and jammed it under his chin sneering into his face. "If I ever hear you threaten her again, I will blow your fucking brains out. I don't care what information they think they can get out of you. I won't torture, but I *will* kill you, and remember I'm a doctor. I know how to do it painfully."

Jeff didn't say a word, but he did piss himself.

Slade tossed him to the floor then walked back to Jill. Everyone just stood watching Slade walk away. "I'm impressed." Sid's eyebrows rose, looking back at Jeff who lay on the floor moaning. "Anyone who can make someone piss themselves that quick is okay in my book."

Sloan walked in looking around. "Where is the little fucker?" His eyes found Jeff on the floor.

"I want him alive." Jared walked out the door with Sid and Damon following.

"Watch yourself boss." Sid nodded toward Jeff. "Slade literally scared the piss out of the bastard."

"Shit!" Sloan walked over grabbing Jeff by the shirt, picking him up to his face level. "You really fucked up this time. Traitors are treated a lot differently from the other scum bastards we catch."

Chapter 26

Pam was walking downstairs with Daniel when someone pounded on the front door. Duncan came out of the kitchen spotting her on the steps.

"Stay there," he ordered as he made his way across the floor.

Nodding, Pam turned ready to run upstairs if she needed to. Hearing Nicole's frantic voice, Pam made her way quickly down the rest of the steps.

Seeing Duncan and Nicole's face, Pam stopped. "What's wrong?"

"Kenny has Tessa." Nicole's voice sounded panicked. "Jeff is involved, and they sold Angelina, and…"

"Oh my God." Pam felt light headed and quickly sat down for fear of falling with Daniel. "When?"

"Nicole, calm down," Duncan ordered, grabbing his phone.

"Tonight. Jared got a text and…" Nicole took a deep breath. "Jared and the rest are on their way here now. Kenny wants to trade."

"Trade?" Pam looked from Nicole to Duncan's furious frown.

"You for her," Nicole cursed. "You can't do this, Pam. He will kill you."

"She isn't doing anything." Duncan's voice was stern and final as more pounding started. Pam just sat holding Daniel in shock.

Duncan opened the door, but blocked Jared as he tried to go to Pam. "She isn't leaving this house."

"Fuck you for even thinking I would suggest it." Jared pushed past Duncan making his way to Pam.

Looking up at Jared, Pam shook her head. "I'm so sorry. This is all my fault."

"No, it's not," Jared replied sternly. "But I need you to tell me what this means." He handed her the paper Kenny had left.

Taking the paper she read it.

One bitch for another. If I even catch a whiff of a Warrior, I will kill her. You know where I am, Pam. Don't make me take another life because of you. See you soon, sweetheart.

She could hear Kenny's voice in her mind as if he was reading it to her.

"Where is it, Pam?" Jared knelt down to take the note from her, handing it to Duncan who stood close. "Where did he take her?"

"I can't tell you." Her eyes rose to meet his. "He *will* kill her, Jared."

"Fuck!" Jared stood, walking away, looking like he wanted to kill something.

Pam looked down at Daniel, his eyes watching her. God, how she loved this child. This had to end, mostly for the innocent staring so intently at her. Until Kenny was stopped, Daniel would never have a normal life, and neither would any of them. Leaning down, she kissed his cheek and nose.

"I love you, Daniel Duncan Roark." She touched his cheek as she stood, handing Daniel to Nicole.

"No, Pam." Nicole shook her head but took Daniel.

"What are you doing?" Duncan grabbed her arm, but she shook it off walking to Jared, who stood talking to Damon and Sid, trying to come up with a plan.

"He isn't lying." Pam stopped in front of Jared. "If he even thinks you guys are anywhere near he will kill her. He wants me."

"We are not making a trade, Pam," Jared replied, his anguish clear in his eyes, a hardness she had never heard in his voice.

"Then you'll never see her again." Pam tilted her head. "Can you live with that? I sure can't."

"Just tell us where she is and we *will* get her." Sid cracked his knuckles.

"You're not going anywhere near that place," Duncan growled.

"Then she dies. I can't live with that." She felt her eyes welling up. "How can I face any of you, especially Jared, when I know I could have done something?" A mixture of fear and determination laced her words.

"*No!*" Duncan shook his head, refusing to listen. "It's not happening. You're going nowhere near him, Pam."

"I want my life back, Duncan. Don't you get it? This is a no win situation for me. If I stay, Tessa dies, and *that* is on my head, my conscience, and I will have to live the rest of my life with that. I can't do it." She shook her head. "If I go…" Pam looked up at Duncan, her face filled with pain, and then she turned to look at Daniel in Nicole's arm. She knew what would happen if she went and was sure so did everyone else, but this wasn't about her getting to live the life she wanted. This was Kenny shoving his will down her throat again, and it had to stop. "If I go, then Daniel has a chance of a normal life. With Kenny after me, he never will get that. Right now, Daniel and Tessa are what's important. This needs to end, and it can end."

Pam wanted to scream at the unfairness of it all, but in order to have the life she wanted, her past had to be put to rest. If that meant her giving up to Kenny, then so be it. Hopefully, she could find her way back to where she belonged, with Duncan and Daniel.

Duncan cursed, pulling her away from everyone and into the kitchen. "You are important to me and Daniel," Duncan hissed. "I won't lose you."

Pam's heart fractured a little at Duncan's words. She knew there was no other choice, but the one she had decided upon. The love and fear radiating from Duncan swelled her heart. Walking up to him, Pam wrapped her arms around Duncan's hard body. "This has to end." She kissed him, a soft small kiss on his lips. "I love you, but this has to end."

"We can get her out," Duncan argued, not willing to give an inch.

"Can you promise me Tessa won't be hurt or killed?" When he just stared at her without making that promise, she laid her head on his chest. "I have to do this, Duncan."

Jared walked in with Sid and Damon hot on his heels. "We have a plan."

Adam followed moments later. "Count me in."

"Shit is about to get real." Sid smiled, a smile that didn't quite reach his eyes.

*****

Sloan dragged Jeff out of the house ignoring his screams of pain. He made sure to run him into a wall when Jeff started screaming threats at Jill.

"What am I going to do with you?" Slade turned Jill's face to his, keeping her focus off Jeff.

"Why?" Jill frowned. "I didn't do anything."

"I keep fixing you, and you keep getting broken," he teased, shaking his head when she snorted. "I need to get that bullet out of you."

"Ugh...really?" Jill looked down at the hole that had already started to close. "It doesn't hurt as much. Can't I just keep it as a war wound...a conversation starter?"

His right eyebrow rose as he looked at her, a slight smile forming on his lips. "We'll see." He stood. "We need to get an x-ray though. I want to make sure it's not close to anything important. You are half human, you know."

Jill let him help her up; her human legs started to shake, making her wobble. "Believe me, I know." She tried to take a step, but her leg gave out. He caught her picking her up. "Sorry." Her voice hitched as his strong arms held her carefully, holding her with ease.

Slade carried her outside to Damon's car he had left for them. Putting her gently in the passenger seat, he walked around and climbed in. "You okay?" He looked her over before starting the car.

"I'm good." She frowned. "Shouldn't you be helping them find Tessa?"

"I'm a doctor first," Slade replied, turning the key. "They don't need me."

Jill stopped him before he could put the car in gear. "But Tessa might. If they find her and she's hurt, then she is going to need you."

"You have been shot, Jill," Slade growled at her in frustration. "We need to see where that bullet is."

"But I'm half vampire," Jill shot back. "Tessa is human, and she was beaten up pretty bad."

"Dammit!" Slade slammed his hand on the wheel. "I can't just choose whom I'm going to help and who I'm not."

"You're not making the decision," Jill replied. "I am, and I'm refusing treatment until this is over."

Slade didn't say a word; he just slammed the car in gear and took off. His jaw clenched, causing the muscle to bunch. Jill turned to look out the window, and then closed her eyes, wondering if she would make it by the time he got back. Catching her breath was becoming harder.

*****

Jill heard her name being called, but opening her eyes took way too much effort, so she just grunted.

"Jill, dammit." Slade's voice was becoming clearer. "Don't you fucking die on me."

"Die?" Jill finally opened her eyes to see Slade standing over her, staring down at her. He looked blurry. She blinked repeatedly trying to bring him in focus. Panic seized her, quickly followed by fear; she tried to sit up. "What's wrong with me? Why can't I see?"

Slade held her down. "Stop before you rip out your stitches."

"Stitches?" Jill blinked again, her vision finally clearing. "Did you knock me out and take the bullet out?"

"No, you crazy little...." He actually laughed cutting himself off. "You passed out in the car. You failed to tell me you were having a hard time breathing. Instead, you talked me into putting you to the side to help someone else. The bullet nicked your lung."

"It did?" She still looked confused, her brain trying to catch up.

"Yes," he hissed, staring down at her. "Why didn't you tell me you couldn't breathe?"

Jill felt so tired. She closed her eyes just wanting to go to sleep. "Because more people would be affected if something happens to Tessa," she mumbled. "You need to help her. She has people who love her."

Slade frowned at her words as he watched her fade. Knowing that she was going to be okay, tempered the building rage that had been forming since he had discovered her with a bullet hole. Touching her cheek, he told himself he was just making sure there wasn't any temperature, but he knew that was a lie. The beautiful, brave little Warrior unconscious before him, had somehow weaved herself into his every thought.

"Dr. Buchanan." A nurse walked up with papers. "I need someone to fill the paperwork out."

"Has anyone called her family?" Slade asked, looking up from Jill's pale face.

"Yes, we have." The nurse looked down at Jill and frowned.

"Then they can fill them out when they get here."

"They won't be coming, doctor." The nurse handed him the papers. "We can wait until she is able to do it herself if there isn't anyone else."

"Why won't they be coming?" His eyes narrowed, realizing he really didn't know anything about her at all.

The nurse hesitated for a second. "One of the nurses in the ER went to school with Jill's sister. She gave me the contact information and…" The nurse looked down at Jill frowning. "They said they do not have a daughter by that name."

"Are you sure you had the right number?" Slade felt his anger return, building, but he kept calm. Surely, parents would never disown their own child, especially someone as remarkable as Jill.

"Yes, sir." The nurse nodded. "We were warned that we would probably get the response we got. It seems after she was turned, her parents and family disowned her. We had to try as they are her-"

"Thank you." Slade had heard enough. He grabbed the paperwork taking a pen off the small table next to the hospital bed. The first line was her name. He didn't even know her last fucking name. Now he knew what her comment meant when she fell to sleep. He'd bet his last dollar none of the others knew her last name either.

"I'm sorry." The nurse turned to leave.

"What is her last name?" It was more of a growl than a question.

"Her legal name is Jillian Robin Nichols." The nurse watched him write it down before she turned, leaving him alone.

Slade wrote the name then looked over at her. "Jillian." He smiled. She looked like a Jillian.

Chapter 27

Pam drove slow enough so that her shaking hands could control the steering wheel. As the men had made their plans - that didn't include her - Pam had left the kitchen saying she had to go to the bathroom; instead, she had grabbed a set of keys on her way upstairs and jumped from the window. She knew Kenny better than any of them, and if he even thought the Warriors were close, he would kill Tessa with no hesitation and certainly no remorse.

Clicking her blinker on, she stared down a road she swore she would never step foot on again. She sat on Kellogg Ave., her blinker lighting up green in the dark car. No cars were coming, but still she sat. Turning her head, she looked' at the street sign, River Row Road. Looking at her hand on the steering wheel, she spotted the ring, warmth and sadness spreading through her. Quickly, she pulled it off, shoving it deep in her pocket. No need to stir Kenny up more than necessary.

A horn blared behind her making her jump. "Shit! Okay!" she shouted. "Okay," she repeated more calmly. God, she had to get a grip.

"Time to put your big girl panties on and end this." Her voice was resolute as she spoke to herself in the darkness, and turned into the road. "One way or another, this ends tonight. Just please, God, let me see my baby and Duncan again."

Pulling up to the house at the end of the road, she flipped off her lights and stared. This use to be one of her favorite places in the world to come, but that all changed. It was filled with nightmares that she'd rather forget. This was Kenny's house of horrors, a place he used for his sickness.

Her eyes quickly looked away from the small white house that stood so innocently against the Ohio River. Rain splattered the windshield. Movement of the curtains caught her eye. Turning off the car, she left the keys in the ignition.

Stepping out, she shut the door and climbed the steps. With one deep breath, she reached out opening the door, preparing herself for his tricks, but instead of walking in as the Pam she had been when she'd last seen him, she walked in with a new purpose. She had to survive this; she had so much to live for.

The door slammed behind her, and she was immediately smacked in the back of the head. Turning around, she came face-to-face with her walking-talking nightmare.

"Can't believe you fell for that again. You always were a dumb bitch." Kenny tsked shaking his head. Grabbing her by the neck, he pushed her the rest of the way in. "Get the fuck in here. Where's my kid at?"

Pam caught herself before she fell. "He's not a part of this."

"Since you pressed charges on me for rape, we need to travel anyway and can't be dragging the brat along. And don't think we won't be discussing the charges you pressed against me," Kenny warned. "But now that I know you can breed, I'll keep you nice and pregnant."

Knowing she would kill herself first, Pam ignored his bullshit as she searched around for Tessa. Spotting her in a chair tied up, Pam ran over to her. "Are you okay?"

"You shouldn't be here," Tessa whispered, her eyes shooting to Kenny.

Pam untied her and helped her up. "You said you'd let her go." Pam walked toward the door with Tessa trying to stay as far away from him as possible, but he caught her hair pulling her away from Tessa.

"I know what I said." Using her hair as leverage, he whirled her into the wall.

Something inside Pam snapped as Daniel's little face flashed in her mind. She had to survive this. She had to see her family again. That's what Daniel and Duncan were, her family. Slowly, she stood up. "Don't ever hit me again, you sick son of a bitch."

Kenny laughed, shaking his head, turning toward Tessa. "Well you turned into a little badass now, didn't you?" He picked up his leg to kick her, but she grabbed his foot, yanking it hard, sending him to the floor.

Fear spurred her forward, but before she could make it to the door, her foot was grabbed making her fall to her knees. With one yank, she was on her stomach being pulled back into the house. Picking up her other foot, she kicked him in the face repeatedly, but his hold didn't loosen.

When Pam noticed Tessa just stood there staring, horror evident on her face, Pam screamed, "Go, dammit!"

"I'm not leaving you." Tessa ran back into the house.

"You are going to pay for that, bitch." Kenny climbed on top of her turning her over. As his fist raised to smash down on Pam's face, she remembered a lesson learned during her training. Thrusting up with the palm of her hand, she smashed it against his nose, just as a loud clunk echoed in the room. Kenny groaned, slumping forward.

Tessa stood over him with a lamp she had cracked him with.

Pam scrambled out from under him to her feet, grabbed Tessa and took off out the door. As soon as both women hit the ground, they slid in the mud, Pam's phone skidding out of her hand.

"Dammit." Pam reached, grabbing her phone out of the mud. With trembling fingers, she went to her messages and hit send, sending the message she had programmed to Duncan with the address of where she went. The click of a gun made her cringe, her eyes closing in defeat. This was it. She would never see Duncan or Daniel again. Her heart broke.

"If you just messaged the Warriors, they're going to be too late. Now get the fuck up, you worthless slut," Kenny spat.

The sound of triple quick beeps of a text alert echoed in the darkness.

"We're already here." Duncan's voice rose out of the darkness.

Pam looked up, her hair plastered to her head and face as the cold rain beat down. She watched as each Warrior appeared, removing black hooded cloaks that blended them into the darkness.

"Well, welcome to the party." Kenny aimed the gun at Tessa. "But you're a little too late for the human."

In a movement so quick, Duncan threw something that whizzed over the women's heads. Pam ducked, then turned to see a knife sticking out of Kenny's arm and the gun dropping to the ground.

Kenny's scream of pain was enough to send Pam and Tessa running. Duncan grabbed Pam putting her safely behind him. She looked around his arm to see Kenny pulling the knife out of his arm.

"You fucker," Kenny screamed, throwing the knife back at Duncan who just batted it away.

"Get her out of here," Duncan ordered, his eyes never leaving Kenny.

"But…" Pam tried to argue, but Sid was there grabbing her.

"Now!" Duncan's tone was low, but the authority made it seem like he shouted.

"Pam, get back here!" Kenny yelled stomping toward her, an insane look in his eyes, the look of a man who knew he was about to die. "Pam!"

Duncan took two steps, punching Kenny in the face. "You're not fit to say her name, you worthless son of a bitch."

Kenny's head snapped back as blood spurted from his nose. He tried to punch back, but missed, landing in the mud. Duncan used his boot, pushing Kenny's head and face into the mud.

"How does it feel to be humiliated, you bastard?" Pushing down hard one last time, he removed his foot. "Get up!" Duncan growled.

"She will never be yours," Kenny grunted, spitting mud and blood. "I made damn sure she would never forget me. Every time you fuck that bitch, it will be me she sees and fear she feels."

Duncan grabbed him around the throat and lifted him in the air. "She is a strong woman and has already moved on." Duncan squeezed harder, making him splutter and claw at his hand. "I will erase you from her memory. After this moment, you will never be thought of again. You will *never* hurt her again."

Dropping Kenny to his feet, he turned him around pushing him up to the house and inside. Slamming the door with his foot, he smacked Kenny in the back of the head just like he knew Kenny had done to Pam.

"What are you doing?" Kenny tripped, catching himself.

Duncan didn't say a word and dodged when Kenny came at him swinging. With one well-placed kick to the stomach, Kenny was down on the ground sucking air. "Making sure you never bring Pam pain again." Duncan punched him again in the face, satisfied when one of his fangs broke.

"You broke my fang," Kenny cried out, feeling it with his finger.

Duncan punched him on the other side of the mouth. When he didn't break that one, he punched him again until it did. "I don't have a file, or I'd file the fucking things down to the gums."

A black-hooded figure came in handing Duncan his cape. Duncan put it on lifting the hood over his head. He took the container, and then nodded at the other figure who turned and walked to the kerosene heater in the corner and lit it. Without looking their way, the hooded figure walked out of the room.

"What is that?" Kenny's eyes filled with fear when the smell of kerosene filled the air. "What's going on?"

Duncan grabbed him, throwing him to the couch and holding him there with his foot. "Don't think I didn't see the faded burn scars on Pam's skin, you sick fuck." Duncan sprayed kerosene on Kenny, making sure he moved his foot.

"You can't do this," Kenny shouted, not looking so sure, the smug confidence finally disappearing off his face. "This is murder."

"No," Duncan replied, pulling his hood back so Kenny's half-breed eyes could see his full-blooded Warrior eyes. "This is justice, the way the Warriors used to exert justice to rapists and anyone who hurt women."

"No, please." Kenny attempted to get up, but Duncan's boot pushed him back down.

"How many times did Pam say those same exact words to you?" Duncan hissed.

Kenny stared at him in horror, realizing the position he was now in.

"That's what I thought, you son of a bitch," Duncan growled. "Any man who raises a hand against a woman deserves to die."

Duncan lit the match with his fingernail, holding it up. "Have a nice sleep…in hell, you bastard." Duncan flipped the match, watching with a morbid satisfaction as Kenny burned, taking all the evil he had ever done to Pam with him. "Fuck you!" Duncan spat, turned and walked out of the house, his hood up.

*****

Pam stood shuffling from foot to foot, her hands rubbing together. They had stopped on the wooded trail next to the river. Damon had caught up minutes before, but Duncan was still gone. A large boom sounded as the night sky lit up with flames.

She went to take off, but Jared, who still held Tessa, stopped her. "Wait."

A shadowy figure appeared on the trail heading for them. When Jared let go of her arm, Pam took off, slipping and sliding in the mud. Without slowing, she jumped into Duncan's arms, almost knocking him off balance, and held him tight.

"He will never hurt you again." Duncan held her firmly, holding her to his chest and breathing in her scent, a scent he had feared never to experience again.

Pam, still wrapped around him, grasped his face in her hands. "Thank you."

"I wish I could have prevented the first part." He looked at the swelling in her face, anger blazing from his eyes. "And we are going to have a long talk about your little 'adventure'."

"How did you know where I was?" Pam frowned.

"Nicole remembered you talking about this place. It was a long shot, but it paid off." Duncan glared at her. "Don't ever do anything like that again."

A moment of guilt flickered through her eyes at his fear. "What happened?" Her eyes looked over his shoulder at the flames.

"It's dangerous to fall asleep with a kerosene heater." Duncan set her down, wrapping her in his cape.

"We need to get out of here." Damon hurried past them as sirens blared in the distance.

Pam felt tears roll down her cheeks. She knew what he had done for her, and the last resistance on her heart broke away. "I love you."

Duncan leaned down and kissed her. "I love you more."

As the police and fire department screamed past, no one noticed the cloaked figures making their way through the woods along the river.

As they made their way quickly through the darkness, Pam reached deep into her pocket, pulled her ring out and placed it on her finger. Rightness settled over her.

"I understand why you took it off this time, but I don't ever want it off your finger again." Duncan kissed the top her head.

"Never," Pam replied with a sigh of pure happiness.

Chapter 28

Everyone sat in the games room, wrapping paper scattered everywhere. The Christmas tree sat in the corner, lights and ornaments twinkling festively. Pam held Daniel who was growing quickly, but not as quickly as they were afraid of. Slade was keeping a close eye on him. The only effects so far of Pam's being a half-breed was that he healed more quickly than a human did.

Her eyes roamed the room landing on Duncan who stood talking to Damon, but his eyes were watching her. She grinned at him; he winked back.

Jill was still recovering from her gunshot wound. None of them could tell if there was something between her and Slade. Time would tell, although Pam had her suspicions from the furtive glances they cast at one another when they thought no one was watching.

"Can I hold him?" Tessa sat down next to Pam.

"You sure can." Pam handed Daniel over to her. "So what did Jared get you for Christmas?"

Nicole heard and sat down across from them. "Yeah, what did Jared get you?"

Tessa looked up at Jared, who was staring at her. "Nothing yet."

Pam frowned. "Don't tell me you guys are still fighting?"

"No, it's not that." Tessa smiled, her face had fading bruises from Kenny's abusive hand. "He doesn't want to give me what I want."

"And what's that?" Nicole glared at Jared. "I know what these Warriors are worth and if he's being a tight ass, then I'll-"

"I want him to change me." Tessa cut her off, handing Daniel to Nicole. "And he doesn't want to."

"Oh, ah…" Nicole looked at Pam, wide-eyed at a loss of what to say.

"Well, Christmas isn't over yet," Pam added. Nicole rolled her eyes at her. Well at least it was better than 'oh, ah' Pam thought.

"What did you guys get?" Tessa changed the subject.

"Damon got me a new coat and a few other things." Nicole grinned. "I didn't want much because I want to work on finding a house."

"What did you get, Pam?" Nicole nodded toward her.

"A wedding." Pam grinned when they both just stared at her. When her words finally sunk in, both women screamed, scaring poor Daniel, making him scream right along with them.

"They give me a heart attack every time they do that," Jared cursed, watching the women hugging each other. "What the hell is going on over there?"

"Guess Pam told them what I gave her for Christmas." Duncan grinned, taking a long swig of beer.

"And?" Jared glanced at Damon with raised eyebrows, then looked back to Duncan. "Can you share?"

"Yeah." Duncan laughed. "A wedding."

Everyone was quiet until an earsplitting scream echoed in the room. Sid placed his hands on his face, and then cut the scream off. "Sorry, just couldn't help it." He raised his beer to Duncan. "Congrats, bro. Really," he added before walking off.

"He's just not right," Jared sighed before grinning at Duncan. "Congrats, my man. When's the big day?"

"March 18th," Duncan replied, still grinning from ear-to-ear.

"I'm happy for you, Duncan." Damon slapped him on the back. "You guys deserve to be happy."

Jared glanced over watching the women talk, but noticed that Tessa was a little more subdued. Putting his beer on the bar, he headed over by the women. "I hear congratulations are in order." He leaned down kissing Pam on the cheek.

"Thanks." Pam smiled.

"Now, may I steal my lady away from you for a few minutes?" Jared grabbed Tessa's hand, leading her out of the room and into another one. Closing the door, he turned. "Hey."

"Hey," she answered back with a blush.

"Are you okay?" Jared brushed her hair off her cheek, loving the pink blush the crept across her skin

"Yeah, why?"

"I haven't forgotten your Christmas present, babe." Jared rubbed her cheek with his thumb. When she didn't say anything, he sighed. "You know I love you more than anything in this world."

Tessa frowned. "Yes, I know."

"No, I don't think you do." Jared looked away. "If I was to change you and something happened, something went wrong, I couldn't handle it. I'm not willing to take that chance with your life." He hated the look of hurt and disappointment that she desperately tried to hide from her face. But the thought of losing her was simply too much.

"It's okay." Tessa tried to smile. "I understand."

"I'm not going to feed from Vicky anymore," Jared reassured her. "And I'm going to talk to Slade about our situation."

"It's not really about Vicky." When she saw his knowing frown, she sighed. "Okay, it is a little bit about Vicky, but I want to be the one to give you what you need. Why can't you understand that? You could feed from a little old man, and I'd still feel that I wasn't giving you what you need."

"I have to feed, Tessa."

"I know that, Jared." Tessa calmed herself, knowing that getting heated wasn't going to help the situation. "But more than anything, I want my blood to be enough for you."

"Let me talk to Slade, okay?" Jared hugged her tight. "We will work this out."

Tessa nodded into his chest. "I know we will."

Jared reached behind him and locked the door. "I think I need to show you just how much I love you."

"If you insist, Mr. Kincaid." Tessa grinned with a sigh as he proceeded to do just that.

Jared could still see the doubt in her beautiful eyes and vowed he would spend the rest of their lives proving to her that she was the only woman he would ever love.

*****

Duncan brought in everything from the Christmas party while Pam put Daniel down for the night. Looking around his home, he smiled. It finally looked lived in. Something he had yearned for.

Heading to the kitchen, he grabbed a bottle of wine and two glasses. Pam liked to have a glass before going to sleep. Pushing open the door, he walked out and stopped, dropping one of the glasses.

"Jesus." Duncan swallowed hard. Standing before him was Pam, wearing only a Christmas-red bra and panties. A red velvet bow graced her beautiful neck. His eyes traveled down her body to the red high heels.

"Merry Christmas," her voice was low and raspy.

In two steps, he was in front of her, his eyes never leaving her body. Leaning over her, without touching, he set the bottle of wine and one glass on the table behind her, his eyes never leaving hers. Taking her hand, he lifted her arm, twirling her around, his eyes taking in every inch.

"Do you like?" Pam smiled when they were face-to-face again.

He could only growl as he leaned down to kiss her, his hands placed lightly on her flared hips. He was still in awe at Pam's ability to bring him to his knees, her ability to strip away the years of wall building that he had carefully erected around his heart. With just one look, he was hers.

"I take that as a yes," she giggled, feeling empowered.

He lifted her, forcing her to put her hands on his shoulders. "I like it so much that I seriously doubt we will be making it to the bed."

Pam wrapped her legs around his waist feeling his hardness. Feeling brave, she slowly rubbed up and down against him. "Take me, now."

He reached down to run his fingers along her sweetness, and sure enough, she was ready. A satisfied rumbled ripped through his body. Unsnapping his jeans, he freed his throbbing cock and moved the wisp of fabric of her tiny panties out of the way. In one sharp thrust, he was inside her. Their mouths were frantic against each other.

Duncan pressed her against the wall, pounding into her. "You are going to be the death of me," he growled. "I can't get enough of you."

Using his shoulders as leverage, Pam slammed down on him, meeting him with every thrust. Pam couldn't answer him if her life depended on it. Her mouth opened in a silent scream. A flash of colors appearing before her eyes as her orgasm pulsated through her.

"That's it, babe, give me everything you have." Duncan bit at her neck as his release followed hers.

They stayed together, neither of them wanting to part. Duncan finally pulled back slightly to look at her. "Thank you."

Pam swallowed hard, trying to catch her breath. "For what?"

"For trusting me and knowing I would never hurt you." Duncan nuzzled her neck.

"I never doubted you, Duncan." Pam hugged him as a tear of contentment slipped down her cheek.

*****

Sid walked into the kitchen flipping on the lights. Adam sat at the table staring at the beer in his hand.

"What the hell are you doing sitting in the dark?" Sid walked over to grab some leftovers.

"Not in the mood to party." Adam tilted the beer bottle at him before tilting it to his lips.

Sid rolled his eyes as he sat down. "So you're sitting in here feeling sorry for yourself, huh?"

"No." Adam frowned. "I just don't feel in the festive mood."

"Ah, so you just sit around in the dark getting drunk." Sid nodded.

"Fuck you, Sid." Adam hissed. "You don't know what you're talking about."

"Well after you're finished drinking your sorry ass under the table, you need to come talk to me." Sid took a bite of turkey. "Right now, get the fuck out of my kitchen."

"What is your problem?" Adam stood glaring down at him.

"My problem, you little shit, is that I just went to bat for you." Sid glared back. "I got permission to head up a new department with you being my second hand man."

"What?" Adam looked confused.

"You want to find Angelina or not, dumbass?" Sid tossed his piece of turkey down.

"What kind of fucking question is that?" Adam hissed.

"Well, seeing that you would rather sit in the dark alone drinking, it's a pretty good fucking question." Sid stood up leaning across the table in his face. "We are now actively investigating the human trafficking and auctioning of young women."

Adam set his beer down. "When?"

"As soon as you sober up." Sid sat back down. "Don't make me regret this," he warned, pointing a piece of turkey at him.

"I won't, man. Thank you." Adam walked around the table, heading deeper into the kitchen.

"Where the fuck are you going?" Sid turned to watch him.

"To get some coffee."

"Pour me a cup. Then let's go torture…I mean interrogate, that little traitor Jeff." Sid grinned at the thought, and wondered if Sloan had made a big mistake putting him in charge of his own department. Sid's eyebrows rose as he thought about that. "Grab something sharp and pointy." Oh, yeah, definitely a big mistake.

A grin split Sid's lips as he ripped a piece of turkey off with his sharp fangs. He was tired of being bored, watching all the lovey-dovey shit going on. It was time he stepped up his game, and helping Adam find Angelina was just the ticket he needed to do something before he strangled one of his fellow pussy-whipped brothers. Yeah, it was time to kill some bad guys.

ABOUT THE AUTHOR

Hey friends! Thought I'd share a little information about myself. I live in a small town east of Cincinnati, Ohio with my husband, son, two crazy dogs and my son's snake, Steve Irwin…'yuck'. I'm a third degree black belt in Taekwondo, a huge Mixed Martial Arts fan and I follow and support my husband's MMA fight team, G-Force, which my son fights for. When not writing I'm either screaming like a crazy woman at MMA fights or reading in some quiet corner with my beloved Kindle. I absolutely love books that are fast reads filled with romance, humor, sexy alpha men and the women who drive them crazy.

Sid Sinclair is the next and fourth book in the Protectors Series. So stay tuned and be ready to follow Sid, who may or may not find that one woman who can bring him to his knees. Okay, maybe not to his knees, but what fun it will be to watch him fight what we all hope will be a losing battle. Oh yeah!! So excited for this story!!! Also find out more about the other Warriors who I hope you love as much as I do.

Absolutely love to hear from you so here's a few links to find me!

Hugs and tons of love to you all!!!!!

www.teresagabelman.com

www.facebook.com/pages/Teresa-Gabelman/191553587598342

Printed in Great Britain
by Amazon